Tom Clancy's

OP-CENTER

FALLOUT

TOM CLANCY'S OP-CENTER NOVELS

ALSO BY JEFF ROVIN

cy's

OP-CENTER

FALLOUT

CREATED BY

Tom Clancy and Steve Pieczenik

WRITTEN BY

Jeff Rovin

ST. MARTIN'S
GRIFFIN
NEW YORK

First published in the United States by St. Martin's Griffin, an imprint of St. Martin's Publishing Group

TOM CLANCY'S OP-CENTER: FALLOUT. Copyright © 2023 by Jack Ryan Limited Partnership and S&R Literary, Inc. All rights reserved. Printed in the United States of America. For information, address St. Martin's Publishing Group, 120 Broadway, New York, NY 10271.

www.stmartins.com

Designed by Omar Chapa

Library of Congress Cataloging-in-Publication Data

Names: Rovin, Jeff, author. | Clancy, Tom, 1947-2013. | Pieczenik, Steve R.
Title: Fallout / created by Tom Clancy and Steve Pieczenik ; written by Jeff Rovin.
Description: First edition. | New York : St. Martin's Griffin, 2023. | Series: Tom Clancy's op-center ; [22]
Identifiers: LCCN 2022058232 | ISBN 9781250901330 (hardcover) | ISBN 9781250868725 (trade paperback) | ISBN 9781250868732 (ebook)
Subjects: LCGFT: Thrillers (Fiction) | Spy fiction. | Novels.
Classification: LCC PS3568.O8894 F26 2023 | DDC 813/.54—dc23/eng/20221212
LC record available at https://lccn.loc.gov/2022058232

Our books may be purchased in bulk for promotional, educational, or business use. Please contact your local bookseller or the Macmillan Corporate and Premium Sales Department at 1-800-221-7945, extension 5442, or by email at MacmillanSpecialMarkets@macmillan.com.

First Edition: 2023

10 9 8 7 6 5 4 3 2 1

Tom Clancy's
OP-CENTER

FALLOUT

CHAPTER ONE

19 miles above the Western Coast of Africa
March 22, 5:45 P.M., Central Daylight Time

"So, Senator?" Colonel Timothy Malo said. "What are you going to tell the press when you land? It's got to be something for the ages."

"Why?" Senator Yvonne Malo replied. "I'm not even the oldest politician who has gone into space."

"True, but John Glenn is not the sitting chair of the Subcommittee on Space and Science. You are. C'mon. Your astutest critic wants to know."

Senator Yvonne Malo smiled. She had no idea—had not even thought about it. Strapped to her couch, forming a circle with her three crewmates, the woman looked up through the large window over her head. The gold tint of her helmet's face mask killed the glare from inside the spacecraft so that all she saw were stars and blackness.

The three days of talking to the scientists, of watching them dry-run equipment, of conducting Senate business from low Earth orbit—*that* was a first—and of learning to eat, sleep, and use the toilet in zero-gravity, all that had been big and preoccupying.

"You've got about thirty seconds until I've got to return the mike," her husband pressed.

"Okay, Colonel. I'll tell those pudknockers that space flight is like sex," the outspoken Arizonan replied. "You can take the classes, you can watch the videos, you can use your imagination. But nothing can prepare you for the reality. What do you think?"

Her husband laughed. "Can I take that as a compliment?"

"You most certainly may."

"Bless ya, girl. That's as good a sign-off as I can think of. I'll let CAPCOM know that our PTC has ended."

"I love you, too, and I'll see you within an hour."

The line went cold for a few seconds as her partner of forty years terminated the private-time communication. It was a chat allowed each astronaut before the fiery and dangerous reentry. The next voice the sixty-three-year-old heard was the capsule communicator letting them know that their automated deorbit burn was just two minutes, thirty seconds away.

Senator Malo settled back into the couch of the *Phoenix One*. The seat was comprised of two sections connected by a flexible joint, assisting blood flow and decreasing the gravitational forces of leaving and returning to the Earth. Its recliner was not so much comfortable as reassuring, holding her space-suited-self snug and plugged in to all communications, air, and the electronic heads-up display. She kept that turned off since the readouts were foreign to the onetime rodeo rider and obstructed her view of space.

She thought about what she had told her husband. It was no exaggeration. The maiden voyage of NASA's new research ship had been a powerful, emotional experience. It was incalculably larger-than-life, from the ferocious thrust of liftoff, through the rattling climb when she feared her bones as well as the rocket would come apart, to the sudden onset of weightlessness. Below the crew section was the science module that was designed to conduct experiments for which the International Space Station was not equipped—or that the Department of Defense did not wish to share with the international community.

"Heatshield alignment in progress," she heard Commander Dick Siegel say. He was in the seat directly to her left in an array she jokingly referred to as "our pie chart."

"Azimuth nominal," CAPCOM answered.

The spacecraft system was fully automated, the exchange simply confirming that both crew and command center were reading the same data.

"Deorbit burn in two minutes—mark," Commander Siegel said.

"Roger that," CAPCOM replied.

It was a surreal moment for the senator, weightless and waiting. With nothing tangible happening and the universe sprawled before her, time did not seem to exist. Except for memory, it was like being a fetus—

And then everything but the stars went away. For a moment, Senator Malo wondered if one of the crewmembers had pushed something by accident. But there was no activity that she could hear or see.

"Commander?" she said into the ominously silent darkness.

She heard her voice in the helmet but not through the audio unit. There was no response, but then everyone was as tucked-in as she was, and she would not have heard anything that did not come through the ship communicator. Her helmet afforded very little mobility, but she turned her head very slightly in Siegel's direction.

"Commander?"

There was no answer. She went immediately to her training, quickly filtering all worries and extraneous thoughts; none of that would help. She wondered if a swarm of micrometeoroids had impacted the *Phoenix One* and damaged its circuits.

"Hello? CAPCOM?" she said. When there was no response, she repeated the call with greater urgency. "CAPCOM? Do you read?"

Save for the hollow sound of her own breath, there was silence—frustrating at first and then, despite her best efforts, it became unnerving. She noticed then that the air was growing warm, that she was suddenly straining to breathe.

You have now *to fix this,* she reminded herself. *Do it! What is your status?*

The air was not being refreshed behind her visor. There

was no communication, no light, no electronics—there had been a catastrophic failure. Even the backup systems had not clicked in.

The senator raised a gloved hand. She touched the right side of her helmet to raise the visor. Its faceplate did not move. That should not be—the suit electronics were not linked to the ship's systems. They should not be nonresponsive.

Fighting down rising panic, she brought her hands to the base of her neck to manually unlatch the helmet. Just then she heard muffled, distant voices.

"CAPCOM?" she asked. "Hello?"

No, she thought. Those were her crewmates. They only seemed distant because of the damned helmet. She realized suddenly that she had to remove the gloves first and did so clumsily but swiftly. She left them floating where they were and hurriedly undid the latches that held the helmet to the connective neck ring. She got it off with a combination of tugging and wriggling in the confined space. At once, the disembodied voices became clear.

". . . batteries are dead!" astrophysicist Dr. John Todd said thickly.

"How is that possible?" Commander Siegel asked.

"I don't know," Todd admitted. "No single radioactive source could do this."

"Sabotage," said embedded technology scientist Dr. Bart Singh. "That's the only explan—"

"Save that for later!" Siegel interrupted. "Jason, we've got about a minute before the reentry maneuver!"

"I'm engaging manual thruster control," said pilot Jason Goodman. "I'll use the angle of the stars to time the burn. We may end up in Iceland, but we'll be down!"

Senator Malo knew that the problem was more complex than that. This low, if Goodman did not fire the rockets at exactly the right moment to reduce reentry to idle velocity, the *Phoenix One* would clip the outer edge of the Earth's atmosphere at 17,500 miles an hour and go skidding off into space.

No one spoke after that, and the dwindling air supply made it incumbent to be still and silent. She relaxed back into the seat, trusting Goodman to get them out of this. He had trained for it. She had observed him, marveling at his instincts. If anyone could pull this off—

Suddenly, there was a spine-rattling jolt from below. The cabin filled with a yellow-orange glow as the spacecraft's four hydrocarbon-fueled rockets ignited. After the period of deep blackness, the flare was so intense that Senator Malo felt a sharp burst in the back of her head.

Through the unexpected movement and light, the woman heard Goodman shout, "*That wasn't me!*"

It was the last articulate human voice she would ever hear. Shrieks came from all four mouths as the burn sent the *Phoenix One* into the atmosphere at an improper angle. Instead of skipping into the void, the spacecraft plunged Earthward with its heatshield improperly aligned. The reaction was severe as the atmosphere poured around it, friction igniting everything that was not the concave steel, fiberglass, and basalt bulwark. The fire melted or vaporized every structural piece of the ship that it came in contact with on its way to the cabin. That process took under three seconds, during which time the passengers experienced heat rising swiftly to 2,750 degrees Fahrenheit—three seconds in which they were able to scream their last mortal sounds.

The flames quickly immolated the chairs, the controls, and finally the crew. The one mercy is that all four astronauts were already dead, their chests having burst from the rapid expansion of heated air in their lungs.

After just seven seconds, no trace of the *Phoenix One* remained.

CHAPTER TWO

Watergate Apartments, Washington, D.C.
March 22, 8:13 P.M.

Chase Williams had just begun streaming a documentary on one of his favorite topics, the history of the Catholic Church. He missed the traditional Latin Mass, and he missed the rest of the old days, the old ways.

"Talk to me, old fellow," he said as an image of Pope Paul VI flashed by. "Explain yourself."

Paul had eased the hold of Latin and was the first pope that Williams had been aware of. But Pope Paul was also the sobriquet that had been applied to his scrupulously honest predecessor at the helm of Op-Center, Paul Hood.

Those tangled thoughts remained jumbled when his work phone chirped. He considered ignoring the call; he was in the mood for saints. But the secure mobile device insisted.

It was a pleasant enough sound: spring chickens, a reminder of his youthful summers on Grandpa Eban Chase's farm. But the innocence of the tone belied what was usually a crisis call from the Oval Office or one of his trusted sources.

The sixty-one-year-old director of the National Crisis Management Center—informally known as Op-Center—paused the show, turned from his wall-mounted TV, and stretched his arm across the sofa to where he had plopped the cell phone on a deep cushion. It was Matt Berry. The former deputy chief of staff was now managing director at the Trigram Institute, a Georgetown-based think tank. Berry had been one of Williams' biggest boosters during the previous Midkiff administration and had been instrumental in the downsizing of Op-Center from a largely redundant, soon-to-be-eliminated intelligence agency to a strike force that went on highly secretive missions for the president of the United States.

Williams' lean, six-foot frame slumped a little into the cushion as he thumbed "accept" and touched "speaker."

"The *Phoenix*?" he asked.

"Yes. Are you watching?"

"No. You know how I feel about conspiracy theories and that's all any talking head would have this soon."

"Would you accept the intel of a Chinese informant?"

That got Williams' attention. He sat up slightly. "One of yours?"

"Yes. You've probably seen him. He shows up now and then down the hall from you at the DLA."

"Down the hall" was not quite as cozy as it sounded. Williams had a belowground office at the McNamara Headquarters Complex at the Defense Logistics Agency at Fort Belvoir, Virginia. This basement was not only balmy with recycled air but was mute with unnatural silence, a disconnect scrupulously maintained by the deep-state workers and black ops who worked there. Nods of recognition, when they were exchanged at all, came without a spoken salutation.

"He doesn't know who you are or what you do, of course," Berry added.

"Of course. We're all intelligence agents over there. Why should we know anything?"

Williams' sarcasm covered a deeper discontentment. Throughout his naval career, the retired four-star admiral had worked in the big open spaces of the sea or in busy military nerve centers. The original Op-Center was housed in a largely subterranean complex. But it was a hive-like environment where the seventy-eight full-time employees mingled, shared information, had meetings, talked about their private lives.

Williams' professional environment was no longer like that. Unless there was a mission, weeks might pass without Williams engaging with what were now just four other members of Op-Center. Seconded from different branches of the military and code-named "Black Wasp," members of that group, at least, were out in the open, quartered, and trained at the adjacent military compound at Fort Belvoir.

"Who's the source and what's he telling you?" Williams asked.

"His name is Dylan Hao. He's a Taiwanese, about forty, who works undercover in the Chinese consulate as a representative of the chief of staff of the Politburo."

"A double agent. He works for Taipei," Williams clarified.

"Right. And us. Gave me reliable information when I was in the West Wing."

Williams reached for the remote and shut off the TV. God, clearly, had other plans for this night. "All right, Matt. What does he say?"

"He says the spacecraft was shut down and then reprogrammed to fire its rockets by commands sent from the Tiangong space station," Berry said.

The newly inaugurated Chinese orbital base was roughly one-quarter the size of the International Space Station and soared at an average of 230 miles above the Earth. It was designed and equipped for military activity and intelligence gathering.

"They've been mucking around with our communications and spy satellites for years," Williams said. "Homeland Security, the CIA—none of the daily updates had any red flags on this kind of escalation."

Even as he was speaking, Williams felt the answer in his gut. China would respond in space to an action committed in or against space. And Beijing's retaliation, whatever the battlefield, was exponential.

"According to Hao, they destroyed the *Phoenix One* and its crew in response to the abduction of Dr. Dàyóu," Berry told him.

Williams felt sick.

Dr. Yang Dàyóu had been the chief engineer on the *Qi*-19 project, Beijing's hypersonic missile program. One month ago, Black Wasp had grabbed him from the Taiyuan

Satellite Launch Center in China's Shanxi Province. It was an ugly but effective exit with collateral damage, which included the assassination of General Zhou Chang, the project director.

Williams' current distress arose from the fact that the abduction had not been part of the original mission, which was to reconnoiter. That action was taken spontaneously in the field by Lieutenant Grace Lee of Black Wasp. Though President Wright had ultimately supported both the mission expansion and the outcome, Williams could have aborted the revised initiative. He was not a stranger to the global stage and the characteristics and psychology of its political and military players. As the former combatant commander for both Pacific Command and Central Command, he had met with his Chinese counterparts and their civilian leaders on many occasions.

"Chase?" Berry said.

"Yeah."

"I know that silence of yours," Berry said. "The grab-decision was the right move. This escalation is on Beijing."

"Cause had nothing to do with effect."

"We can carry that back to Cain and Abel if you want."

That was true.

"Now, you done?" Berry asked. "Because there's more."

Berry was right. Williams shucked the self-reproach.

"I assume Mr. Hao also communicated to you that the Chinese want their man back," the admiral said.

"They did, which was to be expected in some form or another. But—and President Wright doesn't know this yet—there's one more piece to this."

"It wouldn't be financial compensation," Williams said. "That's not Beijing's style."

"No. Beijing is actually running two operations concurrently. One is threatening to knock down American spaceships, satellites, and missiles one after another—and they can do it, too, unless Wright gives them what they really want."

"And he'll fold, if he hasn't already," Williams said.

"He has, at least internally among his brain trust."

"So what else does China want?" Williams asked.

"They insist that the man who headed the American incursion be the one to hand him over."

That was as unexpected as it was unwelcome.

"They want to use me to give them face," Williams said.

"That's part of it," Berry said. "I believe that Beijing's insistence on your presence may be threefold. First, yes, it's a face-saving gesture. They want some top Chinese official, some favored son, to stand tall and look into the eyes of the American who had overseen their defeat. They want you to lose face as that achievement is undone. The second option is—they may want you on the plane when it packs up and leaves."

"Kidnapping."

"Yes."

Williams was about to say, *On American soil?* but then realized how fitting that would be. It was exactly what Op-Center's Lieutenant Grace Lee had done with Yang Dàyóu.

"They'd take you to China and lock you deep in the maximum security Qincheng Prison," Berry continued.

"Where Lieutenant Lee beat the hell out of General Chang," Williams noted.

"The Chinese like their vengeance served with irony," Berry said.

"All right. Then what's the third part?" Williams asked.

"That would be the least welcome part," Berry went on.

"Less welcome than hauling me to Qincheng," Williams said.

Berry nodded. His face looked like it did in the West Wing whenever he had bad news—like a hanging judge. "The Chinese probably haven't identified any of the people who were involved in the abduction. They've certainly gone through their local resources—surveillance cameras, eyewitnesses, fingerprints—and come up empty. At the very least, this transaction will expose your identity, and probably the rest of the team—and not just to Beijing. You name will be leaked to *all* your enemies. You will live the rest of your life under the threat of retribution."

That would not be long in coming. On Black Wasp's first mission, Williams had personally killed a top lieutenant of Mohammad Obeid ibn Said. It was only a question of time before that Yemen-based terrorist came after him.

"All of this presumes that President Wright will agree to turning Dr. Dàyóu over," Williams said. "China has fired the first shot of what could be a war in space—"

"What *might* have been a war, what *should* at least be a firm retaliation against the space station," Berry said. "Seven months ago I delivered the Comprehensive Orbital Aggression,

Situations, and Tactics white paper to President Midkiff, over twenty-five hundred pages of 'if this, then that,' ranging from cyberattacks on a corporate streaming service to technological aggression against international missions—to murder."

"Midkiff would have responded with equal or upticked pressure," Williams said.

"Served warm," Berry agreed. "*Very* warm using the X-37C and FILE."

Williams was familiar with both assets. The X-37C was the newest iteration of the Air Force's robotic space shuttle. Managed by Space Force and placed in orbit just before the last year of Midkiff's second term, the spacecraft was nearly as large as the crewed space shuttle and was equipped with sophisticated "brake and turn" for rapid orbital orientation adjustment. It was also armed with an array of deterrents including the Fast Ignition Laser Emission. The beam could generate up to two petawatts for as little as one picosecond— one trillionth of a second. The damage could be done before the target knew what hit them.

Under Midkiff, the orbital drone would likely have targeted the Tiangong with the FILE, disrupting the space station's orbital integrity and sending it not into the atmosphere, like the *Phoenix One* with its quick-death result, but on a chaotic journey away from the Earth. The world would listen as the connected modules drifted from Earth, the solar panels turning from the sun, the crew freezing as their battery power failed with accelerating swiftness.

"But President Wright is not President Midkiff," Berry

said. "He's the architect of the Sinophobia Is Counterproductive policy and will seek to tamp the situation down. Assured that the intelligence community has squeezed every drop of useful information from Dr. Dàyóu, the White House will return the scientist to his keepers to forestall future attacks on American spacefaring interests. They have already moved the Dàyóu family from their safe house in Silver Springs to your place, the Watergate."

"He's wrong," Williams said. "Conciliation here, now, will have just the opposite effect. The next attack will not be just a retaliatory strike—"

"*May* not be," Berry said.

"No, it will be big," Williams said. "I'm navy, Matt. I always assume there's a next Pearl Harbor, and the one that concerns me based on this event is a coordinated attack to control low Earth orbit. If China does that, they will own us."

"Very possibly. What do you propose?"

"I want to meet with Hao."

Berry was thoughtful for a long moment. "And do what?"

"China has gone beyond planting false data in weather satellites and corrupting National Reconnaissance Office images," Williams said with new urgency. "They used my team's actions as an excuse to establish mass murder and catastrophic destruction as their new baseline in space."

"That's a leap," Berry said. "Your team's actions included the murder of a top general in the People's Liberation Army Rocket Force. This could be payback. There is no indication that this attack marks a new policy."

"You're not seeing the big picture," Williams pressed. "Putting aside the morality of it, killing *Phoenix One* was a technological and tactical triumph. Beijing does not retreat. They're not going to go back to inconveniencing us. This was a complex operation, one that required spies at NASA, planted in the ranks of subcontractors. It had to be in the works for months, possibly years before Black Wasp set foot in China. We need names, and we need their white papers. I want Hao to get me as much of that as possible, as quickly as possible, or to put me in touch with someone who has that access."

"I can handle that interrogation," Berry said.

"Will the president listen to me telling him what you said about what someone else told you? I've got to convince him to use the FILE or other tools already in place and to use them against China *now*. If he doesn't, we will be at Beijing's mercy."

"They have none."

"Exactly. What do we do if they start using Tiangong to attack our aircraft carriers or nuclear arsenal? Either we make our stand now or we face mass casualties and defeat later."

Berry was silent. He was obviously weighing the potential exposure of a valuable intelligence asset against Williams' hypothetical worst-case scenario.

"That was your DEFCON three voice," Berry said.

"I know. I'm scared. I've been feeling that old force-readiness status since Black Wasp got back, waiting for Beijing's boot to drop. Two days, I'm guessing. That's how long I've got. There are logistics to arrange. The family needs time, the site has to be chosen."

"Two days seems about right," Berry agreed.

"That gives me a very narrow window. There's no way Wright keeps me around past a handover of Dr. Dàyóu, especially with January Dow whispering in his ear."

"Probably not," Berry agreed.

Dow was formerly the director of the State Department's Bureau of Intelligence and Research, now assistant to the president for national security affairs. She was the architect of the administration's pro-China stance as well as an outspoken critic of Williams and what she referred to as his "brash and impulsive" unit.

"If I'm going to argue on my own behalf, not walk willingly to the scaffold, I need information. I need to see Hao."

"All right," Berry went on. "I'll talk to him. I doubt he will want to meet you at the DLA."

"Anyone talking to anyone there would attract attention," Williams agreed.

"Make sure you have some of that cash I left you. If he agrees, the down payment will be about 20K."

"Same price as a hitman, more or less."

"Life and death, two faces of one fat gold coin," Berry said. "I don't think I should give him your name."

"You gave me his."

"I know you a lot better than I know him."

"All right," Williams agreed. "Use Mr. Chase. If someone recognizes me, calls my name—"

"Right. It's a surname."

Williams thanked his old friend and hung up. The expression of gratitude carried weight that went beyond this call. When Deputy Chief of Staff Berry had set up the new Op-Center, he had given Williams four essential codes. The first was to operate the food and beverage vending machines at either end of the corridor. The surest way to spot a spy was to see someone insert money without using the code. The second password was to get into the lavatory. The third was to access Williams' Op-Center files, which had been "officially" shut down but were warehoused in a White House subdirectory. The fourth was to a series of wall safes that contained large denominations of cash, the currency of all nations. Until now, Williams had used it sparingly, on missions. This would be his first big buy.

Williams did not want to think. He put the documentary back on, hungry for stories about evangelism and martyrdom and the importance of ideals.

CHAPTER THREE

Fort Belvoir North, Springfield, Virginia
March 22, 10:00 P.M.

Standing under a dark, moonless sky, Jaz Rivette fingered the puffy, steel gray vest he had just been handed. It was too dark to see, but his sense of touch told him all he needed to know.

"This is not Kevlar," he said disapprovingly.

"This is not Kevlar, *Captain*," Captain Ann Ellen Mann firmly corrected him.

"Sorry, Captain, sir," Rivette said.

The new commander of Black Wasp regarded the lance corporal. She wore a Beretta M9 service pistol on her hip and a look that said she expected discipline and respect.

"No, Lance Corporal," said Captain Mann. "The vest is cotton with polyamide pockets."

"With respect, Captain, a bullet will go right through this," the twenty-three-year-old lance corporal replied. "In fact, with respect, a twenty-two-caliber bullet will go right through this. And what's in these pockets anyway, sir?"

"Lance Corporal Rivette, you will put that on and you will

stop talking before you become Private First Class Rivette," the officer said.

The rebuke was sharper than any Rivette had heard from the officer and a little *kaboom* went off in his head. He felt like a dummy target for radar-guided seeker heads.

"Yes, sir," the Marine Air Ground Task Force sharpshooter replied. He slipped his wiry arms into the garment then took a long moment to make sure the fit did not inhibit his handling of the silenced Osprey .45.

"Are you satisfied?" Mann asked.

"Sir, I am."

"I will inform Combat Capabilities Development Command that their efforts have not been in vain," she said.

The two members of Black Wasp were standing on the South Post Golf Course near the wooded water trap. A third member, Major Hamilton Breen, stood several feet away holding two pair of virtual reality goggles. Beside him was the fourth teammate, Lieutenant Grace Lee. The twenty-six-year-old had already donned her vest and sleek, black goggles and was waiting impatiently.

Captain Mann turned to the other woman. "How is the night vision capability?"

"Much sharper than standard issue," she replied. "I can see Jaz still frowning at six feet."

The young man mouthed an oath.

"You forgot 'Lieutenant,'" Grace told him.

"If we can return to the exercise," Mann said. "We were just beginning distribution of these AR 4.0 HoloLens units when I left Naval Support Activity, Philadelphia," Mann said. She was not accustomed to bickering among personnel but overlooked it. In the month since she had been seconded to the unit, the officer had learned that Black Wasp was unique in many ways. "You will drill as you did in the tactical response training structures, but with real-world terrain and—this."

The officer raised a tablet and touched the screen. There was a simultaneous hiss and pop and Rivette's left shoulder jerked backward. Lieutenant Lee instinctively rushed over; an instant later, acrid white smoke seeped from Rivette's vest.

"Victim response *and* support response," Mann said. "I'm impressed, Lieutenant."

"Simulated impact pellets," Rivette said admiringly. "I should've known. Are they waterproof?"

"That water trap will reach nearly to your chin and nothing will get wet but you." Mann handed the tablet to Breen and took her set of goggles. "The SIPs contain compressed biofuel that simulates the impact and disorientation of enemy fire without the pain," Mann said. "I controlled that one. The program will control the rest."

Rivette donned his glasses and Breen watched the scenario on the tablet. For the next hour the two members of Black Wasp drilled against figures moving through the dark in a simulated base invasion. Rivette fired blanks; Lee attacked with kung fu skills and her ten-and-a-half-inch fixed blade knife, virtual bodies bleeding and falling as they would in actual combat.

Not another gas pellet burst in the vests of Rivette or Lee. The captain was pleased to be able to put the concussive shells back in her armament bag.

"That was first-rate," Captain Mann told the team. "Thank you."

This was the first time Captain Mann had taken charge of the team's training. Major Breen had been happy to surrender the standing assignment. The thirty-eight-year-old was a JAG attorney and criminologist who preferred tactics and logistics to combat drills. Mann had desperately missed the field. The U.S. Naval Academy veteran spoke thirteen languages, including Pashto, and had worked as an interpreter in Afghanistan. During a clandestine effort to find and destroy Taliban fighters who had shot down a Chinook, the then-lieutenant took a bullet in the hip. After several surgeries that left her with a limp, Mann was given a promotion and her command position in Philadelphia.

"Active desk retirement," she had called it.

After aiding Black Wasp in their mission against the anarchistic Black Order, she had been offered a spot in Op-Center. The offer had not come from Director Chase Williams but from President Wright's chief of staff, Angie Brunner, with a strong endorsement by January Dow. Mann would not have accepted if Williams had not signed off on it.

The team returned to Dogue Army Family Housing residence on-post, where they lived in what was listed as a "non-traditional domestic arrangement." That became even more nontraditional when Mann moved into the house and Rivette relocated to a rapid-deployment military shelter erected in the small backyard. The young man had not minded. He grew up in an overcrowded apartment in San Pedro, California; this was the first time he had his own private residence.

On the way, Captain Mann received a call from Williams on her secure Mil-Spec smartphone.

"Were you watching the drill, Admiral?" she asked.

"No, I was on a call."

"That's one helluva team you assembled," the captain said.

"Those three built it," Williams replied. "I just observed."

Mann knew that Williams was being characteristically modest. The best commanders often did nothing except course-correct.

"Captain, it looks like I may have more to do on the China mission," Williams said.

Mann stopped walking. "Oh?" She motioned the others on.

"I've heard that China wants their man back and I'm to make the delivery," Williams said.

"That's idiocy!"

"It's the dark side of diplomatic chess," he said evenly.

"No. No, this doesn't rise to that level of statecraft." She stopped short of saying it was a death sentence. She did not have to.

"That's the privilege of kings," Williams said. "If it's true, I'll have to sever all ties with Op-Center immediately. The Chinese have no way of identifying anyone I worked with, and we've got to keep it that way."

The captain had no words to express her outrage. "Let's . . . let's hope it isn't true," she said.

"I'll let you know. In the meantime, I wanted you to be prepared to take over all operations, including interface with the Oval Office."

"Yes, sir," she said.

"Op-Center is still about national defense, not Chase Williams."

Captain Mann did not reply other than to say, "Good luck, Admiral," as Williams clicked off. But standing alone in the chill, bleak night she felt a kind of rage and mortification she had never felt in her years of wearing a uniform. It had the stink of King David sending Uriah the Hittite to die in battle because his presence was inconvenient.

The captain continued walking. At her worst moments, when the wounded warrior, the so-called "wonder woman," was brought out for public relations tasks because she checked necessary gender and combat boxes, Ann Ellen Mann had toughed it out. She understood the process. She was embarrassed but never ashamed.

Until now.

Only now did she consider the fate of Dr. Dàyóu and his wife and daughter when *they* returned to China. She briefly wondered what would have compelled President Wright to make such a deal—and then the stars above gave her the answer. The *Phoenix One*. Its destruction had been China's doing.

And suddenly right and wrong did not seem so clear to

her. Williams' thoughtful comments suggested he understood the situation as well.

Maybe Dickens said it best, she thought gravely. *"It is a far, far better thing that I do, than I have ever done . . ."*

CHAPTER FOUR

Embassy of the People's Republic of China,
Washington, D.C.
March 23, 12:04 A.M.

The black sedan pulled up to the high iron gate of the Chinese embassy complex located at 3505 International Place NW. Joseph Kebzabo was the sole passenger of the state vehicle, his large frame lost in the darkness of the back seat. His clear eyes peered from beneath the brim of a brown fedora as they took in the imposing, brightly lit complex spread before him.

The Chancery building was comprised of a two-story East Office Wing, a matching West Office Wing, and a central, three-story-high Entrance Pavilion. The structures were a blocky interpretation of traditional Chinese architecture constructed of beige French limestone. The design and materials created a simultaneous impression of strength and warmth.

Where is the hint of madness? Kebzabo wondered. Without a hint of disorder, of errant geometry, the building was not alive. Like the Sahara where he had been raised, the environment that had forged him, a great construct—anything, any*one*—required some chaos or it was just big and mute and ineffective.

Both the car and driver were known to the two sentries and were swiftly ushered inside.

Kebzabo was anything but ineffective. Sloppy men had to be propped up by others. Sloppy assassins endangered others.

The forty-one-year-old had learned responsibility early. He belonged to the Toubou, an ancient people of Little Borkou in the Sahara. He grew up in the shadow of great basaltic peaks and ancient volcanic caldera. There, generations of Kebzabos had harvested dates from a lake oasis. Each basketful was precious, and the extremes of weather made vigilance imperative: a frost on unpicked fruit meant the family would go without necessities.

It was a lonely, very provincial existence. Small groups of tourists came through every week, and once-a-week fig processors sent planes from the capital city of N'Djamena. Kebzabo was too busy harvesting or mending baskets or resting to engage with outsiders.

Then, when Joseph Kebzabo was seventeen, helicopters from the China National Petroleum Company arrived. They were looking for oil and were hiring strong young men to help with the heavy equipment, men who were inured to the temperature extremes of the desert. Kebzabo eagerly volunteered and was permitted to go, promising his family he would send home most of his earnings. He went seamlessly from carrying crates of pipe fittings to carrying crates of Beijing-sponsored arms throughout Chad, Sudan, and Libya. He began with bipods—

two-legged supports for assault rifles—then moved easily to the type 56 assault rifle and type 57 carbines, Chinese copies of both the AK-47 and Russian SKS. He learned to demonstrate the firearms to prospective buyers. He had an uncanny eye and his muscular build was unaffected by recoil. He earned money on the side by betting that he could shoot the prey from the talons of hawks in flight. After his boss was shown a video of his skills, Kebzabo quickly graduated to collecting late payments and exterminating competition.

And then, in his early thirties, Kebzabo went global. To this day he continued to send the bulk of his income to his family in Little Borkou.

Beijing was impressed with the young man, not just his skills and reliability but his silence. They had secretly watched him in private. He did not drink or carouse. He read, he exercised, he wrote then texted then FaceTimed with his family. Two years ago, he went to work at the Embassy of the Republic of Chad on Massachusetts Avenue NW. Officially, he was attached to the consulate as a security officer. Unofficially, he answered to a small group of handlers in the Second Department of the People's Liberation Army, the intelligence unit of the Chinese military. The American attack on the Qi-19 compound fell directly under their jurisdiction.

Kebzabo did not hate. He did not have the visceral contempt for Americans that the Chinese possessed. Even after they had told him about what the American special forces had done in China, he was not outraged. Angry people made mistakes and a man who handled sensitive arms and explosives could not afford even one. But the assassin respected his superiors and held deep, deep gratitude for the opportunity they had given him. He did what he was told.

The car circled round the Chancery and pulled up to a darkened door behind the East Office Wing. The big man moved easily from the shadows of the sedan to the shadows of the recessed entranceway. There, he was met by a man he had worked for twice since coming to the United States.

"It is good to see you," the tall, lean Chinese said quietly.

Kebzabo lowered his head in silent greeting as Dylan Hao welcomed him inside.

CHAPTER FIVE

Lady Bird Johnson Park, Washington, D.C.
March 23, 9:00 A.M.

Williams woke at six after a restless night. It was not the unknown that agitated him. Rather, it was the cruel predictability of the known. He had used the chess analogy for a reason: there were a limited number of moves at this late stage of the *Qi*-19 game.

Berry had phoned at eleven to tell Williams that Hao had agreed to meet him. The spy had suggested Lady Bird Johnson Park, formerly Columbia Island, a public place on the Boundary Channel across from the Virginia coast. Williams had agreed. The park was close enough so that he would not need his car. The vehicle, the plates, his route, and his destination were four fewer things he had to worry about being compromised. The meeting was set for 9:00 A.M.

Williams went to the curbside coffee cart before getting his car from the underground garage. He drove through the light morning traffic to the DLA to get the cash he would

need. He stuffed the large denominations in a leather portfolio and was back by 8:30 then walked toward the Potomac.

The park had opened at six and Williams waited outside for Dylan Hao. He did what everyone did who did not
want to seem conspicuous: he placed his portfolio between his
legs and checked his personal cell phone for messages. The
government-issue secure phone remained in the inside pocket
of his blue blazer, on mute. Only Matt Berry and Dylan Hao
knew where Williams was; in case anything happened to him,
the GPS function was still operative.

It was a warmish weekday and there were college students,
nannies, and others coming to enjoy the sun and the sounds of
the returning birds. There were four other people just waiting;
one young couple and two women checking their cell phones.
None of them was Dylan Hao. Williams was certain that one
of the women was a "spook," probably just a courier. She held a
thin vinyl folder tightly under one arm but no separate carrier
for a tablet or laptop. By Washington standards, she was naked.
The woman was trained but inexperienced, tense and carrying a
few select documents—although nothing that could be picked
off electronically.

At any given moment there were probably, collectively,
more intelligence operatives in D.C.-area parks than anywhere else on the planet. Part of this was because bars and
restaurants had nearby ears—and security cameras. Police
surveillance cameras were mounted high on streetlights and
announced themselves with red lights. The facial recognition
software with which they interfaced in real time was easy

to avoid by looking down. The big benefit of the parks was that no automated aerial systems were permitted within a fifteen- to thirty-mile radius of Washington Dulles International Airport and there were few surveillance cameras. The National Park Service kept their budget up by insisting that rangers, not devices, be on-site. Given the number of protests held routinely in places like the National Mall and Lafayette Park, which was adjacent to the White House, the presence of deputized personnel was also practical. Ironically, the uniqueness of park security actually added to the congestion of spies, since watchers from the FBI, the CIA, and foreign governments were themselves on-site, clandestinely surveilling clandestine activity.

Williams looked out over the river, at the pedestrians walking across the Arlington Memorial Bridge from Ohio Drive SW.

"Mr. Chase?"

The voice came from inside the park. Williams turned and saw Dylan Hao standing directly behind him. He was a head taller than Williams with slumping shoulders perched atop a lean form. The admiral made him out to be about fifty, judging by the lines on his forehead and longish, graying hair. He wore a loose-fitting green windbreaker, deerskin gloves, and he carried a cell phone. It was a Prochase model, judging from what Williams could see of the logo; a Taiwanese manufacturer.

"I hope I did not startle you," Hao said in a soft, high voice. He smiled thinly and jerked his head across the park. "I live in Virginia. The other side of the river."

"Yes, I know where Virginia is," Williams said, offering his hand.

Hao looked down at the American with bold, brown eyes as he shook his hand. "I'm sorry, Mr. Chase. I had hoped to be amusing. Is it not like the saying 'the other side of the tracks'?"

"I suppose it is, in a way," Williams replied. "I guess people from Washington think that everything comes from Washington."

"You see my meaning," Hao said, his smile broadening with apparent relief. The man extended a hand toward the park. "Shall we walk?"

Williams nodded. He picked up the portfolio with his left hand, held the cell phone in his right, and the two headed toward an expanse of lawn that sprawled gently upward from the entrance. The hardwood trees were just beginning to show renewed life and the daffodils were plentiful, awaiting the arrival of the bountiful tulips.

"Actually, I work in Virginia," Williams said.

"At the Defense Logistics Agency," Hao said quietly. "I've seen you there."

"I don't recognize you, Mr. Hao."

"I consult with a number of organizations. I only go there when I have something of an extremely . . . *delicate* nature to impart." Hao smiled slightly.

The way Hao said the word "delicate"—with the smile as a coda—suggested that the man was not talking about geopolitical intelligence but about something more personal, like sex and blackmail. Williams himself had nothing to hide in his private life. He was divorced and there was nothing scandalous in his behavior.

"Mr. Hao, why don't we get to the reason I asked to meet you—"

"You want me to furnish proof that the abduction of Dr. Dàyóu was just a pretext for the attack on the *Phoenix One*," Hao said. "You want to persuade President Wright that Beijing had been planning to make a dramatic move against America in Earth's orbit well before your actions at the Taiyuan Satellite Launch Center. Proving this intent, you hope to convince the president not to turn over the engineer and to respond to the attack in kind."

"Essentially, yes."

"All of that is not just to demonstrate American resolve and capability, but it will also save your job."

"My job is not a hot item on the list."

Hao's easy smile returned. "You've had a bellyful of government?"

"My career is not what I'm here to discuss," Williams replied. He was becoming impatient. Hao was behaving as if he were paid by the hour. "I was told to bring this." Williams raised the little briefcase.

"Yes," Hao said without reaching for the valise. "Thank you."

"That bench." Williams nodded ahead. "We'll sit there. I'll put this down, and you can tell me what you know. When I'm satisfied, I'll walk away."

"I know a great deal," Hao said. "For example, I know

that you came to this meeting to offer a bribe to a diplomatic official of the People's Republic of China."

Williams stopped. He replayed the words in his head and swore. "Triple goddamn agent," he said. In Washington, intelligence was the backbone of any operation. But disinformation was the heart and Berry had been taken by this man.

"I would say, rather, I'm a patriot," Hao told him.

Williams was angry. Angry at himself for having jumped into this, angry at Berry for having been duped, and angry at the bloody seat of power that had lost any semblance of ethics and virtue.

"Before you think of leaving," Hao said, "please note the fellow at your nine o'clock, the gentleman on the footbridge."

Williams glanced to his left. Roughly one hundred yards away a man was leaning in the rail, facing them. Hao waved to him. The man waved back. Hao turned his hardened gaze on Williams.

"My associate is carrying an automatic weapon," Hao said. "It will be discharged at the picnic grounds unless you come with me."

Williams did not doubt what the man was telling him. An experienced intelligence operative did not go through this kind of trouble to bluff. Williams had no choice. His capture could well lead to exposure for the rest of the team and he had no way to warn them. But their sworn job and privilege was to protect American lives even at the cost of their own.

"I don't appear to have a choice, do I?" Williams asked.

"We always have a choice," the other man observed.

"Come where?" Williams asked.

"For a short ride."

"That never ends well," Williams said.

"You have seen too many American crime dramas," Hao said. "There is a gentleman coming from Beijing—Mr. Jing. He will be the one to receive Dr. Dàyóu when your government has agreed to his return. And they will. He wishes to meet you."

"He could have done that at the handover."

Hao shrugged. "Mr. Jing has his ways."

"Maybe *he's* seen too many American crime dramas," Williams suggested.

Hao's humorless eyes drifted impatiently to Williams' cell phone. "I'll have that and the government-issue phone."

Williams handed him the personal device then carefully reached for the one inside his blazer. He did not want to make any movement that the assassin might take as threatening.

At Hao's urging, the men continued to walk. The personal phone went into Hao's pocket. The other was tossed in a trash can.

"Mr. Hao," Williams said, "if you're thinking that holding me and this cash 'payoff' will embarrass the administration, you've gravely miscalculated."

"I have not miscalculated," he said confidently.

Williams was about to press his captor with "*Then what . . . ?*" when his tactical mind, racing through possibilities, gave him the answer. Hao would report to Berry that

Williams had never shown up. That would preserve Hao's cover as a double agent. Berry had no way of contacting Black Wasp so he would contact the Oval Office. Someone there would notify Captain Mann.

They walked toward a van parked by the river, followed by the assassin. The vehicle had diplomatic plates and was artfully parked between street cameras on that side of the park.

For the first time in his career, Williams felt his legs unsteady. The cause was the sudden realization that he was not the objective of this maneuver. Nor did it have anything to do with China's ambitions in low Earth orbit. This was about saving face after what had happened five weeks earlier at the launch center in Shanxi Province . . . in the Chinese homeland. The ultimate target was the team that had attacked that facility and taken Dr. Dàyóu out of the country.

The goal was to use him as bait to destroy Black Wasp.

CHAPTER SIX

The White House, Washington, D.C.
March 23, 10:50 A.M.

Working for the president of the United States was not just an overwhelming job, but each of its many hungry hydra heads had conflicting needs. Whenever there was a crisis, the president's team did not have time to be shocked or sickened. That would come later. A disaster, either natural or international, had to be dealt with while, simultaneously, the nation—the people and the economy—needed its collective hand held. A press secretary could only plug the dike for a few hours. The president had to be heard from.

Before moving to the West Wing, Brunner, an attorney and former Hollywood studio head, had studied the crisis addresses of the previous two administrations. The brief talk required the commander in chief to promise, "We will hunt down these perpetrators" or "This will not stand" or "The climate has spoken and we *will* listen," and then get back to finding a way to restore equilibrium rather than satisfy the natural, national fear and bloodlust.

Both of those responses had been present in the Situation Room meeting Brunner had just attended.

The moderates—the bulk of the attendees, from the vice president to the ambassador to China who appeared via videoconference—had spoken first. And then the two figures most directly affected were called on.

"Mr. President," NASA administrator Dr. Ulla Endfield had said, "our vulnerabilities are baked into the Outer Space Treaty that China has not only broken but stomped on."

The Treaty on Principles Governing the Activities of States in the Exploration and Use of Outer Space was the 1967 document, still technically in force but brazenly ignored by signatory China. Endfield's blunt remark was met with dismissive calculation by national security advisor January Dow.

"Dr. Endfield, you were personally very close to the astronauts who have passed," Dow said. "This situation must be met with the cooler goal of stabilization and renormalization."

"Capitulation, you mean," said General Michael Buthelezi, Space Force chief of space operations. "The crew did not pass, Ms. Dow. They were murdered."

Dow might have replied—without stability, Brunner judged from her expression, had the president not immediately asked General Buthelezi to support his accusation. The officer furnished telemetry that proved the *Phoenix One* systems had failed in sequence, and on a direct course, with a hypothetical attack from the Tiangong space station. Buthelezi then urged the president to use the X-37C robot shuttle to knock out the navigational system of the Chinese orbital asset for a few hours, or to destroy a few solar panels so the base would become dangerously cold and dark until replacements could be lofted into orbit.

There had been a cacophony of responses that the president silenced by raising his hand.

"Prepare that plan, General Buthelezi," the president had advised, throwing a bone. "But I want our immediate actions to be on economic sanctions and the ramping up of unrest and dissent in the Chinese provinces, Hong Kong, and Taiwan. That remains our long game."

Angie did not disagree with that policy. China had two soft underbellies: its reliance on the United States as a consumer market and its costly, spirit-crushing anti-dissident programs. The administration believed that creating financial and domestic rot was a safer and ultimately more enduring means of dealing with Beijing.

The meeting ended there as the president needed time to address the nation. Brunner asked to be excused from that Oval Office meeting so she could apply herself to the cornerstone matter of Dr. Yang Dàyóu. Besides, she knew that the speech would not point an incriminating finger at China; not yet, probably not ever. Wright would be describing an active investigation by NASA and full cooperation from the space administrations of other nations—including "our colleagues" at the Guójiā Hángtiān Jú, the Chinese National Space Agency. He would also announce that he planned to attend a memorial service for the "heroic crew" where he would also visit with the grieving families.

As large and dangerous as this crisis was, Brunner's piece of it suddenly became a small hydra in itself. Her office was two doors from the Oval Office. Walking back, she saw that she had a text from Matt Berry flagged as urgent. The former deputy chief of staff had run both the old and new incarnations of Op-Center for President Midkiff. The only individual she and Berry had in common was Admiral Chase Williams.

The man who had approved the abduction of Dr. Dàyóu.

Brunner's deputy assistant was waiting for her but she raised an index finger as she closed her office door. Sitting on the edge of her desk, she called Berry. The woman welcomed the brief respite while the call connected. The sunlight was just beginning to appear in her southwest-facing window. After the forced-air chill of the Situation Room, daylight provided a welcome moment of normalcy.

"Angie, sorry to interrupt what I know is a busy morning," Berry said, diving right in. "Chase Williams is missing."

It took a moment to process that. "What happened?"

Berry told her about the intelligence he had picked up from China regarding Chase handling the turnover of Dr. Dàyóu, and Williams having gone to meet the source of that information. Brunner was surprised to hear all that, then annoyed.

"You've called, texted his government and personal phones, of course."

"Yes and—"

"All right, back up a bit," she said, reaching around for a yellow pad and pen on her desk. "What is the name of your source?"

"That is confidential Trigram Institute data," Berry replied.

"You're playing that card *now*?"

Berry responded with silence. Brunner had faced stone-walling in Hollywood too, but only careers were at stake there.

"All right, Matt. Keep your goddamned secret. Why didn't you let us know about the Chinese development?"

"Again, that is—"

"Screw your proprietary information." Brunner cut him off—at the knees. "You might have been more concerned about protecting your friend with backup before sending him into a risky situation."

"It was Williams' idea and that is what he does for a living."

"At the pleasure of the president."

"Williams is only answerable to the president if and when he is called in on a mission, not before," Berry said. "Look, Angie, this has been a bad morning for you, for all of us—"

"No, you don't wriggle out that way. The Op-Center charter does *not* permit its director to engage in a rogue mission—"

"Fine," Berry said. "Williams has autonomy on intelligence-gathering until and unless it involves Black Wasp. He has considerable leeway when it comes to fact-finding, which is what this meeting was." He added, "As to your point about my own actions, I don't answer to either of you."

Brunner felt marginally better for having vented. "I assume you've been in touch with the asset he was to meet?"

"I tried contacting him but he's not answering calls or texts either," Berry told her.

"Then how do you know they aren't holed up somewhere?"

"As I was going to say a minute ago, the GPS on Williams' secure phone is still active," Berry told her. "I pinpointed it in the park and I went over to see if I could spot either man. I found the phone in a trash can near a food stand. It could just as easily have been tossed in the Potomac."

"We were meant to find it."

"Yes. And discover that its owner is missing," Berry said.

"You have it now?"

"I do. My assistant Jay Paul is former CIA. The only fingerprints on the phone match those on Williams' security clearance."

Brunner let Berry's possession of government GPS codes and privileged documents slide for now.

"Why would Williams have been taken?" Brunner asked.

"Interrogation about the China mission is my guess."

"Very few people knew of his involvement," Brunner said. "He was not even *in* China. Did your source turn him over?"

"Not impossible, but he's been reliable for years. For all I know my guy was under surveillance. Perhaps he was taken too."

"All right. I've got to let the president know."

"Can you hold off at least an hour or two? He's got a lot on his plate and I want to try to find my source. Maybe Captain Mann has heard something. She and the team should at least be put on alert."

Brunner did not like Matthew Berry. She did not like the man, his style, or his deep-state ways. But unlike January Dow or some of the other career opportunists President Wright had inherited, she was smart enough to listen to the advice of even people she could not stand.

"I will call Captain Mann," she said. "I do not want you interfacing with her or her team."

"I've been where you are," Berry reminded her. "My input would only complicate things."

Brunner ended the call, let her arm fall to her leg, and sat for a moment more in the sunlight. It had not become the balm she hoped for.

"Southern California sun fixed so many problems," she said to the window. "Or maybe the problems there were not really as big as I thought."

Slipping from the desk, she made sure there were no messages from the president before placing the call to Captain Mann.

CHAPTER SEVEN

*The Officers' Club, Fort Belvoir North, Springfield,
Virginia
March 23, 10:58 A.M.*

Captain Mann was having a late breakfast at the Officers' Club,
a three-story, antebellum-style structure scenically situated at
5500 Schulz Circle, Building 20. Mann had helped herself
to the self-serve breakfast bar that offered coffee, juice, and a
selection of pastries. She sat with the tray at a rear table of the
near-empty room. This was the time of day when she reviewed
the digitized files on Op-Center, not just the current incarna-
tion but the storied past under Director Paul Hood, Deputy
Director General Mike Rodgers, Chief of Intelligence Bob
Herbert, and nearly three hundred other members.

She felt a particular kinship with these people as she
lived through moments in their lives and careers. They had
either moved on or passed; she wondered, this morning, what
they would have made of the attack on *Phoenix One.*

They would have been motivated, she knew. Intelligence

work was more than just a job to them. To a one, it was a tangible expression of their deep patriotism.

Their achievements were extraordinary, from infiltrating North Korea to prevent a new war to shutting down neo-Nazis in Europe. She was particularly impressed with the activities of the field force Striker, which came into its own when the military unit was stranded between India and Pakistan during a period of hair-trigger tension.

The four-member Black Wasp unit was a stripped-down version of Striker, the larger Joint Special Operations Command out of Fort Bragg, North Carolina, that had served Op-Center for most of its twenty-nine-year history. Like the U.S. military, both JSOC and Black Wasp uniquely answered to a civilian leader.

The highly mobile and—according to Williams' own confidential comments—at times headstrong quartet was on "extended leave" from their commissions in other branches of the military: Captain Mann from the Naval Special Warfare Development Group, Major Breen from the army's Judge Advocate General's Corps, Lieutenant Grace Lee from the Army Special Operations Command (Airborne), and Lance Corporal Jaz Rivette from the 15th Marine Expeditionary Unit. Major Breen jokingly referred to Black Wasp as "a wholly owned subsidiary of Op-Center," and the description was not inaccurate.

The team was exceptionally skilled and effective. As far as Mann could see, the only hole was in the increasingly significant

area of T-PAW—Technologically Planning and Warfare. The
virtual reality glasses she had brought to the training session
the previous night had been developed by Jessica Hawk at
Naval Support Activity in Philadelphia. Mann had under-
written its development from a Department of Defense fund
allocated for black ops technology. It was one of the perks the
captain received for allowing herself to be a poster child from
the very small pool of older women wounded warriors still in
the armed forces.

Mann had not gotten too deeply into her reading when the
phone pinged. The caller ID read "West Wing." It was Angie
Brunner; the president's ID was "Oval Office." The origin of
the call was surprising; mission directives were supposed to
go from the White House to Admiral Williams.

"This is Mann."

"Captain, it's Angie Brunner. I'm sorry to report that
Chase Williams is missing after what was supposed to be a
meeting with an intelligence source. His government phone
was found in a trash can in Lady Bird Johnson Park but we
have no information as to his whereabouts."

"What about his private phone?" Mann asked.

"It wasn't there and the voicemail folder is full."

Mann's mind was racing through the Op-Center charter.
Command falls to the ranking officer but missions must be
authorized by the president.

"What are my orders?" Mann asked.

"Captain, we've been up all night and I have to be with

the president for his remarks about the spacecraft," Angie said. "We'll revisit this later. Right now, my instructions are to make sure that Black Wasp takes no action. Any hint of aggression would be in no one's best interests."

"With respect, is it in Chase Williams' best interests for them to stand down now—"

"Captain, must I get the president on the line to make that an order?" Brunner threatened.

"No, ma'am," Mann replied.

Brunner hung up and Mann went to both her phone and laptop to see if there was a message from the admiral. Finding none, she sat silently staring intently at the list of emails as though willing one to show up.

Brunner's threat carried no weight and the question *What are my orders?* remained officially unanswered. The chief of staff did not have command authority regarding Op-Center. Even so, it had been replaced by another: *What am I supposed to do?* The answer: no soldier is left behind in war or in peace. What Mann had to figure out was how to investigate the disappearance. She did not want to involve the two younger members of Black Wasp—not yet. They would want to rush out and do something . . . anything. That was never a good idea. The response to even major events, like Pearl Harbor and 9/11, took planning.

The captain texted Major Breen and asked him to join her in the Officers' Club at once. She needed her tactician. Breen might also know who to contact for additional information. They needed to put a few red flags on a map. Mann was new to Op-Center and to Chase Williams. She did not know the admiral's professional or personal circle.

The major responded that he would be there in five minutes.

Her movements rote and disinterested, Mann absently finished her breakfast. China loomed large in her thoughts. For weeks she had been wondering not if but when and how Beijing would strike back. Was this their response? Had they learned about Op-Center and its mission, ferreted out the name of the director?

The officer strode in as if he were walking into a courtroom. His uniform was neatly pressed and the combination of military discipline and law gave him a bearing that was unique to JAG. It was not just shoulders back and head erect but eyes sharply attentive, a mind alert to examine evidence, to read the signs of innocence or guilt.

He carried a tablet under his arm. He put it on the table and slid into a seat across from Mann.

"Captain," he said, acknowledging her rank informally.

"I just received a call from the president's chief of staff," she said. "The admiral is MIA."

She had not intended to use that term; it reflected the fear she felt and it just came out. If Breen was surprised or concerned it did not show in his face. "How did she find out?"

"From Matthew Berry."

"What happened?" Breen asked.

Captain Mann revealed what little she knew up to checking for a communication from Williams. Breen did the same. There was nothing.

"Another BAM," the major said thoughtfully.

"What is that?"

"It's the name the admiral gave to his private sorties after meetings with Berry—Budget Activity Missions."

"Tell me about their relationship," she urged.

"If you're thinking Berry might have played fast and loose with the admiral's safety, that's never been the case. He was a professional politician, a canny player, but he always looked out for the admiral and Op-Center."

"That was before he went to the Trigram think tank," Mann said. "That's a for-profit organization."

"Berry is loyal to Chase Williams," Breen stated. "The admiral has been a mentor and a father figure."

"So the leak wasn't with him. The source?"

"A likely possibility."

"What I don't understand is why abductors would discard the admiral's work phone," Mann said. "They wouldn't know we burn stored data and communiqués before and during a mission."

"The admiral actually goes further," Breen said. "Chase is the only one of us who makes official calls during the course of his day so it autoscrubs every hour. The only value of the phone would be to us, pinpointing his location. Which it's done."

"Berry went there," Mann said. "He was apparently not molested or approached."

"Berry's position with Trigram was announced in political

journals and on intelligence websites," Breen said. "If someone wanted him they already knew where to find him. No, it appears that Op-Center is the target."

"We have to assume someone is watching the park where the phone was found," the captain said.

"Watching for whom? None of us is known outside of the president and the chief of staff."

"Then perhaps we should go and have a look around," she said. "We watch any watchers."

Breen shook his head. "Black Wasp tends to cause collateral damage wherever they go. I don't like it, but that's the nature of the missions and the team. We can't risk that."

"Then—what?"

"The others will have to be briefed at some point," Breen said. "In the meantime, I'd like to put on civvies and go to where Berry found the phone. I've been to crime scenes and presuming this is one, I may pick up something Berry missed."

"Will you be armed?"

He shook his head as he stood. "That's something a park ranger might pick up on. It wouldn't do to be stopped and questioned." He grinned. "I'll wear my lucky bomber jacket. UV has never let me down."

"All right," the captain said. "Would you keep an open line, though?"

"Of course."

Mann did not have to say it; Breen understood.

If the same thing happened to him as happened to Chase Williams, she wanted to know who, when, where, and how.

CHAPTER EIGHT

Wang Jing prided himself on being a man of sharp, shifting contrasts. It kept his friends and adversaries unsteady.

His appearance alone was a visual statement of that. He was pasty-faced and soft, a tall, bulky man who got little sun and no exercise. But his eyes were those of a predator and his other senses were alert to every sound, smell, touch, and taste—poison was always dangerous background noise in his line of work. His expression was supernaturally calm, as though the man who wore it had no opinion about anything.

Only that last part was misleading. He had iron-firm views about everything from nations to the people that ran them, dwelt in them, served them.

Over a period of twenty-seven years, Wang Jing had earned a reputation as one of the most methodical and effective interrogators in the People's Liberation Army. His conscientious analysis of prisoners and his careful conduct during interviews was balanced by extreme measures that solved emergent problems without delay. His methods were so highly regarded that he was permitted to bypass his immediate superiors to report directly to the intelligence division of China's Central Military Commission.

Now, the forty-nine-year-old was a deputy director of the CCMC. And this journey he knew—*knew*—would be the peak of his career. The trip on the CCMC 737 aircraft would deliver the directorship to him and from there the path to supreme power was clear. The power to ensure that China never again suffered a humiliation like the one that struck the missile facility. Ironically, that disaster would be the backbone of his ascension.

For three weeks, under his direction, two branches of law enforcement had been investigating the matter of the men who had stolen a truck carrying thirteen women being trafficked between Mongolia and China. The men had set the young ladies free then abandoned the truck. The women claimed to know nothing about their saviors, and the People's Armed Police, Jinzhou, had released them. At the same time the Border Defense Corps canvassed the Jinzhou neighborhood where the truck was spotted. They were looking for anyone who had seen the men. Those interviews turned up nothing. Two days later, during a scan of traffic flow videos, images were found showing the cab of the truck; a high-definition image was rendered of the two occupants. One of them was a white man, the other a Black man—neither of them Asian. Their identities were unknown and still of low priority. Publicly, the Ministry of State Security did not approve of human trafficking. Privately, they received kickbacks and did not want the trade interrupted. The image was sent to Chinese and Chinese-affiliated agencies in the region, a routine procedure that typically turned up nothing.

However, one month after the incident, the Procedure and Documentation Section of the Mongolian Civil Aviation Authority sent the Chinese minister of state security a surveillance photo from the International Airport in Ulaanbaatar, Mongolia. It showed Dr. Dàyóu, his wife, and his daughter in the company of two other individuals: one was a white man, one was a Black man. Their identities still were not known.

The case was immediately given top priority and was booted up to the CCMC. Wang Jing's task was to identify the two American agents. That would be a part of the larger move against the team that had staged the murderous attack on the Taiyuan Satellite Launch Center. Beijing wanted those operatives dead. All of them, and their leaders. Wang Jing intended to make that happen. Now that they had faces, if not names, the focus of the investigation was expanded to include the United States.

The man tasked with the American search was Dylan Hao. Hao was a Taiwan native who fervently believed in the one-China policy. He had gone to school at Georgetown University in Washington, D.C., in 1996 to study political science. Going to work at the Chinese embassy as a double agent—actually working for Beijing—he had managed to insert himself in the good graces of the intelligence community by spreading minor truths—what the intelligence services rightly called "chicken feed"—to gain credibility. All the while he was picking up as much information as he could about counterintelligence activity against Beijing.

Jing knew that this was a risky undertaking. The enemy was far from helpless and, this time, they would be on their home territory. Yet he felt youthful eagerness balanced by seasoned confidence as he sat in the VIP lounge at Beijing Capital Airport. He was waiting to board an Air China flight to Washington, D.C. Officially, Jing was going to meet up with a delegation from the consulate to collect Dr. Dàyóu and his family. Beijing was confident that the handover would be accomplished within days. That mission was for the nation, for its pride.

Unofficially, however, Jing was going to Washington to put an end to the humiliation China had suffered. Through Hao, who had a reliable source in the private sector, Jing had learned that the operatives were based in or near the American capital. Through a simple ruse—insisting that the team leader was required for the handover—Hao had taken the man prisoner. Now, armed with the two photographs, Jing was hopeful Hao would find the others. Jing wanted the leader interrogated, humiliated. He wanted to make sure that the two men in the photograph died. He wanted the woman who had attacked the missile center to be identified and killed— only after she had suffered. He wanted everyone involved in the operation to be wiped out, their headquarters razed, an example made that would not need to be made again.

An aide informed him that the pilots had checked the aircraft and were prepared to take off.

"The military guard?" Jing asked. The returning heroes must be met with ceremony, not just shadows in the night as these handoffs usually went. There was great propaganda value in this.

The aide informed her superior that the ten-man squad were in their seats. Jing acknowledged and said he would board shortly. Jing dismissed her.

"Hold!" Jing said suddenly.

"Sir?" she turned back.

"It is a momentous journey we are about to undertake," he said. "Leave-taking does not occur with cavalier haste."

"Yes, Mr. Deputy Director," the young woman said, bowing.

Jing dismissed her again. He stood and inhaled the air of his homeland. Most of all he wanted to witness the suffering of the man who had masterminded the attack on his beloved homeland, Hao's prisoner, the man named Chase.

CHAPTER NINE

Embassy of the People's Republic of China,
Washington, D.C.
March 23, 11:46 A.M.

If there was a time to be philosophical, this probably was not it. Yet Chase Williams had nothing to do but pray, muse, or regret. There were no plans to make, no actionable input, and prayer had always come automatically and silently. That left just detached contemplation.

Williams had been shown to a black sedan on the Virginia-facing side of the park. The individual who had been described as a gunman did not join them; he remained where he was. Hao sat beside Williams in the back while the driver—a young woman in a black suit and red tie—looked ahead, watched the road, and spoke only into a radio when they started out, her voice a clipped, undisturbed monotone.

The admiral did not have to ask where they were going. The driver started her short call with the words *dàshǐ guǎn.* Williams knew enough Mandarin to know that meant "embassy." It was a stronger expression than *shǐguǎn* which meant "diplomatic mission." *Dàshǐ guǎn* was not an outpost. It was a place "of the homeland." The compound *was* China.

What had Williams thinking in abstractions was the wasteful process of thought. A few hours ago—hell, thirty minutes ago—if the president or Captain Mann had said, "Admiral, under what conditions do you think you will go to the Chinese embassy?" he would have replied, "To hand over Dr. Yang Dàyóu."

He should not have been surprised. Did any mission with Op-Center ever go as its considerable brain trust had planned? Did *any* shopworn expression about plans ever advocate for them?

"Life is what happens to us while we're making other plans."

"The best laid schemes o' mice an' men. Gang aft a-gley."

"No plan survives first contact with the enemy."

"Man plans and God laughs."

Even victory, the success in China—not just nabbing Dr. Dàyóu but giving renewed life and hope to thirteen trafficked women—seemed like nothing more than a staging area for defeat.

Williams watched as Washington, D.C., loomed through the dark window. He wondered if Hao had sat to his right on purpose, affording the admiral a clear view of the familiar landmarks as they approached. A pane of glass was all that separated him from his beloved heritage, from a do-over: a fresh chance to get this right . . . or at least better. It might just as well have been an ocean.

In less than ten minutes they were at the embassy and then behind its great iron gates. Williams had seen them before—from the outside. Then, the gates had seemed functionally decorative. Now they seemed—they *were*—prison doors.

"I want to show you something," Hao said as they pulled up to the main door of the central building, the one that looked like a church with its steeple lopped off.

Williams sat with disinterest as the car stopped. He did not bother looking over as Hao removed a glove, slipped his left hand into the windbreaker, easily withdrawing a pair of photographs. He handed them to Williams. The admiral accepted them, his arms and hands unwilling clay. He looked down without interest.

The color images were heavily pixelated and fuzzy. It took him a moment to make them out. One showed a small group at an airport. The other was a picture of two men in a truck. It took him a moment to realize that the two men were in both photographs.

They were Hamilton Breen and Jaz Rivette.

Williams screamed from deep in his chest; he heard the cry before he even realized it was coming from him. He turned in his seat, was on Hao a moment later, his hands reaching for the man's face. The door behind the admiral opened, admitting bright sunlight and two pairs of hands, one set belonging to the driver and the other to a guard.

The strong, coordinated attack yanked Williams back, dragged him from the car, and dropped him on the cobbled road. He heard Chinese voices and shoes on the stones around him. He was looking up at faces moving in silhouette against the blue sky until dark plummeted into view—a black leather glove with the heavy butt of a CZ75 Phantom service pistol. The next thing Williams saw was a flash of fat red lightning, followed by pain that shot from the front to the back of his skull, followed by oblivion.

CHAPTER TEN

Lady Bird Johnson Park, Washington, D.C.
March 23, 12:01 P.M.

Hamilton Breen took a cab to the South Arlington Boulevard on the city side of the island. He was dressed in jeans and leather jacket, no baseball cap or sunglasses—the giveaway tools of a government operative.

He walked at a leisurely pace toward the park as though enjoying a spring noon. The lunchtime crowd would afford him cover as he made his way toward the spot at the food pavilion where Williams' cell phone had been found.

Breen did not leave the base very much. He shopped there, ate there, and did not have any local friends. He used to walk a great deal around the University of Virginia campus, home of the JAG Legal Center and School, where he taught up-and-coming JAG officers and, during summers, corps newbies. He had a motorcycle that he rode on weekends, close friends like Chief Bob Fender of the UVA Police Department—and then there was Inez Levey, an American history professor. The two had a strong romantic relationship—which, unfortunately, did not survive the first few months Breen spent with Op-Center. It was not just distance that came between them—the campus was not so far away—but Breen's globalized concerns. A college campus was a neatly kept garden; the world was a weedy mess. The chaos changed him. Strong, constant effort was required to stay ordered and sane amidst the bloodshed and chaos.

Stepping into Lady Bird Johnson Park was both a balm and a shock. It was neat and safe, at least on the surface. The experience was different from walking the streets of Yemen or Trinidad where he did not speak the language or resemble the locals, where survival required him to assume that everyone was a potential threat. He was not overly distracted as he tried to put himself in Williams' place, figure out where the admiral might have walked for a private meeting. Or did he hide in plain sight at the food stand or on the footbridge or on a bench? Breen would go to each of them, methodically look for something that did not belong, some clue Williams might have dropped like the lucky Indian Head nickel he carried or the silver-and-black onyx navy ring he wore.

Breen spotted the trash can where Matt Berry had found the admiral's phone when his own Op-Center device buzzed in his pocket. Only Williams and Black Wasp had this number. His heart kicked up a notch as he retrieved it.

There was a text message from Captain Mann. ID'd anonymously as #2 in the event the phone was taken:

WH says CIA watcher at Chinese embassy
reports man pulled from official vehicle.

> There was a scuffle behind the gates. From
> observer's description it could have been our
> party. Return to base asap.

The major's heart continued to hammer as he reread the message twice. He was surprised to find his finger unsteady as he acknowledged receipt of the message and put the phone back in his jacket pocket. His heart continued to hammer.

From the start, theirs had not been the kind of military association Breen was accustomed to, what he called the "civilized wood-paneled relationship." Breen and Williams had been shoulder to shoulder on all of those dangerous, improvised Black Wasp missions. They had also looked out for each other and for the two younger members.

This hurt.

It also changed things. The major now knew three things: where Williams was, who had him, and the reality that President Wright would not spend diplomatic coin trying to get the admiral back. Williams was a casualty of his own unilateral decisions, judgments that did not reflect U.S. policy.

Dammit, Chase, how many times did we have this discussion? he thought. The descending chains of command never had all the information required to make a fully informed decision.

Breen understood the reasons the Chinese might have taken the admiral. They were sound, even justified. The whole situation stank.

The major shoved his hands in his jacket pockets to stop

them from shaking. He stood there and looked out at the Washingtonians and tourists smiling, reading, going about their leisurely business. He reminded himself that each member of Black Wasp understood what they were risking when they signed on. He also knew that behind him, in the marble, granite, and steel buildings of the nation's capital, literally thousands of stories like his were playing out, each one weighing oppressively on someone. That was the nature of any center of power. That awareness did not make Breen feel any better about their leader being gone, but it did help him to feel not so alone.

He turned to leave the park and retrieved his phone to call a car service. The good news was that alone among Black Wasp, he was not entirely helpless. He was a military attorney. There was still a mission. The embassy *was* China, and American law held no sway over Beijing. But there might be something he could use in the International Prisoner Transfer Program legislation passed in 1977—something to pressure the administration not to return Dr. Dàyóu without the surrender of a prisoner of equal importance. He began scrolling through 18 U.S.C. §§4100–4115, searching for the definition of "cornerstone value" that would place Chase Williams on par with—

Breen felt himself pushed back as if he were struck by a powerful gust. An instant later the screen of the phone went red. Major Breen steadied himself, was about to damn the spotty reception when he saw red running down the right side of his jacket.

"What the hell—?"

The next punch pushed him back again only this time his legs folded. He was aware of dropping the phone and falling but those were his last mortal thoughts as the second bullet opened the back of his head, pinged off the trash can behind him, and scudded across the short spring grass.

Around the dead man a single scream became a chorus of shouts that became a stampede of running parkgoers and voices shouting "911" into voice-activated phones.

•   •   •

Joseph Kebzabo was not yet among those fleeing the scene. He was squatting behind an oak tree, waiting. He had taken a cell phone picture with his left hand after the first shot, then with his right, he made the killshot and now waited to take another photo. They went into the same folder as the images Dylan Hao had emailed him showing this man in Mongolia and in China.

The assassin stayed where he was, ducking as if he were fearful and hiding, and shoved the compact, silenced .22 caliber Long Rifle into the open computer bag on the ground beside him. Kebzabo waited as park rangers converged on the picnic area before crawling, then running off as though fleeing the scene.

The rangers ignored him. Police always did. In his plain brown suit and fedora he looked unthreatening. Kebzabo made himself skittish, ordinary, fitting no go-to profile for law enforcement. Killers—whether trained or simply homicidal—tended toward extremes, either too slick or too wild. This man seemed like he belonged wherever he was. Law enforcement would also assume that the shooter would have been the first to flee and blend in with the mob. He would not still be nearby, among them.

Knowing that the target would begin his search at the trash can where Hao's unwitting ally Berry had found the phone, Kebzabo had chosen this spot so that he could move from tree to tree—not furtively but fearfully, appearing to seek cover. When he was away from the proximate circle of park rangers he would vanish on the other side of a rise. Moving out, the assassin listened as the Washington Police Department cars arrived, followed within moments by the unmarked vehicles of the FBI. He quickened his pace so he could be out of the park before a wide, outer cordon could take shape.

And then he was gone.

He did not secure a cab on the other side of the Arlington Memorial Bridge. Records of all hired vehicles going to and from the park would be collected by investigators. Instead, he walked just over a quarter mile to the National Mall. There, out of view of any surveillance cameras, he removed his hat, slung his jacket over his arm, and continued on foot roughly one-third of a mile to the embassy. Even if a park ranger saw and remembered the man in the brown fedora, he would have vanished in the Mall and surveillance cameras would only show Joseph Kebzabo hatless, in a dress shirt, walking to an appointment.

CHAPTER ELEVEN

The Officers' Club, Fort Belvoir North,
Springfield, Virginia
March 23, 12:05 P.M.

When Major Breen left, Captain Mann had remained in the Officers' Club. There was no reason to return to the residence. Lieutenant Lee would be talking to her parents in New York and Jaz would be catching up with his friends in San Pedro. They merited this downtime and deserved their privacy. The two came from wildly different backgrounds but they worked harder than any enlistees she had ever known.

Lieutenant Lee was the only daughter of a father who published the *Mulberry Community* newspaper and a mother who was his fact-checker and compositor. The weekly was pro-reunification with Taiwan but against the Chinese Communist Party. Grace never struggled with that apparent conflict because all her *sifus* in a lifetime of martial arts training were fierce patriots who felt the same.

Lance Corporal Rivette was of Cajun descent. He grew up on the opposite coast, raised in a poor section of San Pedro.

Though he had an extended family he was closest to his friends and mentors at the Los Angeles Police Department. Rivette had discovered a talent for marksmanship at age ten when he stopped a bodega robbery with the proprietor's .38. The LAPD enrolled Rivette in a junior marksmanship program. Since joining the Marines at age twenty, the young man had won a Distinguished Marksman Badge, a Distinguished Pistol Shot Badge, numerous other citations and medals.

Mann admired them both, even when their impulsive go-get-'em nature had—according to Williams' reports—caused mission creep in the field and created diplomatic problems at home. Like the one with China and Dr. Dàyóu.

Mann had been trying to concentrate on the files but continually checked the time, told herself this is when Major Breen left the base; this is when he will arrive at the park; this is how long a quick surveillance would take. Her patent attention to every passing instant had been interrupted when Angie Brunner called.

"The Chinese have Chase Williams," she had said in an open rage. "A CIA spotter saw him struggling behind the gates of the embassy."

Mann had felt as though she were kicked in the throat. Not that she had anything to say; words, even thoughts were frozen in her head. When Mann had finally freed them and was able to speak, her voice was low; two other officers had entered the room.

"Has—has there been any confirmation from his captors?"

"None," Brunner had snapped. "If and when such information is received I will notify you. It may be a while."

"Of course."

Brunner went on, like a tank. "I want to reiterate that Op-Center, Black Wasp, are to do nothing. Any action you might take will only make matters worse. Do you understand, Captain?"

Mann had not had a chance to answer before Brunner hung up. As though in a stupor, the captain had immediately texted the information to Breen. As soon as he had acknowledged she felt some of her tension leave. The captain was no longer aware of the seconds that he was potentially in danger.

The captain gathered up her things and smiled blankly at the two unfamiliar officers as she passed. She put on her sunglasses and let the sun wash over her as she breathed the fuel-tinged air that to her was the smell and taste of home. The sense of being rooted did not dispel the dark, dark feeling that Williams had not been taken as a hostage but as a prisoner. But that had not been her immediate concern. She was thinking, first and foremost, about how to contain the two other members of Black Wasp. The ones who would not so easily accept the edict from Angie Brunner.

• • •

Jaz Rivette hated phoning. He loved talking with his "three ladies"—his mother and two younger sisters—but it felt unnatural not to videoconference. Unfortunately, Zoom and Skype and every other service were not permitted.

"It might give away some clue to your location," Major Breen had told him when he first arrived at the residence.

"A bedroom?" Rivette had questioned, before quickly remembering to add, "They'll see—a wall, sir. Or I can drop in, y'know, some old photo."

"Regulations," Breen had replied. "Pretend you're still at Camp Pendleton, Marine."

The lance corporal came around, in time. There were bad people "out there" in the hacking world, some of them sophisticated enough to see through window shades or match the time and the angle of the sun to pinpoint a location or even see what time he got up by seeing the closeness of his shave. Still, just pressing the green phone icon when the phone wanted him to engage video felt—

"Lame," he muttered.

Rivette lay on his back on the bed after ending the call. He was sorry to hear that one of his childhood friends in their low-income housing complex near the port had been wounded in a stabbing attack. The lance corporal was not surprised; Little Guillermo, who was actually about six foot four, was in the massage parlor business that the Russians wanted. It was only a matter of time before they moved on his three locations. He wondered if Guillermo would sell the storefronts or fight back.

"What would you do?" he asked himself as he removed the earbuds and went to his Instagram account to see if the Mexicans had posted about the incident.

Rivette did not answer his own question, distracted by a

selection of images showing women walking pigs on a beach in Tonga.

"I don't know where you are, Tonga, but you have fine ladies," he muttered as he thumbed through the crisp, sunny images.

And then he came on a "suggested post" from someone named BloodyLBJ. It was uploaded within the last minute, a short video shot by a phone in a trembling hand with the comment: "the Johnson name gave us Vietnam and that MF keeps bleeding."

Rivette did not get the reference but the images were from a park with people running and crying and slamming into each other. What was left behind was a body on the grass, legs and arms akimbo in a way that Rivette had seen before. The person on their back, on the ground, had been shot. The camera zoomed in.

"This post ain't lasting long," Rivette said when he saw the blood on the leather jacket, on the grass, and then on the forehead. "Social media overlords are gonna—"

Rivette sat up hard. He looked at the video with fresh, clarifying scrutiny as it ended.

"*Lieutenant!*" he shouted. "Shit, goddamn—*Grace!*"

The lieutenant did not charge into the room but cracked the closed door, stepped back, and kicked it open with a heel.

"No, we're cool!" Rivette said. "Nobody here. You gotta see this. I think it's Major Breen!"

The woman appeared in the open door and relaxed her

fighting stance. Her expression shaded from disapproval to curiosity as Rivette held up the phone.

"Quick!" he urged. "Before it's pulled!"

Grace took the phone from Rivette and he swung off the bed to look over her shoulder. They watched the short video together twice. Though the dead man was missing the top part of his head, they recognized the jawline and bomber jacket.

Grace swiped away from Instagram and went to the local news on Fox 5. There were breaking headlines about a shooting in Lady Bird Johnson Park.

AN UNIDENTIFIED MALE REPORTEDLY IN HIS MID-THIRTIES . . .

HE WAS SEEN USING HIS PHONE JUST BEFORE . . .

LAW ENFORCEMENT HAS SEALED THE PARK . . .

THERE IS NO SUSPECT OR MOTIVE . . .

The front door of the residence clicked and Grace simultaneously flipped the phone on the bed, crouched, and went to the bedroom door.

Rivette dropped to a knee and retrieved the M1911 semi-automatic from the nightstand where he had placed it after training. He flicked off the safety.

Black Wasp is under attack, he thought as, duckwalking, he joined Grace at the jamb. She was listening with Rivette tight behind her. A moment later she relaxed and stood.

"It's the captain," she said and walked out.

Mann's face was without expression as she entered the foyer. She did not offer a greeting as she usually did.

"It's true, isn't it?" Rivette asked.

Mann stopped. "How did you know?"

"It's on social media," he replied. "There's video."

The captain was confused. "Of the embassy?"

"No," Rivette answered. "Of Major Breen."

Mann stopped breathing; her chest just locked up on her for a long, long moment. She flashed back to Afghanistan, to a handful of missions were nothing went right and losses were high. The captain inhaled hard through her nose.

"What about Major Breen?" she asked.

Rivette went back to the room to get his phone.

"There was a shooting in Lady Bird Johnson Park," Grace informed her. "The victim is dead."

Rivette returned with the phone. The video had not yet been taken down. He held it so the captain could see.

There was no doubt: it was Breen. Mann took the phone and zoomed in. There was a bloody University of Virginia patch on the shoulder.

"You two have to leave, at once," Mann said. There was no time to mourn, not now.

"You were about to tell us something else," Grace pressed. "What is it, sir?"

"Admiral Williams," Mann said. "He was seen being off-loaded from a vehicle behind the gates of the Chinese embassy. There was a struggle." She looked from Grace to Rivette. "The Chinese are hunting Black Wasps. The admiral won't tell them anything, not willingly, but the Chinese use a potent form of scopolamine, SP-17. They'll find out where we are."

"Understood," Grace said.

"You can take the ISV."

The ISV was an Infantry Squad Vehicle, a light utility transport that seated four.

"If it's all the same, sir, I'd prefer to be on foot," Grace said.

"I'm with the lieutenant," Rivette said. "I like my rides but quick pivots are better when you're being hunted."

"All right," Mann said. "And Lieutenant? If we communicate for any reason do not tell me where you are or where you're going."

Mann did not have to explain why. She might be taken as well.

"Come on," Grace said, grabbing some of her martial arts tools and their tactical uniforms before Rivette had finished processing the information.

"Where?" the lance corporal asked.

"We'll figure that out when we're off base," she said. Grace stopped to adjust the garments in her bag and turned. "There are not many people we can trust."

"The admiral relied on Matt Berry," Mann said. "Major Breen and I were discussing him—"

"Berry," Grace cut her off. She did not want to think of the major right now. She had to stay focused. "It's an option. Are you coming, Captain?"

Mann shook her head. "Sooner rather than later the White House will learn the identity of the shooting victim. I suspect I will not be asked to present myself; I will be escorted over."

"All the more reason to get out!" Rivette said.

"I'm in command," she reminded him. "You have your orders. My place is here."

Rivette pressed his lips together and saluted the captain as he followed Grace to their respective rooms. Being off duty they were already in civilian clothes. In less than five minutes, with backpacks slung over their shoulders, they were simultaneously saluting the officer and fighting tears and anger as they left the house.

Behind them, with the door closed, Captain Mann surrendered to the horror, turning to the wall, putting her arm stiffly against it, and sobbing for a lifetime of death and loss and anguish . . .

CHAPTER TWELVE

Embassy of the People's Republic of China,
Washington, D.C.
March 23, 12:59 P.M.

Chase Williams woke with a severe headache. His forehead pulsed beneath a raised lump, possibly the result of a concussion, but it was the back that hurt from the middle of his neck to the top of his skull.

He was on his back, in a bed, one with a hard mattress. The pillow was not much softer. He was still in the clothes he had been wearing—

In the park, he remembered. *In a car.*

The admiral opened his eyes in darkness, heard nothing but muted conversation. He heard a mechanical whisper from somewhere overhead. He tried to raise his head but gave that up when a lightning flash exploded in the bump and drilled through both eyes.

He lay back. His mouth was dry. The air tasted mechanical—forced air. That was the sound he heard. He turned his head just a little from one side to the other, saw no telltale signs of daylight or of a window.

He remembered arriving at the Chinese embassy. That was probably where he was now. There was a scuffle, a blow on the head—

The photographs.

The fight had been triggered by two images of Major Breen and Lance Corporal Rivette that Dylan Hao had showed him. Williams had wanted to kill the man, not because Hao worked dutifully for an enemy government but because he had taken pleasure displaying the pictures. Williams still wanted to beat the man until his own fists were raw but in addition to the pain in his head there was unfamiliar pressure on his wrists.

He shifted his body from side to side, and the bed moved enough to rattle the bars on either side. Williams was tied to them with leather straps. He tried to call out but his throat was raspy, his mouth dry.

Jesus wept, he thought suddenly.

He bent his right arm as much as he could, then the left. There was a bandage in the bend of the elbow. He had been drugged—and not to sleep but to talk. From the soreness there he knew that his interrogators had not given him an injection but an intravenous drip.

He did not think the blow on the head caused all the cloudiness and pain he was feeling. God and the Chinese alone knew what he told them.

Williams could not call out. He did not have enough spit

to swallow. There was nothing to do but try to shake the bed harder. The effort was enormous and the pain great, but he wanted to see someone, anyone. Spit might come, then.

There was a door at the foot of the bed. When it opened Williams saw the silhouette of a man framed in yellow light. A lamp flicked on in a far corner of the room. It revealed Dylan Hao with the same self-contented look he had been wearing in the car.

Hao entered and shut the door behind him. He grabbed a wooden chair from another corner and sat beside the bed. A blackjack hung from his belt. It had a rubber grip, a heavy plastic spring on top, and a heavy rubber club affixed to that. He smiled.

Hao noticed Williams' eyes fall to the weapon.

"In my line of work, one needs protection that won't set off alarms," he said. "It's become a part of me."

Williams did not reply. He did not yet have the energy to speak.

"I'm sorry about the restraints," Hao said. "You had a lot of fight outside."

"Have," Williams corrected. It was the only word he could push from his dry throat and papery lips.

"Yes, rev away," Hao said. "But you're set in idle now. You won't be going anywhere unless it is to serve our needs."

Williams was not one for forced bravado and he did not respond. There was no avoiding the reality: lashed to a bed, on his back, in a dark room, stripped of his secrets and sub-sisting on water, a man was not worth very much. He did not allow himself the luxury of self-pity but neither did he pretend things were better than they were.

Hao took a cup of water from the nightstand and offered the straw to Williams.

The admiral refused.

"Take a sip," Hao insisted. "Not for me but for your own—let's call it your recovery, body and spirit. There are things you'd like to tell me, I'm sure. Not *work*-related. I mean about how you feel. *What* you feel."

Williams felt woefully incomplete and took the sip. "Who—who is handling the negotiations with my government?" Williams asked, with effort.

"Ambassador Qiang herself."

"Would you tell her—" Williams began, with effort. "Would you—tell her that whatever you're planning, don't." The admiral's tone was not belligerent but was almost conciliatory.

"Why not?"

"It's a zero-sum game," Williams said. "You lost face, you'll get it back by humiliating us, me."

"Humiliate . . . you? How?"

"By having me present at the handover."

Hao actually laughed. "That was never a consideration. We have asked for January Dow to be present and she has agreed."

Williams felt like an amateur. And an ass. That story was only to draw him out. And he, and Berry, had fallen for it. And Dow—that was a brilliant, careful choice or compromise or whatever it was. China got a high-profile administration official to eat crow and Dow, in the limelight, would be grateful for the meal.

Hao shook his head. "Do you know what losing face is? For over a year now I had to let Mr. Matt Berry think that he is a trusted friend. I had to sit across from him over coffee or beer. I had to take the cloth or paper napkin in which he had folded hundred-dollar bills. And then—here is where it hurt— and then I had to pull my mouth into something resembling a smile. The way that becomes a zero-sum game for me is to smile for real each and every time I strike. I have waited for this since you came to my country to kidnap, sabotage, and murder. You cannot reverse course."

"That's true," Williams said. "But believe this, I implore you. I'm a fighting man who prayed, on my knees, for the day I might not be needed. I would rather see us fight, if we must fight, with ideas instead of bullets."

"The biography of history is against you," Hao said. "All of this might be a stimulating dinner's conversation if you were not already too late."

The words chilled him, once again casual and devoid of regret. Williams dared not imagine the scope of what "too late" meant. He had no thoughts, no threats to throw at the man.

Hao unhooked a cell phone from his belt. He brought up a video from social media. Williams did not want to look at it but, anticipating that, Hao leaned forward suddenly, slapped an open palm on his prisoner's forehead and pressed upward, forcing Williams' eyes open and keeping his head firmly in place. Hao's demeanor changed in that moment from the bored host to the enraged captor.

"You will not turn away!"

Williams' eyes became a battlefield and he tried to pull the lids shut. Hao pressed harder on his forehead, on the gash left by the gun. The searing pain forced his eyes wide and he saw, through the flashing bolt of pain, a video image of Hamilton Breen lying on grass, in two growing patches of blood.

Regret and sorrow crushed Williams' will. His chest heaved.

Hao moved the phone away and bent close. He looked directly into the anguished eyes of his captive.

"*That* is what my friends General Zhou Chang and Captain Shen Laihang looked like on the ground outside Qincheng Prison, where your operative left them," he snarled. "The general died of his injuries two days later. The captain was stripped of his rank for having survived. If these are 'games of state,' then it is a new game."

Hao rose. Williams lay limp.

"Those two photographs I showed you," Hao said. "We knew from the timing that someone else attacked the satellite launch center and then Qincheng. We knew from reports out of Taiyuan that the raider was a lone wolf, a young woman. A highly skilled woman who dishonored her heritage by turning her skills against her people. A woman whose name, thanks to you, we now know."

Hao nodded toward the bandage.

Williams prayed that Hao was lying, that this was a ruse to get him to say her name. But it was a foggy, empty hope.

"Lieutenant Grace Lee, one of five members of a special ops team known as Black Wasp," Hao went on with a satisfied expression. "Excuse me—four members, now. Three members if we include the fact that you are never going back to them. The others are Lance Corporal Jaz Rivette and Captain Ann Ellen Mann. They are based at Fort Belvoir. That location makes our objective difficult but hardly insurmountable. Unlike the gullible Major Breen, it's too bad we cannot make them come to us. But we have to be done with this quickly since President Wright is suing for a truce."

It was the hellish cost of doing business, Williams told himself. *The men they had attacked were key pieces in a program of world domination.*

"It *will* be done, thanks to you—Mr. Chase, or rather, Mr. Chase Williams." Hao continued. "Grace Lee is going to suffer before she ends up under a flag like your major. She will know pain in proportion to her misdeeds. The others will die as well. You met their slayer, in fact. You were drugged and found his name amusing—'Tang.' Like a space drink, you said. Nonetheless, you pointed him in the direction he needed to go."

"You're dirt." It was all Williams could think to say and he packed as much venom in the word as possible. "We all do our duty, on both sides of this conflict, but you're *enjoying* this."

Hao smiled. "Two corrections, Admiral. First, you *did* your duty. Your responsibilities are ended. Second, what a fool a man would be if he did not enjoy his work."

Williams was out of arguments, reason had fled.

Hao smiled one last time before shutting the door behind him.

The admiral had mourned fellow soldiers before. It was a terrible inevitability of their trade, a possibility that came with any uniform. Breen was a good man and a fine officer. He would have been grateful for that epitaph.

As for Williams, he might be defeated but he was not broken. A practicing Catholic, he asked God to watch over the soul of Hamilton Breen and the three others he had failed, insisting that whatever sins they committed were ultimately his. Then he recited Mark 11:25, begging forgiveness for those sins.

Though God had to know, and hopefully understand, that Williams would have traded his stained soul to the devil to be upright with a carbine.

CHAPTER THIRTEEN

The Mulberry Community *Office, Mulberry Street,*
New York, New York
March 23, 1:13 P.M.

Rosamund Lee hung up the landline, took a moment to center herself, then left her small, fire hazard of an office and walked to where her husband was conferring with his reporters. It was an informal gathering, the older man with his even older journalists standing around the teapot on a hot plate in the composing room. They still called it that, and the old wooden floor still bore the discoloration of where the Linotype machine had once stood. But there were now three computers on three desks, and they were wired directly to the printer in Brooklyn.

Kent Lee was standing in the small reception area of the *Mulberry Community*. He did his writing and editing in the storefront, where he felt he was in constant touch with the pulse of his neighborhood and his friends in adjacent Little Italy. He was making a point with passion and spilling tea from the Styrofoam cup as he did. The fifty-year-old was emphatic about everything, even when he said good morning.

Kent Lee turned when he heard the floor creak, saw his wife standing just inside the main office where Rosamund worked with the two reporters and the photographer. Kent had seemed annoyed at the interruption until he had a moment to explore his wife's expression. Without a mid-sentence pause in his discourse—about the rising number of Chinese youths turning to crime—he dismissed the two reporters, put the cup on a desk, and walked over to her.

"What is it?" he asked. "We spoke to Grace"—he looked at his watch—"ninety minutes ago."

"She called again," Rosamund said.

Kent moved closer. "Is she all right?"

"I don't know," the woman admitted.

As much as the Lees were devoted to their community in Manhattan's historic Chinatown, nothing came before their daughter. They had embraced her lifetime study of martial arts and accepted the inevitability that she was going to grow up to be a warrior. Grace had never furnished many details about her life at Fort Bragg in North Carolina. She trained fighters there in hand-to-hand combat and occasionally went overseas—to train more fighters.

But since she had been handed "a new assignment," Grace had been aggressively secretive about her work. The Lees knew that with her skill set the understatement meant she was probably working in or around a place that was sensitive and dangerous.

"What is it?" Kent asked, touching his wife's cheek.

"She was not at whatever base she calls home," the woman said. "She was calling from Washington, D.C., and said that she may not be able to call for a while."

Kent's eyes scanned the room, considering possibilities. "She has done that before."

"She was walking. There was no video. *Why* wasn't there a picture?"

"Did you ask her?"

"She said she was holding things but—"

"Did she say *why* she was walking?"

"No." Rosamund shook her head. "It was more than what she was doing—it was how she sounded. Her voice was different. I think she was scared."

Her husband forced a smile. "She hasn't been scared since those New Year firecrackers went off outside her window. She was three."

"Kent, I'm serious."

"So am I. Grace is a professional and she can take care of herself. Meanwhile, we have our own work to worry about. Hark and Leung have some new poll numbers on the election in Taiwan. I sent them out to—"

"We don't even know how to contact her."

Kent exhaled. "You worry about our daughter. I will go to my desk and worry about Taipei."

The woman nodded and turned back to her computer station. As she did, her husband looked toward the street. The daylight pouring through the big storefront window seemed to vanish, swallowed by a fast-moving black van. People outside ran from the vehicle and an instant later she felt the entire two-story structure shake.

Just inside the computer room, Rosamund thought she heard Kent cry out but there was a crack that sounded like a garbage truck ramming a dumpster. She turned just as a van rammed through the façade. Shards of glass, from large to particulate, were the only source of light as the front of the van plowed over Kent Lee and his desk. The glistening fragments fell around the van as it raced unchecked through the reception area, jumped over the crushed desk and broken body, and careened into the plasterboard back wall. Even before she could scream, Rosamund was scooped up by the fender and thrown up into the drop-down ceiling. She fell on top of the van, rolled over the side, and landed under the rear wheels as they slowed and came to rest.

The driver of the van was blocked on that side by the wall of the building. Scrambling over the armrests, he tumbled into the passenger's seat and pushed at the door. He heard glass tinkling as the roof of the van shook from the effort. The heavy door was not bent by the impact with the desk but the chassis was. Still, putting his shoulder to it, he managed to force it open. The man emerged headfirst and landed on his open hands.

The bloody top half of the body of Kent Lee was under those hands.

The driver hurriedly drew his feet out of the van, got his

legs under him, and staggered toward the street, pulling off his bloody gloves so they did not leave telltale spots on his saddle-color field jacket. He was shaken but unhurt and still had on the baseball cap and sunglasses he had been wearing.

He was unconcerned about the van. It had been stolen an hour ago from a construction site near Hudson Yards. By the time the theft had been discovered and reported, the van would have been found.

Concerned pedestrians had begun to gather. The driver dropped the gloves, pulled the brim of his cap low, hunched down, ignored people who asked if he was all right. He just wanted to get away and, in the process, appear in as few cell phone videos as possible. Though he had diplomatic immunity, he did not want to be here when the police asked what had happened and how it had happened. He could not very well tell them the truth: that he had been told to kill the owner of the newspaper.

The other victim was either an added benefit or an unfortunate bystander. He would find out soon enough.

People were still coming to the crash site from all sides, more and more of them ignoring him the farther he got. Taking a moment to pull off the jacket and throw it over his arm, he hurried on to the nearby Canal Street subway station. He did not care which line he caught there as long as it took him away from the scene of the crash.

Eventually, the counterterrorism officer of the elite People's Liberation Army Special Operations Forces, turned courier, would make his way back to the Consulate General of the People's Republic of China in New York on Twelfth Avenue. By then, of course, they would have learned that his mission had been a success.

The affront to China by American commandos took another step closer to being avenged.

CHAPTER FOURTEEN

The White House, Washington, D.C.
March 23, 1:55 P.M.

When he was governor of Pennsylvania, John Wright had discovered that compromise was easy.

He had not learned that in business, of course, as founder of the organic Wright Farms. There, he had had a single mandate that was also his advertising slogan: Produce Healthy Produce. As governor, though, he had to recognize that the needs of a state were not homogenous. What Germantown or Scranton wanted was not the same as what the voters in Lancaster or Blue Ball required.

He swiftly learned to compromise. That was how he won Hershey, Pennsylvania, after a record loss in his first term.

The goal of compromise was to not lose as much ground as you gained. The equation was that you gave up something you wanted for something you needed. In most cases, that meant pork barrel politics. If you need senatorial votes or mayoral support for your social agenda or harbor project or clean-air bill, you upped the budget—and thus taxes—to give cities or counties or towns money. The process ended up being a lumpy, ponderous wash because it simultaneously cost and earned taxpayer votes. As far as Governor Wright had been concerned, it really came down to one question: Did I do the right thing?

President Wright had asked himself the same question after the chairman of the Joint Chiefs of Staff reported the clear hand of China showed up in the demise of *Phoenix One*. No one in his circle had doubted it but L-TATS—laser tracking and triangulating systems—and the micro-debris path left by laser irradiance at the time of the incident pinpointed the Chinese space station as the point of origin.

"It works better as a right-wing conspiracy theory than as reality," Wright had said at the Oval Office meeting of his top staff.

There was no question that the Chinese had also taken Chase Williams or that Major Breen had been a targeted hit. The only party the major had aggrieved was China.

The rapid-fire unfolding of inflicted pain reminded Wright of mob and gang activity in Philadelphia and other large cities across his state. Violence continued until the participants had had enough and called a truce.

However justified, however well-meaning, the actions of Op-Center in China had triggered this "platform war," as the Department of Defense called it. A destructive exchange that took place on and around just one issue. In this case, the issue was the kidnapping of Dr. Yang Dàyóu. The proactive retaliation suggested by the more hawkish members of the Joint Chiefs—a "platform response" against the Tiangong—would have kept the situation accelerating until such time as it "jumped platform" from something space related to shipping or civilian flights or population centers. Or to the refusal of China to sell the U.S. electric car batteries. That would put Wright's Green Advance Program in the compost heap.

Wright wanted none of that.

Yes, he had agreed to the capture of Dr. Dàyóu after the fact; the mission had been for Black Wasp to reconnoiter. Yes, the Department of Defense had learned a great deal about China's hypersonic missile program, enough to improve on their own designs and also begin a crash program of ballistic countermeasures. As an added benefit, Space Force had learned a great deal about China's Lunar Farside Settlement from Dr. Dàyóu based on the kind of surface transports, communications structures . . . and weapons Beijing was developing. China was building a colony out of view from the Earth with the intention of owning the moon.

The value of that information was underscored by what appeared to be China's overreaction, the destruction of *Phoenix One* and its crew. When Wright considered the matter dispassionately, that strike was in proportion to the magnitude of the security breach.

Plans were still evolving as to how to respond to the hypersonic and lunar intelligence. Right now, however, as Angie Brunner put it, "We need to allow the angry dragon to save face."

She should know. As a Hollywood mogul she had personally seen to it that Hollywood did not openly criticize Beijing's open use of slave labor or systematic genocide against the Uyghur people. China was too big a movie market to insult. Losing face, they would respond with lopsided vengeance—in the case of Hollywood, releasing bootleg copies of films to flood the international market and destroy theatrical revenue.

Wright agreed, and he had resolved to find a quick diplomatic solution, even as the Chinese kept up collateral pressure through what was clearly an effort to uncover and destroy the team that had offended them on their home soil. The decision was not just to surrender Dr. Dàyóu and his family but to agree that the return of Chase Williams was not a quid pro quo. That had to be negotiated separately. There was no indication of what concession Williams might cost. Wright could not afford to worry about it now. The bloodshed had to stop.

A morning filled with Oval Office meetings and video-conferences with Chinese ambassador Chin Qiang and her staff had apparently resolved and quieted the matter. Even Dr. Dàyóu would come out on top. Before the kidnapping he was going to be scapegoated for the explosion of the hypersonic missile. Now he would be a returning hero. The authorities would want to know what Washington had been eager to learn. To the extent that those plans could be changed, the information rendered useless, they would be. The only outstanding matter was Black Wasp.

Now that the secretary of state, chairman of the Joint Chiefs of Staff, national security advisor January Dow, and other high ranking officials had left, Wright was alone with his chief of staff.

The president looked again at the intelligence tweet from the Office of Intelligence and Analysis of the Department of Homeland Security. The message was just over a half-hour old.

Van incident in Manhattan Chinatown struck
local tabloid weekly, *Mulberry Community*. Husband
and wife owners were killed. Investigating
publication politics as potential trigger.
However, flight of panicked driver appears
to be a vehicle theft gone wrong and not a
retributive attack against the Chinese
people.

A tired Wright set the phone down. "More payback," he said.

"Without a doubt," Angie agreed.

"My God, this has got to *stop*!" The president's voice was raw from talking and exhausted from this entire matter. He chucked a thumb toward the tablet. "Damn report got the heart of it wrong. Makes me wonder about our intelligence services."

"In fairness to HS, we're the only ones who know about the Op-Center connection," Angie said.

"You forget the Chinese," Wright said. "How the hell did they find out Lieutenant Lee's identity? And Major Breen . . . Chase?"

"January Dow is looking into that," Angie said. "Beijing had a month of in-country forensics to explore."

"Matt Berry will also see this and understand what's going on," Wright said. "So will Captain Mann and her two special ops. That's six people. Spread that across every scrap of intelligence this government processes and how many wrong conclusions are the result?"

"Fair point, sir. In this case, at least, we have control over five of them." Angie checked her phone for messages. There was nothing from Ann Ellen Mann. "I suggest you call Captain Mann."

"What's the status of Op-Center?"

"I told her to keep the team in the residence."

"But they know about Chase Williams and Major Breen?" Wright asked.

Angie nodded. "And they will learn very quickly about Lieutenant Lee's parents, if they haven't already."

"Yes, of course. She'll need leave to go—"

"That's not what I mean, Mr. President," Brunner interrupted. "Grace Lee is the one who made the field call to take Dr. Dàyóu. She has been singled out for special punishment."

Wright made no comment on whether that was merited. The buck in China stopped with Chase Williams.

"Black Wasp is a rogue operation," Angie went on. "We have to decommission them—that isn't in dispute."

"You were one of their biggest boosters."

"*They* changed, Mr. President. Williams pushed us the way

he never pushed against the previous administration. Bringing in Captain Mann obviously did not change that. Sorry if this sounds callous, but she allowed Major Breen to go on an adventure that led to his death."

"He seemed a good man," Wright said.

"He was a rock," Angie agreed. "If we shut them down now, and advise Ambassador Qiang of that fact, we may be able to save the three surviving members, perhaps their families, and maybe Chase Williams."

"Fair points," Wright agreed. "I'm thinking of something beyond that, actually."

"What's your concern?" Angie asked. She was usually on top of Wright's concerns; she, too, was tired.

"Saving the deal we just worked out regarding Dr. Dàyóu," the president replied. "God only knows what Lieutenant Lee will do when she hears the news about her parents."

"Should we conference with Captain Mann?"

"No," Wright said. "I don't want any two-way communication logged. Draw up a condolence message to Lieutenant Lee and copy the captain with an order to resist-in-place. I don't want the team off base but I also don't want to leave them defenseless."

Angie brought up the president's Op-Center dossier and accessed the file marked "personnel support." This was the back-door method of communication that the previous administration had used to send orders without appearing to send orders. Though the command was secure on the president's end, he wanted plausible deniability of unlawful military action in case Chase Williams'—now, Captain Mann's—files were ever breached.

"Done, sir," Angie said a minute later. She looked across the desk at the president. The sun was coming in over Wright's right shoulder. It threw long shadows across his face, making him look tired.

"Thank you." He leaned back in the chair. "This is Black Wasp we're talking about."

Angie was confused. "Yes, sir?"

"What I mean is, these are the people who put us in this situation by going off mission. Do you think they'll follow this order?"

"I don't know," Angie admitted.

For the first time since coming to the West Wing, the chief of staff experienced something more worrisome than the destruction of the *Phoenix One*.

The fear of what came next.

CHAPTER FIFTEEN

Fort Belvoir, Springfield, Virginia
March 23, 1:56 P.M.

"It's been over an hour," Jaz Rivette said. "My feet already had their workout today and I want to know where we're going."

Grace Lee looked directly ahead. At this moment she seemed, to Rivette, more like a jungle predator than when they were on a mission or drilling. Her black hair was worn in a very short military style, tufted on top and buzzed on the sides; her dark brown eyes had an intensity that made them seem almost black.

"Where does the leopard go when there are hunters afoot?" she asked.

"I had a feeling you'd ask something kung fu like that," Rivette said. "He'd go somewhere they are not."

The woman nodded. "Right now we're just staying mobile south and then east. I want to put distance between us and any pursuit."

Jaz Rivette was on her right, on the street side of Keene Road. In case they needed to get off the road, there were trees and buildings to the east. They were walking slowly, partly so as not to attract attention and partly because they were emotionally spent.

"What makes you think there'll be MPs?" Rivette asked. "Captain Mann isn't going to give us up—will she?"

"Jaz, I don't know what's coming next. I truly do not."

"But *if* there're guys chasing us, they got Jeeps. We got Adidas."

"You said you wanted to be able to pivot," Grace reminded him. "You can."

"I'm not gonna shoot my own people," Rivette said.

Grace was looking straight ahead but listening for the sound of traffic coming from behind—in particular, the high growl of the light Jeeps favored by military police. So far, she had not heard or seen any.

"We'll be okay," the lieutenant assured him. "The DES will figure we're headed directly to a population center. They'll concentrate their efforts in Alexandria, and D.C."

The DES was the Directorate of Emergency Services, the base unit responsible for law enforcement, base security, and fire emergencies.

"They'll get support from the police, the FBI," Rivette pointed out.

"Not for us," Grace answered confidently. "Fort Belvoir will handle its own."

Rivette did not seem convinced. "We keep heading this way we're gonna be knocking on George Washington's door. Then what?"

"We won't go that far. There are tour buses along this route."

"Why would they stop for—"

"The military? Flash your ID and salute," she said. "They'll stop. It was in the orientation manual."

"Last manual I read was for the first gun I owned," he said.

Grace had not turned toward him since they left the base. "Jaz, I don't feel like talking now if you don't mind."

"Sure," he said. "Just answer me this. Are we going to try and get the admiral?"

"I don't see how we can't," she said.

Rivette unraveled that statement and nodded in accord. Such as it was, the lieutenant's plan had been revealed. It was not a bad one. It was definitely different from any he would have come up with. His inclination would have been to hide. Back in the day, before he discovered firearms, Rivette was a spotter for gangs. They would hide and wait for their contacts delivering stolen goods. He would watch for their partners to arrive. In concealment, none of the boys ever got caught. It was only when they were out, looking suspicious, that the police stopped them.

"It was them versus us," Rivette said under his breath. There was a wistful tone in his voice, almost a longing. "We knew who the bad guys were. How the hell is it that more than a dozen years later I am once again ducking dudes in uniforms?" He swore. "I can't believe the major is gone. How the hell did any of this even happen? We were all just doing our jobs, defending our country."

Grace responded despite having asked for silence. She knew—because Rivette liked to talk—that he had grown up in a small, crowded apartment on a street that was noisy 24/7. The only way he ever got to think was by saying things aloud.

"Nothing is ever clean," Grace said. "The admiral killed that terrorist. I had to stop myself from killing the Chinese general. Both times we were murdering people who were in their own lands, doing jobs they thought were right."

"But they weren't right. They murdered other people."

"I love objective morality too but try and find it in this world."

Rivette was not sure what she had just said and his question still had not been answered. He took out his cell phone to look for sense and stability. He did not feel like answering texts from Los Angeles or looking at anything on social media; the video from the park had poisoned that for a while. Instead, he went to Bing to look up videos from the international marksmanship competition in Tokyo.

"Y'know," he muttered to himself. "The contest you would have attended if you had not been in freakin' Mongolia and had been given leave, which was not likely because you're a secret agent."

Before he could write in the search bar, Bing news came up. Rivette froze. "Oh shit. Hit the damn brakes."

Grace stopped and looked back. "What?"

Still looking at his screen the lance corporal came forward. He handed her the phone.

The headline read DEADLY CRASH IN NYC. Grace

saw the words but only in passing. Her eyes went directly to
the image, vivid on the bright screen. It showed the wreckage
of her parents' office behind haphazardly strung yellow police
tape. There was glass on the street. Above the shattered window the top floor sagged.

On the second floor was the Lee apartment, the home
where she had grown up.

Grace did not notice Jaz carefully watching her expression. She did not feel him lightly put his fingers around her
right arm. She touched the headline and read the first lines of
the story:

> A van lost control on Mulberry Street this afternoon
> and tore through the street-level office of a local
> newspaper. Pedestrians fled as the vehicle turned.
> The only victims appear to be two individuals
> who were inside what locals say is a century-old
> structure. They were identified as the owner and his
> wife. Their bodies have not yet been recovered due
> to the instability of . . .

That was as far as Grace got. Her insides were burning but her muscles were numb. Her flesh seemed like dead
weight. Sounds were muffled.

Jaz held off a moment and then went to embrace her. The
instant he moved, fire broke through Grace's lifeless exterior.
She pivoted ninety degrees, facing him, and stiff-armed him
back.

"You have to do something for me, right now," she said urgently.

Her move had surprised him. Her kung fu always did. He waited.

"I want you to call whoever you have to in L.A.," Grace said. "Gang members, smugglers, Little Guillermo, all of them. Mobilize people to protect your family."

The warning took a moment to sink in. "Shit. God bless you, Lieutenant."

Rivette placed his call. As he did, Grace Lee walked a few paces into a parking lot that belonged to a strip mall. The Taoists would have said this heinous act was the universe balancing its energies. By her actions in China, she had caused yang, aggression, to rise within her sphere. The execution of Major Breen, and the murder of her parents, was the result.

She knew that to be true, and she knew that cosmic Tao would inevitably be restored. But not through her yin, her peaceful energy. Balance was going to have to wait.

For at this moment, as the fire rose, Grace did not give a goddamn about the universe, its coherent ways, or its symmetrical energies.

She only wanted to complete the war she had left unfinished.

CHAPTER SIXTEEN

The Trigram Institute, Georgetown,
Washington, D.C.
March 23, 2:13 P.M.

Matt Berry felt as though he had slipped backward in time about a decade. He had been reviewing surveillance images on his laptop when a call came to him through the company's automated switchboard instead of on his cell phone. The caller ID told him it was the lobby of his four-story brick office building on Canal Square. In the two months he had been here, Berry could not remember anyone coming to Trigram unannounced. Takeout meals were delivered to the rooftop by DronEats.

"Yes, Mr. Polkhorne?" he said.

"Mr. Berry? Sorry for the interruption but there's—"

The announcement was interrupted by Polkhorne's shout of protest as a female voice took over. "This is Grace Lee. You know my name?"

"I do."

"Jaz and I are coming up."

"Hey, tell him I rang some bells at security," Jaz shouted to be heard. "Dude wants to call the cops!"

"Grace, put Mr. Polkhorne back on," Berry said.

There were shuffling sounds as the phone was handed over.

"Mr. Berry, one of the visitors does appear to have a weapon—" Polkhorne began.

"He's active military."

"Yes, sir. He showed his ID, sir. But—"

"I'll take responsibility," Berry replied. He had already opened a page on his tablet, brought up a building pass, and put his thumb to it. He sent the document to the front desk. "Send them up."

The document was returned a moment later with a photograph of Grace Lee and Jaz Rivette. Berry stored the pass and brought up the security camera at the front door. Trigram did not have a receptionist. The thirteen partners—of whom Berry was the newest—preferred the automated safeguards in their smart office. The think tank had the entire fourth floor. The doors of the stairwell and elevator were steel-reinforced and able to withstand direct contact with the most powerful kinds of explosive devices, from military-grade Semtex—commonly known as C-4—to ammonium nitrate and fuel oil. The windows were not just bulletproof, they were two-way mirrors; catching the sunlight and bouncing it back made observation from surrounding buildings impossible. Thermal cameras on the roof registered any living creature larger than a cat and PSR—portable surveillance radar—swept the skies for drones. Electronic webwork built into the walls foiled the efforts of acoustic listening devices, whether aerial or adhesive. The Russians used bugs designed practically and with a sense of humor: they were mechanical cockroaches not only capable of listening but of directed movement. Even if those got inside, none of their signals got out.

The office was secure. Though there was nothing good about this day, Berry was encouraged by the old-school approach of another bug, Black Wasp. Initiative was not dead.

He sent out a company-wide notice that two individuals not on the day's guest list were about to arrive. He attached the pass and then went to the front door to await their arrival.

In the past, Berry's contact with Black Wasp had been exclusively through Chase Williams. He knew the director had spoken of him to Major Breen and, clearly, his name was known to the others. He was unconcerned by their arrival. Given the events of the day he knew what they were looking for. It was the only reason anyone came to Trigram. To sell or secure names and information.

The security camera at the front door flashed green indicating that the people who had arrived were the two who had been photographed in the lobby. A palm pressed to a panel opened the door from the inside.

Berry stepped back to admit them. The newcomers arrived like their namesake: an outwardly serene queen wasp and a buzzing drone. Neither spoke. Berry shut the door behind them and indicated that they follow him.

"You don't look like the picture on the website," Rivette noted as they walked along a thickly carpeted corridor.

"That's an old White House photo," Berry said. "We spies like to keep people off-balance."

"Thank you for seeing us," Grace said, surprising him. Though her expression was resolute there was something vulnerable in her voice.

"I'm sorry for the circumstances that brought us together," he said as he ushered them into his office.

Berry shut the door behind him and indicated the two armchairs in front of his desk. The two Black Wasps unshouldered their backpacks as Berry popped the door in the base of a large bookcase. There was a refrigerator inside. "Help yourself."

"Thanks," Rivette said.

The lance corporal helped himself to a bottle of water and offered one to Grace. She shook her head. Rivette left it on the desk anyway. Grace placed her backpack on the floor and sat. Rivette sat with his grip in his lap.

"I'm guessing you are here without leave," Berry said as he settled behind the desk.

"Captain said we should go, so we went," Rivette said. "We walked around till we heard about . . . about New York," he said, softening his words. "Then we got an Uber."

"Does the president know where you are?"

"Nobody knows where we are except you now," Rivette said.

Grace had been gazing blankly at the water bottle. "Mr. Berry, we know where Admiral Williams is. So do you, I'm sure."

Berry nodded once.

"We want to know who put him there," Grace said. "We also want to know who shot Major Breen. And I want to know who killed my parents."

"I have my suspicions about the first one and I can answer the last one based on the MO of the—the incident," he said. "But I don't think you'll like what I tell you."

"I have not liked anything about this day," she said. Her eyes rose. "And you can both stop being careful about your words. 'New York,' 'incident.' My parents were murdered, crushed to death, and I want to know everything."

"Fair request," Berry said. "The New York killer was not an assassin. He was a driver. The van was stolen shortly before the crash. It was only driven two dozen blocks or so. To onlookers, to the NYPD, it was meant to look like the thief lost control and fled. That is not considered an assassination. It's—and I don't mean to minimize the impact—it's considered a message."

"Like the friggin' gangs leave?" Rivette said.

"The Chinese *are* a 'friggin' gang,' Lance Corporal, a gang one-point-three billion members strong," Berry told him.

Grace thought back to the brutal death of Dr. Dàyóu's son in the Chinese prison. The former deputy chief of staff was not wrong.

"Well, I want to send a message back to them," Rivette said. "You don't kill and kidnap our people."

"Don't do what we did," Grace said quietly.

Rivette shot her a critical glance. "What we did was for a good reason, to keep them from building a nuclear weapon that can hit us before we can even turn on a siren. What they did was payback. It wasn't gonna bring their missile back."

Grace regarded Berry. "Did China shoot down the spacecraft? The *Phoenix One*?"

"It appears so."

She turned to Rivette. "*That* was payback. This was revenge."

"What the hell's the difference?"

Berry answered. "Payback is political. Revenge is personal."

Rivette fingered the straps of his bag. "Little Guillermo asked about that when I called to have him look after my family. He wanted to know what line a marine could possibly cross that would make things personal. I told him the line was duty and country. Far as I'm concerned, the Chinese crossed that line. My question is—questions *are*—what do we do to stop them and protect ourselves?"

"Thank you . . . Jaz," Grace said. It was the first time this morning her voice had cracked.

Berry settled deeper into his leather chair. "Before we look at that, you have to understand that up till now you are just AWOL. Defensible, given the morning's events. But anything you are contemplating, anything you do when you leave here will be considered a rogue action. When—not if—you are apprehended, you can expect a court-martial and prison time."

"Without Major Breen to defend us," Rivette added poignantly.

Berry regarded Grace. "Some frank questions need to be answered. First, are you willing to try and get into the

Chinese embassy to secure the release of the admiral? Keep in mind, the place is a fortress. And before you answer, I want you to consider something. Were you able to get Dr. Dàyóu's son from prison?"

Grace seemed surprised by the question.

"I know about Wen Dàyóu's death, yes," Berry said. "I read the admiral's report. We keep each other informed. The answer is, you would likely have died in the effort."

"Better to die trying than hiding," Rivette said.

"Second," Berry said, "isn't that what the major did? Tried rather than hid?"

"All he did was go to the damn park," Rivette said. "Just to look."

"What he did was walk into a trap set and sprung by the Chinese," Berry replied.

"Man, you're talking to us like we're kids in boot camp," Rivette complained.

"Not at all, and I'm sorry if you think that," Berry replied. "I'm talking to you like troops who are close to Chase Williams and who are contemplating a course that may end in their deaths or, at the very least, prompt the Chinese to amp up their response."

"Let 'em amp up," Rivette said. "They should've left this at killing four astronauts."

"But they didn't," Berry said sternly, "and here we are."

"All right," Grace said. "We hear you."

"We don't," Rivette replied.

"We *do*," Grace said, "unless you want us tearing at each

other the way the Chinese are hitting us. Or do I have to order you to stand down?"

Rivette slumped and fell silent. He was verbal and headstrong but he invariably respected the chain of command.

Grace turned her attention back to Berry. "The person who shot Major Breen. That was a hit, an assassin, yes?"

Berry nodded. "Classic, old-school."

"It was done to send a message," Grace went on. "All right. We're not going to sit around waiting for the Chinese to pull in their claws. I want to send a message too. I want to find the individual who pulled the trigger on Major Breen. How can you help us? *Will* you help us?"

Berry considered the requests. "My trade is geopolitical intelligence, not murder."

"I did not say anything about murder. I'm asking for geopolitical intelligence," Grace said.

Berry almost smiled at that.

"Nice one, Lieutenant," Rivette said.

"There must be surveillance cameras," Grace said. "Do you have access?"

"Not in the park," Berry said. "Outside."

"Do they tell you anything?"

"The assassin was a man, middle-aged, and he has done this before." Once again Berry thought about what to do. He input a password. After a moment he turned his laptop around. There were six panels of street scenes, three in each row.

"This is the from the FBI's Office of Law Enforcement Coordination," he said. "I was looking at these when you arrived. The basic data is on the top—six-footer, mid-thirties, about two hundred and twenty-five pounds. The first six images were culled from digital recordings of someone who left the park with a computer bag."

The pictures showed a man with a brown Fedora, his face carefully hidden by the brim or because he was looking down.

"SOB knew what he was doing," Rivette said.

"Tap the image in the middle, top row," Berry instructed.

Grace did so. The image filled the screen.

"Touch the computer case."

Grace obliged. At once a wireframe overlay defined the contents of the case. It held a water bottle, a cell phone . . . and a handgun. The weapon was red.

"The color is a thermal assessment that was part of the original surveillance reading," Berry said. "That's what flagged the man in the first place."

"You said these are the first six images—" Grace said.

"Swipe to the next screen," Berry said.

There were six additional images. They showed the man holding the same case, only now his hat and jacket had been removed.

"Clearly, he left Lady Bird Johnson Park, went to the Mall, did a nominal makeover, and continued on his way," Berry said.

"Where to?" Grace asked.

"The FBI does not know," Berry said. "After putting distance between himself and the crime scene he was careful to stay away from surveillance cameras. The man was no longer in a rush. He had time to be careful."

"Not careful enough," Rivette said.

"What do you mean?" Berry asked.

He leaned forward and wagged a finger at the monitor. "I know that head, the way the guy's walking."

"What do you mean?" Berry asked.

"Give me a second," Rivette said, leaning into the laptop. "What happens if I touch each picture?"

"It's like peeling an onion," Berry answered. "You get different layers of information."

Rivette began poking the fifth of the second group of six images. While the lance corporal watched the screens change, Grace moved several steps down the tactical road. If nothing else, it kept her from thinking about what had happened to her parents. Rivette's pronouncement caused an unexpected response from Matt Berry. Grace did not know the intelligence expert. He had not seemed particularly sympathetic when they arrived. Perhaps, out of loyalty to Chase Williams—if there was such a thing in this business, in this city—he had made no move to curry favor with the present administration by turning them in. But for the first time since Black Wasp had walked in the door, Berry seemed engaged.

"What's this?" Rivette asked, swinging the laptop toward Berry. "Looks like one of those butcher shop posters."

"You're nearly correct," Berry said. "It's a re-creation of the body under the clothes. If you touch the limbs, the abdomen—"

"I can see what muscles he uses most," Rivette said, turning the computer back around. He touched the lower legs. "Upper body development but he doesn't walk a lot."

"Bench pressing would do that," Berry said.

"Or lifting heavy equipment. Once upon a time, anyway. That shit gets baked into your body."

"You said you know him?" Berry pressed.

Rivette sat back. "Yeah. How about that. The Hawk."

"Name? Nickname?" Berry asked.

"What they called him on YouTube about three, four years ago," Rivette said. "Saw a video of this guy—this head, these shoulders—using a Ruger 10/22 rifle to shoot fish from the talons of hawks in flight. Somebody posted that he shot a poacher. Shot him off a moving Jeep as he was chasing down a cheetah."

"Do you know his name?"

"Nah," Rivette said. He went back to the computer. "But if it hasn't been pulled I can show you the video."

The item had been taken down. Since there was nothing illegal in what Rivette had described, Berry assumed that the man's tracks had been scrubbed—either by himself or his employer.

"You said he saved a cheetah, Lance Corporal," Berry continued, undaunted. "That narrows things somewhat."

"Let me think," Rivette said. He shut his eyes. "There were a lot of posts. People saying 'fawsome' and posting heart emojis and eyeball-wasters like that. The cheetah thing—" Rivette said, then suddenly sat up. "Someone replied to that, all about how they were endangered in Chad."

Berry took the computer back. He began typing.

"What're you looking for?" Rivette asked.

"I'm going to a database for the Department of State, Bureau of Consular Affairs, searching for diplomatic visas from Chad going back two years. That's the typical period of rotation for embassy personnel. Prevents them from being sought out and used for intelligence gathering by our people."

Four C-3 nonimmigrant visas had been issued for government employees. Berry's practiced eye saw the one that matched best.

"Joseph Kebzabo," he said. Berry began typing.

"You have some way of—" Rivette began.

"Comparing the top of your man's head to his ID photo in our facial and cranial profile software?"

"Yeah, that," Rivette said.

Berry touched the screen once, then again, then swung the computer around so the others could see. The program had not only identified the man as a match but had created a likeness of him in the Mall images aged eighteen months beyond the ID.

"A gunman leaving Lady Bird Johnson Park with a recently fired gun," Berry said. "I would say you have found our man."

"*Our* man, not yours," Grace said. "He killed our superior officer. He is our responsibility."

Berry looked at her disapprovingly. "Lieutenant, if you will please take some advice—"

"I don't think you heard me."

"I *heard* you. You forget, the man behind this took me for a ride as well. I want him, but it seems I'm the only one doing any listening. Leave this to the FBI."

"I'll pass," she said. "What can the Bureau do to a man with a diplomatic visa? Make some calls, have him sent from the country in two, maybe three months?"

"The only numbers I know are calibers, but that's about when he'd be due to cycle out anyway, right?" Rivette said.

"The FBI can follow him, bug him, see who else he meets, communicates with."

"And who earns bonus points for the 'get,'" Rivette muttered.

"Snark noted, but, yes, that's the coin of the realm," Berry admitted. "That has nothing to do with why I'm saying this. Until now, you two have done nothing to jeopardize your future. If you cross this line, you'll be hunted by international and domestic resources."

"You mean the bad guys'll come directly to us?" Rivette said eagerly. "I'm good with that."

"In force," Berry warned. "You two will be on the run for the rest of your lives. That will be your future."

"The *I Ching* instructs us to live in the present," Grace said.

"Besides, that bastard doesn't deserve a future," Rivette added. He grabbed his backpack and stood.

"At least hear me out on *this* point," Berry urged.

The two Black Wasps waited.

No, Berry thought. *They tolerated.* He closed the lid of the

laptop and regarded the two. He felt as though he were looking at an entire generation, one that was staring back at him
with disapproval and impatience.

"Lieutenant, Lance Corporal—if you run off half-cocked
there's no guarantee you'll succeed."

"My firearm is never half-cocked," Rivette replied. "*That*
is indecision. And Major Breen—he said that at least twice
a day."

"He was right. And you respected him."

"True, that. We didn't usually listen, though."

"Give me a better idea," Grace challenged.

"All right," Berry said.

The lieutenant was still seated, studying the man across
from her. There was something different in his eye now. Something she had seen in opponents in kung fu competitions. A
hungry quality.

"Suppose I work with you on this," Berry said. "You can
use help with surveillance."

"You said you don't do murder," Grace reminded him.

"And I'm not about to start. But there *are* other options."

"So you said," Grace answered and stood.

"I don't mean the FBI."

"What, then?"

"Let me work something out," Berry said. "Trust me."

Grace shook her head. "Mr. Berry, I didn't understand
when the admiral executed Ahmed Salehi on our first mission.
Now I do."

"That asshole torched the *Intrepid*," Rivette said. "That asshole died."

Grace's eyes were still fixed on Berry. "You ask me to trust you. Admiral Williams does and that's good enough for me. I trust you not to try and stop us, to warn anyone."

Berry sat back. "That sounded more like a question."

"Maybe it was," Grace admitted.

"Will I make Black Wasp a 'get,' turn you in to curry favor with Wright? Is that what you're asking?"

Grace did not answer with words. Her look—more warning than questioning now—was his answer.

"I will not tell anyone you were here or where you're going," he said. "But you'll be back."

"What makes you sure?" Grace asked.

"Because I told you—I think I know who betrayed the admiral."

The Black Wasps both seemed to appreciate that small gesture of support.

"Thank you for seeing us," Grace said. Then she scooped up her bag, turned, and walked toward the door followed by Rivette.

When the door had closed, Berry flipped open the laptop and began typing urgently:

Plan B. This is all you and R.T. No F.B.I.

CHAPTER SEVENTEEN

Embassy of the People's Republic of China,
Washington, D.C.
March 23, 2:55 P.M.

Chief Sergeant Class 4 Tang Changfu had learned his trade in Afghanistan.

The thirty-two-year-old chemist had graduated from Princeton University with a master's degree from the Institute for the Science and Technology of Materials. He was among the first members of the People's Liberation Army to fly into Bagram Airfield after the American departure. A member of the Strategic Support Force, Tang had been charged with marking roads that had to be cleared of mines and tribal factions before mineralogists were sent in. The lithium fields were critical to China's plan to own the manufacturing market for electric car batteries.

Tang learned about explosives by removing them from the ground—treading lightly, like he observed spiders do— and neutralizing them. With his science background, he spent his spare time coming up with better ways of making them.

He presented his findings to a second lieutenant who passed it up the chain of command.

Three months later Tang was no longer in Afghanistan. He was in the Chinese embassy in Washington serving on the anti-terrorism oversight unit. His job was to create and execute protocols to ensure that everything from mail to vehicles was free of explosives.

After three years in that position, this was the first time that Tang had been ordered to apply his talents to something other than screening. It was shortly after dawn when he was instructed to create an explosive device that could be concealed in a small package and detonated remotely.

The small package was conceived by Dylan Hao. The design he presented to Tang was efficient and credible but with an undercurrent of cynicism: Hao wanted a powerful explosive placed in the base of a potted plant to be delivered to an officer at Fort Belvoir. A sympathy card would be provided in a sealed envelope that would take a few moments to open. The message would take mere moments to read and would be signed anonymously by a friend. By the time the recipient got that far, it would be the last words they would ever read.

"There must be nothing in the item that will trigger an alarm, not metal detectors, not guard dogs," Hao had said. "You will select a delivery uniform from wardrobe and take a motorbike from the garage. The recipient's name will be unfamiliar at the gate, so you will furnish an address in the residential sector. The information will be sent to your phone."

"The target likely will be on guard," Tang had noted.

"But curious," Hao said. "They will be sure to admit you to the base. I will text you a map showing your route. When the job is done, the exits will be secured. You will leave the motorbike and go to Dogue Creek, adjacent the lodgings. Take one of the rowboats and head away from the base. An embassy vehicle will meet you at the fishing pier."

With that, the English speaker set to work assembling a fertilizer-based bomb with a blast radius of thirty feet. It would require a quick triggering when delivered since there was no guarantee the target would stand beside the plant while reading the card. By 1:00 P.M. the bomb was completed and inserted beneath an amethyst sympathy plant. Tang did not know who had died or who would die. He tried not to think about that, to remain clear-eyed about the job he had been given. All he was told is that the delivery pertained to the attack on the Taiyuan Satellite Launch Center several weeks earlier. Tang was aware of that; it had been the talk of the embassy.

The green card he carried was authentic. It was secured in a "bulk buy" arrangement with the U.S. Citizenship and Immigration Services to allow Chinese students to study in America. It had been kept current with annual updates. To the sentries at the army base, he would appear to be a genial, polite, hardworking immigrant.

The bike he selected was a Honda ST1300. It was heavy enough to absorb any bumps and holes in the road and had storage compartments in the back to place four small plants. It might raise suspicions if he arrived with just one.

Waiting until after lunch hour so the traffic would have

thinned somewhat, and with his heart thumping in a way that was familiar from Afghanistan, Tang Changfu set out with a detonator in the pocket of his white shirt and the plant in its solid ceramic planter, which was packed with fertilizer, ammonium nitrate, glass beads, and an igniter.

CHAPTER EIGHTEEN

Fort Belvoir, Springfield, Virginia
March 23, 3:01 P.M.

Ann Ellen Mann had learned, long ago, that waiting is not downtime.

Whether she was eleven years old, holding her mother's hand as lung cancer took her life, or waiting for a unit to return with prisoners from a combat zone in Afghanistan, being alone with her thoughts was miserably stressful. At least, when she was recovering from her injuries, there was physical and psychological therapy to occupy her time and mind.

Today, here, in the family lodgings at Fort Belvoir, she had waited for Major Breen and then for the president and now for fresh word from Lieutenant Lee and Lance Corporal Rivette.

The president had sent her a resist-in-place order. It struck her as odd that an organization as thoroughly committed to personal well-being and newfound sensitivity as the Department of Defense would allow the acronym RIP in reference to a defensive position. Maybe one day she would point that out. Maybe she would not. Right now, it suited her pessimism. She had a brief text exchange with Grace, who assured her they were all right. The lieutenant had heard about her parents and the captain offered her deepest regrets. Mann had resisted assuming a command posture at that moment, which would have been to caution Grace about doing anything in haste or retribution. But it did not seem the time, not then.

By habit, the captain had tried to busy herself with work. She did not return to her go-to files, the history of Op-Center and Black Wasp. Reading reports by Chase Williams that referenced Hamilton Breen was impossible now. She turned, instead, to intelligence reports. Ordinarily these were marked up by the admiral first thing in the morning and then forwarded to her. She used his security code to access the raw data from the Department of Homeland Security, which was updated in real time.

The references to Chase Williams and the update on the murder in Lady Bird Johnson Park—identifying the victim as an active service member attached to JAG but nothing more—were already known to her. The intelligence about China pertained to Beijing's global activities with only one mention of Dr. Yang Dàyóu, using his code name and the map ID for the safe house in Silver Springs, Maryland:

F.B.I. Alert 323–12–29B: Transfer of Booster will require secure zone from Safe House 33T. Drones will be in use, exempted from Special Flight Rules Area from 2300–2400 hours tonight.

In other words, don't jam the signals or overfly with helicopters, Mann thought.

Her reading had been interrupted twice. The first time was to call Grace Lee and inform her about the attack in New York. Grace thanked her and said she had already heard. As they had previously agreed, the lieutenant had not said anything about her plans.

The second interruption was from the north gate. The officer on duty announced a floral delivery. A closed-circuit camera showed a split screen of the new arrival—an Asian man on a motorbike—and his ID.

Mann was not only suspicious—she was surprised by the obviousness of the ploy. An assassin would find it nearly impossible to get a weapon through the metal detector and pat-down. This was something else. The Chinese did not sacrifice their own on suicide missions against the West; according to CIA reports, they hired jihadists from African nations like Niger and Sudan.

An IED? she thought. In Afghanistan, she had seen bombs packed into everything from coffee tins to cadavers left at the side of the road.

But it also occurred to her then that someone—perhaps the admiral—might have managed to give this man a message. Perhaps the messenger had been guaranteed payment of some kind. There was only one way to find out. Captain Mann told the guard to send the young man over.

Mann went to the arms locker in the hall closet. The chest was thumbprint-activated, responsive to each member of the team. She retrieved her M9, held it behind her, and went back to the foyer. She was focused, her mind and eyes sharpened in a way they had not been for years. It was a dangerous, hair-trigger state, the kind she would hear law enforcement try to articulate in interviews. Back in Naval Support Activity, Mann would snarl inside whenever athletes on ESPN talked about how they only had x number of good years, ten or fifteen tops, how injuries and stress affected their bodies and psychology. Earning millions, collecting trophies, endorsements, and press—what the hell did a football player or tennis star know about pressure?

Mann watched through the curtain of the window beside the door. Except for the Infantry Squad Vehicle in the driveway, this could be any suburban street with civilian residences, flower boxes on the windows, and family vans. The ISV was probably the talk of the street, but Black Wasp did not have time to requisition vehicles—

The captain stood very still. There was something subtle but familiar in the air. An odor. She turned in to the residence slightly and felt a ghastly sense of déjà vu: the heat of a desert sun combined with the growling tread of an army security vehicle—and most penetrating of all—the smell of decomposed sheep manure.

The back door, she realized, turning and running even as the thought was still forming.

Drawing the gun with one hand, she used the other hand to push herself off the wall for added speed. As she made the turn toward the kitchen, Captain Mann was once again struggling with the kind of decision she had faced dozens of times in Afghanistan: *Deal with the situation or bail, try to put as much distance as possible between it and you?*

Running had never been an option when she was in country, nor was it now.

The deliveryman had come to the back door, not the front, and had left a plant rooted in a fertilizer-based improvised explosive device. Even as she raced for the door, she mentally replayed the video image from the front gate. The size of the plant—more especially, the plot—suggested an IED with a blast radius of some twenty-five or thirty feet. That would mean the young man had to be farther than that before he triggered the detonator.

Her injured leg moved with the kind of certainty and speed it had not known for years. She peered through the triptych of windows at the top of the back door as she ran. She saw the young man's back, heard the sputter of his motorbike as he rode away.

He looked back over his shoulder as he retreated.

Drop somewhere, anywhere! Captain Mann screamed inside as she closed in on the door. She had seen bombs level buildings, knew this one would certainly take out the kitchen—but only if the attacker cleared the kill zone.

The officer had used the door only two or three times since she had arrived weeks before. Did it open in or out?

In, she remembered as she grabbed the knob and pulled. It was locked. She punched the button in the middle of the brass and pulled again, stepped back to allow it to swing inside.

The plant was on the black rubber mat with the army insignia. She stood above it looking out into the small yard with a natural-wood picket fence. The gate in the back was open, and the young man was rushing toward it across a paved path.

Yelling "Stop!" would cost her time she did not have. He had his left hand on the handlebars. In his right hand was something that resembled a key fob in black plastic. The fence was about thirty feet away and would afford him some protection once he got behind it—

She released the safety, crouched behind the plant, extended her right arm, and aligned the front and rear sights of the Beretta. She fired. Two loud cracks filled the air and she lived each fraction of the ensuing seconds as if each were a full minute. The young man's right shoulder erupted in side-by-side splashes of red, the impact of the hits spun that side forward, and the front wheel of the motorbike twisted to the left. The bike started to fall to its right and the rider made a move as if to brace himself. Mann put a third shot into the man, this one in the center of his back just below his neck. His head went forward then snapped back as the bike continued to fall. Still in motion, the motorbike and rider hit the grass and then the fence, pushing over a complete section and skidding awkwardly across it, carried by their own momentum. The tires had kicked up dirt and old, brown grass as they continued to spin for a moment longer.

Then everything fell very still but only for a few moments. As real time returned, neighborhood dogs that had gone silent began to bark. Neighbors who were home looked warily out windows. Ann Ellen Mann rose slowly, her bad leg complaining from the effort she had asked of it. Realizing that she was dressed in sweat clothes and not her uniform, and that members of the Directorate of Emergency Services would be arriving presently, she put the Beretta on the counter just inside the door.

The smell of the gun covered the stench of the fertilizer in the plant at her feet. Also inside the door was a local landline with a laminated directory below it. She glanced at the number of the bomb squad, punched in the code, and asked for assistance with an "active package." Then she called the Fort Belvoir Community Hospital to report an enemy combatant down and furnished her address.

Then, finally, she went to see about the man she had shot. Her legs were surprisingly steady as she made her way over.

The man was dead, there was no question of that. His eyes were open and lifeless, his mouth twisted into something ugly—a dying look of pain she knew too well. Blood had continued to pulse from the three wounds.

Sirens closed in from two different directions as Captain Mann collected the detonator. It *was* a key fob, adjusted to trigger the bomb as if the bearer were starting a Honda. She opened the back with a fingernail and popped the battery. It sickened her all over again thinking back to her tours of duty, the anguish of the wounded, the carnage of death, the three enemy fighters she had killed. Those shootings, like this one, were justified. But they were no less final for that, no less a stain on her conscience.

Mann turned away. She inhaled through her nose to clear the smell of the bomb, the gun, of death from her lungs.

"You wanted a war," she said to no one in particular. But in her mind she visualized Major Breen, alive; Admiral Williams, wherever he was; her two subordinates. "You wanted a war, you bloody bastards. Now you've got one."

CHAPTER NINETEEN

Embassy of Chad, Washington, D.C.
March 23, 3:13 P.M.

Grace Lee and Jaz Rivette were on Twenty-Fourth Street NW across the street from the square, beige edifice at 2401 Massachusetts Avenue NW. They were walking along the row of stately if bland façades, structures designed with security rather than pure aesthetics in mind.

"Technically, that place is on S Street NW," Rivette said, looking at the map on his phone. "But that's not sexy, right? Ambassadors gotta be classholes."

Lieutenant Lee let her companion monologue. They were both wired and this allowed him to vent slowly. It also kept him from dwelling on the loss they had suffered that morning. She wished she could put her own grief aside. The loss of her parents seemed impossible and untrue, and she did not fight that denial. That disbelief was all that kept her from waiting until the gate opened and charging in, seeking blood. Anyone's blood.

In the sharp light of the spring afternoon, the urgency of their mission ran headlong into the practicality of pulling it off. The "safe" they wanted to crack was formidable.

"An' who would want to attack Chad anyway?" Rivette went on. "Why do they need a blockhouse?"

Because states have changing fortunes, Lee thought.

They neared the end of the street and turned back. There was a black iron gate outside the compound and long but very narrow windows. She would stop short of describing it as impregnable but not far short.

What are you doing? she asked herself. It was strange. When she did not have time to think, in the field, strategies always revealed themselves. Here—

"It won't work."

The voice came from a man who was walking toward them. He was approximately five feet tall and built like a weight lifter. He wore jeans, a tight white V-neck sweater, and a black bow tie. His features were concealed behind large reflective sunglasses and a blank, khaki baseball cap. A pair of black leather gloves were tucked in his belt.

"What the hell?" Rivette murmured. "Is he on the phone with somebody?"

"Doesn't look like it," Grace said. She moved her left leg casually so that it was behind her. If the newcomer meant them harm, she did not want to be facing him flat-footed.

"And what's with those sunglasses," he critiqued.

The lieutenant was alert but not tense; the man did not

"read" as private security for any of the government buildings along the street. And a single passage in one direction would not be enough to trigger any kind of security watch.

"I am Jay Paul," the man said as he approached. "I work with Mr. Berry."

Grace studied the man closely. Paul's breath smelled of mint and he was clean-shaven down to the follicles, even this late in the day; the man used a straightedge. Vanity or did he have the blade on him? Or both?

Your mind goes to concealed weapons too quickly, she cautioned herself. *Not every government agent practices ninjitsu.*

Rivette clearly had a similar idea and was looking the man over. There was a slight bulge at the bottom of his trousers on the outside. Rivette dropped then raised his eyes inquiringly.

"Glock?" the lance corporal asked.

"You know your weapons. A Glock 43."

"You followed us, Mr. Paul?" Grace asked.

"No, no," he said. "He told me you were coming here. My car is faster than the buses you took." The man stopped a few feet from them. "What you're thinking, an incursion or stakeout, won't work. There's a better way."

"Like?" Rivette asked.

"Let's walk," Paul encouraged. "Standing here too long *will* get the attention of the security officer surveilling the outside of the embassy."

The three began walking abreast with Paul in the middle.

"I'm parked just ahead," Paul told them. "I'd like to take you somewhere and tell you what I've been thinking."

"Say, Paul, just so you know—I got a firearm too."

"Osprey .45," Paul said. "Building security told me. But it's still in your bag."

"You sure?"

"Very. There was no tell," Paul told him. "Your hand didn't move when I approached. Lieutenant Lee, on the other hand, assumed a deflective fighting stance."

"Are you former military?" Grace asked.

"FBI," Paul replied. "Critical Incident Response Group. Oh, and Lieutenant Lee—I was sorry to hear about your loss. Matt said not to remark on it, but I do not believe in conspicuous avoidance. Especially if we are to be working together."

"Thank you," she said, then turned her mind from the subject. "What makes you think we're—"

"We have the same goal and Trigram has resources you lack," Paul said. "For example, we own a row house condominium on P Street NW. It's a safe house, not on any books. It's imperative we get you there."

"More imperative than before?" Grace asked.

"An IED was left at your residence," Paul said. "Captain Mann shot the man who brought it, precisely and decisively. Two bullets in the shoulder of the arm holding the detonator, then one through the heart. Trigram received word just before I called out to you."

"Captain Mann," Rivette said as though the words were an exaltation and not a name. "Distance?"

"I don't have that information," Paul said. "My point is, the Chinese are determined to get as many of you as possible before their self-imposed deadline."

"But she's all right?" Grace asked.

"As far as I know."

Grace was grateful for that and proud of their commander. Their world was in utter confusion and, at that moment, Mann embodied professionalism and hope. It reminded Grace of her own training, not just military but going back to her childhood. Though Berry and Paul appeared to offer stability, the lieutenant had the feeling that she and Rivette were being hustled.

"What if we decide to remain on our own," Grace asked.

"That's your choice, of course," Paul said. "But then your chances of getting inside the embassy and putting your hands on Joseph Kebzabo will be considerably diminished."

The comment got their attention, as Paul had known it would.

"You can do that?" Grace asked.

"We can. And then, Lance Corporal, you can personally let Mr. Kebzabo know how much you enjoyed his video."

"I would like that," Rivette said.

They reached Paul's car, a Mercedes C-Class Cabriolet convertible.

"Nobody had a ride like this back in my neighborhood,"

the lance corporal said. "But then, they're only criminals, not spies."

"In this line of work you learn to enjoy life while you can," Paul said.

Grace hesitated. She was a soldier, the handpicked member of an elite team. She had not just taken an oath of enlistment when she joined the U.S. Army, she had proudly memorized it.

> "I, Grace Lee, do solemnly swear that I will support and defend the Constitution of the United States against all enemies, foreign and domestic; that I will bear true faith and allegiance to the same; and that I will obey the orders of the President of the United States and the orders of the officers appointed over me, according to regulations and the Uniform Code of Military Justice. So help me God."

She was on a mission ordered by a commanding officer, a counterattack. By her oath, she was still on-task. She did not suddenly want to morph into something adjacent, a part of Berry's and Paul's patriot-for-pay "line of work."

Then, as it did so often, the voice of Jaz Rivette brought her back to the moment.

"I wonder what Kebzabo drives," the lance corporal mused as he looked back at the embassy.

"When he's not on foot he's in a chauffeured Chinese sedan," Paul replied.

That remark was a cannon shot. The woman's misgivings were sincere but Paul had reminded her of the larger enemy they were facing, one who killed not just Major Breen and her parents—and had abducted Admiral Williams—but who had just tried to murder Captain Mann. They would be hunting Black Wasp even as Grace and Rivette sought their own targets.

Decided, she opened the door and the two Black Wasps climbed in.

CHAPTER TWENTY

It was, briefly, a circus complete with braid, brass, and service members packed into cars. There were also gawking crowds, residents who were understandably concerned about whatever had happened.

No one knew. No one would know, Mann suspected.

As word of the shooting spread through the base, officers from virtually every division arrived at the residence, not just permanent units but also tenants: a van from the local Donut Glaze showed up to provide support.

Captain Mann had expected to see the head of the Directorate of Emergency Services, but she was not expecting the rest. Most of them went directly to the crime scene to "observe and report" but she was personally sought out by the head of the Civilian Personnel Advisory Center—who was wearing her support hat rather than waving the empowerment flag—to the Protestant Youth Coordinator from the Religious

Support Office. The cleric did not know Captain Mann or her faith but was on duty and came, arriving with a Watchcare spiritual wellness booklet in case the captain was not permitted to use online services during the shooting investigation.

Almost as quickly as the military roustabouts had staked their tents, the carnival ended. The captain knew why.

Mann was seated at the window of the small living room, with the PYC and CPAC officers throwing "grieving and trauma space" blocks against encroachment, when the staff vehicle of the Garrison Command Sergeant Major arrived. The CSM was carrying orders from garrison commander Colonel Juliana Gee, that everyone—including DES investigators—was to stand down and depart.

The influx had taken about fifteen minutes. The exit took one-third as long, hindered only by the jam of vehicles as they tried to leave. The only personnel left behind were four "physical security" officers from the DES. Mann wondered whether their instructions were to safeguard her or to make sure she was not unstable and would begin firing at adjacent homes.

The quick dispersal could only have been the result of a call from the commander in chief. And as she went to the kitchen to make tea—the only thing she felt she could keep down—and set a cup and saucer at the table where she intended to plant herself, Mann received a text notification on her secure phone.

Videoconference with WH1 and WH3 at 15:45.

That would be the president and the chief of staff, in ten minutes.

Enough time for the water to boil before they boil me, Mann thought humorlessly.

The president had ordered this stand-down, of course, and Mann knew why. No one on the base knew her or Black Wasp or why they were there. Any investigation would reveal their identities, and there would be blowback in Congress and in the military and public sectors: the new president has his own private military strike team.

She could almost feel the painful reluctance with which Angie and the president made this latest move. The RIP order was private, essentially "innocent." This was public. Though the garrison commander and her subordinates would wonder why, no one would venture to ask. Not unless they wanted to be transferred to someplace cold and unwelcoming.

Captain Mann set up her laptop on the small kitchen table, a rickety affair Rivette had picked up in a tag sale. None of the housing on base was furnished and everything in this house was from IKEA or some curbside.

She had just finished her tea when an email arrived with a secure link to the videoconference. The officer experienced a sense of disharmony inside herself. In Afghanistan, she had been a follower—a "truster," she had preferred to call it. No mission was undertaken without two essential qualities: clear parameters and also veteran eyes out front. Those eyes and their judgment were referred to as "the supreme court," trumping even protocol. At NSA Philadelphia, Mann had taken the same tack: follow the playbook, it had your back. If she had to step outside of regulations—as in the matter of the Black Order—she did it only because she knew it was right for that moment.

That reluctance to break rules was the reason the captain was here. Even under President Midkiff, the White House had regarded Chase Williams as something of a rogue. She had been seconded to Op-Center to furnish stability and accountability. On her first assignment with them, she could not have designed a result less in line with that objective.

The president and Angie Brunner appeared in separate side-by-side images. Both were in the Oval Office. The president did not look relaxed.

"I have been informed by Colonel Gee that you are the only member of Black Wasp on the base," Wright said thickly.

"That is correct, sir."

"Where are the other two members?"

"I don't know, Mr. President. They departed shortly after the hour."

"Get them back," the president ordered. "Now."

"Sir, with the execution of Major Breen it became clear that Black Wasp had been compromised. On my orders, Lieutenant Lee and Lance Corporal Rivette departed as a matter of safety. I do not believe they will follow an instruction to return. It clearly is not safe to do so, and I will not put them in a position to disobey a direct order."

It took a moment for the president and his aide to digest that.

"Did you just say 'no' to the commander in chief?" Angie asked incredulously.

"With respect, Ms. Brunner, that is a simplistic reduction of what I said."

Mann was not sure where that low-level defiance came from, but there was no withdrawing it. The "supreme court" had spoken.

"Captain Mann," the president said, "you understand that your stated course will cost you the Op-Center command and earn you a court-martial."

"I understand, sir."

The woman had said the words clearly but with regret. Angie's lingering gaze seemed to recognize the officer's struggle. Then either the chief of staff or the president muted the call. The two faced each other from opposite panels, open hands blocking the possibility of Mann reading their lips.

The president returned after a short discussion.

"I want to remind you, Captain Mann, that we are in a delicate situation with the Chinese, and we must do everything to preserve our ongoing negotiations."

"Sir, they just tried to kill me," Captain Mann said.

"I am not defending them, Captain, and their action underscores the point that we must de-escalate this conflict as quickly as possible. You and your team have endured a great deal today, and so I offer you this alternative—at Ms. Brunner's urging, I might add. Black Wasp can remain wherever they are, but you must inform them that they are to take no hostile or aggressive action except in a clear case of self-defense."

Mann was surprised by the softening of the president's position. It only took her a moment to consider the option.

"I will do that at once, sir," she said. "Thank you, Mr. President . . . Ms. Brunner."

The screen went black and just like that Mann's career had been salvaged. She would live to fight another day—or two or three hours. It was impossible to say, but at least she was still in a position to help her team.

And just like that, too, the death of a young man was absorbed into the belly of this geopolitical monster.

She made more tea, wondering if she wanted more than that hour or two as a strike force commander.

CHAPTER TWENTY-ONE

P Street NW, Washington, D.C.
March 23, 4:00 P.M.

P Street NW is a major artery in the life of Washington, D.C., running west from North Capitol Street all the way to Georgetown University. The surface of the street was cobbled; cars were stuffed fender-to-fender along the curb; and pedestrians and dogs were out enjoying the pleasant late afternoon.

Jay Paul drove past a long row of pricey residences that stood adjacent to the beating pulse of the nation's capital. They were hidden behind fat, orderly trees whose branches were just showing the first signs of spring. The limbs seemed to be saluting, flashing daylight, then shadow, then daylight through the open top of the Mercedes.

Paul slowed at a stately, three-story town house that sat at the corner of P Street NW and Fourteenth Street NW, just past Logan Circle. The circle, a former gathering place for junkies and derelicts, was now a showpiece, as were all the once run-down structures around it. There was a chest-high stone wall out front of the safe house. It was covered with winter-brittle ivy and ended in an iron gate that opened onto a short, curved drive.

"This city loves its iron bars," Rivette said.

It was this barricade that had prompted Rivette to make his first remark. He had been to the city only a handful of times since transferring to Black Wasp, and then only to go to a bar. Embassies and town houses were well outside his small social orbit.

The façade looked pink in the sunlight that spread across the rooftops of the attached, adjacent homes. It was majestic but foreign to the lance corporal, and he did not aspire to live here. It was that thought that prompted Rivette's next remark, heavy with nostalgia.

"I'll take the worn-down Rivette apartment with the dead bolt my mom installed herself."

The other two passengers were silent, as they had been throughout the short drive. Paul was listening to texts through earbuds and Grace was deep in reflection. The lance corporal did not have to wonder what she was thinking about. She was stone-faced behind her sunglasses, sunk in the contoured seat, as distant as Rivette had ever seen her.

That got to him. Until Major Breen, the only death Rivette had experienced firsthand were ODs or gang members, doomed-to-die punks from San Pedro. The major was a new experience, so new that it did not seem real; and though they trained together and went on missions together they were not really close. Not the way he was with Grace. Even her pain now was his pain. The comments he made about the city as they drove through it, about the street they were on—that was habit. He did not feel as buoyant as he thought he sounded.

The car stopped in front of the stone steps that led to a heavy white door.

"Whose poor ride is out front?" Rivette asked, jerking a thumb at a Kia minivan on the street.

"Ours," Paul said. "Armored, in case we have to move cargo or passengers that someone else might want. It also doubles as a barricade in case someone tries to ram the wall."

"Has anyone ever done that?" Rivette asked.

"Twice, though not on purpose," Paul said. "One of them was a Speaker of the House coming back from a rendezvous. Washington likes to drink, especially the power brokers. Worked out for us, though."

"How so?"

"Another official in our pocket," Paul said.

That was something Rivette understood. It was no different from the drug dealers and human traffickers in Los Angeles.

They entered the town house, passing through a narrow mudroom with coat hangers. It opened into a large living room that had a lot of shiny wood Rivette could not identify. He felt self-conscious stepping on the highly polished floor and avoided altogether the expensive-looking white rug in the center of it.

"This is *not* like safe houses in the movies," Rivette said.

"Those are FBI or intelligence services," Paul said. "This is private enterprise."

"I guess you're used to people being impressed," the lance corporal added.

Paul stood at the foot of the stairs. "Truthfully, most of the people who come here are too afraid or too eager to get off the first floor to be impressed."

Stopping on the fringes of the rug made the lance corporal think of the threadbare carpet in his home, which made him think about his family. He excused himself, stepped into a corner beside a plant that was taller than he was, and texted Little Guillermo.

"Eye on the window behind you," Grace cautioned.

"It's bulletproof," Paul said.

"Thanks. Watch it anyway," she told Rivette.

He gave her an okay sign, faced it, and resumed typing.

Grace looked around. She was not admiring the furnishings and staircase but noting the other windows and exits.

"I didn't mean to interfere with your command, Lieutenant," Paul said.

"You didn't," she said. After determining the ways out—she was wary of the Chinese but not entirely trusting of Berry or this man—Grace faced Paul. He remained by the staircase, waiting patiently for his guests. "We'll stay downstairs, if it's all the same to you."

"The computers are upstairs."

"Laptops?"

He nodded.

"You have Wi-Fi?" Grace said. It was not so much a question as a next step.

Paul smiled. "It's a wash down here, isn't it? They can see you, but you can get away."

"It's the kind of tactical balance I prefer."

Paul nodded once. "Help yourself to a late lunch," he said. "I'll be right back."

Grace glanced at the artwork on the wall, geometric confusions that seemed to fit the trade of the owner. Rivette had finished with his call and said that everyone was all right.

"They think it's just some old gang grudge against my old man and I left it at that."

Rivette's father, Jackson, had been a short-order cook who handled numbers on the side. He was fatally stabbed in a dispute over revenue.

As they headed to the kitchen to help themselves to whatever was there, Grace received a call from Captain Mann. She put it on speaker.

"Captain, how are you?" Grace asked. "We heard about the IED, the shooting. We were—are—glad you're okay and also proud."

"Thank you."

There was a brief hesitation on Mann's end. Rivette shot the lieutenant a pained look. It confused her.

"Heard from whom?" Mann asked.

Then she understood. Grace was still looking at Rivette, who shrugged, held out two fingers, and pointed them twice—the field signal for going forward along the existing track.

"Matt Berry told us," Grace replied.

"Where did you see him? Where are you?" Mann asked.

Rivette repeated the gesture.

"We're at a Trigram safe house," Grace said.

"I didn't know they had one."

"Neither did we, sir, until Mr. Berry offered it," the lieutenant replied.

"Where is it?" Mann asked.

Something compelled Grace to answer vaguely, "In town." She did not think Mann would press her; that would signal mistrust.

"All right," Mann said. "You'll be staying there?"

"For now, Captain."

Once again, Rivette made a face. He mouthed, *I should have taken this call.*

"Lieutenant, I just got off the phone with President Wright," Mann said. "He wanted me to recall you both and I refused. The Chinese know this location and will be watching it. I did not want you trying to get here."

"Thank you."

"But I assured him and Angie Brunner—who I believe is our only ally in the West Wing—that we will not take independent action."

"What is the president doing to recover Admiral Williams?"

"I don't know," Mann admitted.

"Or arrest the killer of Major Breen. Or whoever drove a van over my parents."

"I don't know that either, Lieutenant. And I'm sorry I

don't have any answers. But I appreciate the delicacy of the negotiations that are ongoing to stop the killing."

Grace had to lock down her mouth to keep from responding.

"Can I count on you both to resist-in-place?"

Rivette nodded. Grace relaxed her jaw as memories of Mulberry Street—the neighbors, the shops, the scooter she rode as a little girl—flooded forth. Rivette snapped his fingers to bring her back. He repeated the nod with emphasis.

"Captain, it is the duty of an officer in the field to make calls as circumstances change," Grace said.

"Lieutenant, don't paraphrase Doctrine 2015 initiatives to me," Mann said sternly. "You will resist-in-place."

"Sir, Black Wasp—yourself included—are under attack. The president will do what he must do to cover his retreat. Until then, we are still vulnerable."

"Ride this out!" Mann said. "That is an order."

Rivette's head had stopped moving. Whether he was responding to his own inner voice or reacting to Grace's challenging, then defiant expression, his head began shifting slowly from side to side.

"Captain Mann, Black Wasp—and its two surviving veterans—only know one direction." She made the same motion toward Rivette that he had used moments before, two fingers ahead. When she was done, she turned those two fingers toward the phone. "I'm sorry, sir," she said and ended the call.

"That was unpleasant," Rivette said.

"Necessary," Grace replied.

"You understand that we just went rogue. If the captain informs the president—"

"She won't. She will support the unit."

"Okay, but if she does tell the president, he will send more than the DES after us."

"Where?" Grace asked. "They don't know about Joseph Kebzabo or the Chad connection. If anything, Wright will want to protect the Chinese embassy—which, under the circumstances, is itself obscene."

"What if the captain or the president call Matt Berry?"

"The White House doesn't know about his involvement and Captain Mann won't tell him."

"Lieutenant, you have a lot more faith in our commander than I do. Actually, scratch that. You have *less* faith. She's a lifer. I think she'll put the chain of command first."

"If that's true," said a voice from the living room, "I'll know about it."

Jay Paul had returned with his laptop.

"You heard?" Grace asked.

"I did and I'm impressed with you both. Duty before cover-your-ass."

Rivette finished his personal mission, which was to find orange juice in the refrigerator and an apple on the counter. He tossed the latter to Grace and grabbed an oatmeal cookie from a glass jar.

"How do you operate, Mr. Paul?" Grace asked.

"At the Bureau, I was all about duty. Then I found something larger."

"Oh?" Grace said before she took a bite of apple.

"I would think about the next word that came from your mouth," Rivette cautioned. "Duty and patriotism are two of the biggest words in our line of work."

"Are they really?" Paul asked. "I've read your files. There's one other word. Admiral Williams demonstrated that one in Yemen."

"Unafraidness?" Rivette suggested.

"That too, but the word, the idea I'm thinking of is *justice*. When the admiral foreswore his oath to put a bullet in a terrorist."

The Black Wasps were silent. Thinking about the admiral brought their duty into laser-sharp focus. While he was still a prisoner, their work—their duty—was open-ended.

"What's your plan?" Grace asked, nodding toward the laptop Paul was holding.

"Embassy records show that Joseph Kebzabo lives in the compound with other security officers and will likely remain there until the heat on Major Breen's killing dies down. Our document officer is preparing a letter of introduction for Lance Corporal Rivette, along with a corroborating ID. Both will represent that he is a graduate student at the Université de Moundou, in particular the Faculté de Droit et Sciences Sociales."

"My grandma was Cajun and your French is terrible," Rivette noted.

"Not a linguist," Paul admitted as he set the laptop on the counter and slid into one of the three bar stools. "The point is, you have come to the United States to study solutions to the challenge of lower-income housing. You have been denied the help of local authorities and have gone to the embassy for assistance."

"Back up," Rivette said. "I'm supposed to be from Chad?"

"You are, but don't let that concern you."

"Man, I don't even know the capital."

"N'Djamena," Paul informed him. "But you won't need to know that."

"Why not?"

"Because you won't be talking to anyone once you're inside," Paul said.

"Okay," Rivette said, "so full disclosure—my French isn't perfect either."

"Again, not a problem. The real reason you're there is to admit Lieutenant Lee and, together, to find Joseph Kebzabo."

CHAPTER TWENTY-TWO

35,000 feet, Airways First, Apartment 2
March 23, 5:33 P.M., Eastern Standard Time

Wang Jing had been dozing while he considered what he had labeled, in the notes on his tablet, "The Problem and the Possibilities."

The deputy director was more than halfway through the thirteen-hour flight when his phone awakened him. It took him a moment to recall where he was: in a first-class cabin suite on his flight from Beijing to Washington, D.C. His tablet was still on the bedding, on his lap, plugged into the wall socket. He set it on the small shelf and reached for his phone.

The only individuals who had the deputy director's number were those who had security clearance from China's Central Military Commission. The only people who called this number were those with urgent information.

The caller was Dylan Hao. That meant there had been developments, probably not good, or the agent would not be calling.

"Yes?" Jing answered curtly while he drew himself up slightly in the bed.

"I'm very sorry to disrupt your sleep, Deputy Director, but the agent dispatched to the enemy target failed to destroy it and perished in the attempt."

"Is he clean?"

"They will not trace him here," Hao assured the official. "He had only his green card on him and the motorbike was newly purchased by him."

"But the Americans know."

"They will surmise, of course. But they will do nothing. He could be a lone wolf," Hao said. "That will be our position."

"The woman who beat General Chang is still alive?"

"Alive and at liberty, her whereabouts unknown," Hao said.

Jing considered the situation. "You cannot attack their leader again. She will be on her guard and protected. And the third member—"

"A lance corporal, his location also not known to us."

"The problem and the possibilities," Jing remarked.

"Sir?"

Fully awake now, Jing retrieved his tablet, looked at his notes. "Any situation, even one that is unexpected and seemingly disadvantageous, is an opportunity to learn. To probe, find a new weakness, a new direction. At this moment, President Wright is an unknown quantity as a leader. It's been just two months—we don't really know him and he doesn't really know himself. Let's find out."

"What are you thinking?"

Jing looked at his notes, a mass of half-finished thoughts and even less complete sentences.

"You've been living there, moving among several tiers of bureaucrats, reading their press. Tell me, do you think this failed effort will affect the American position on the return of Dr. Dàyóu?"

"I do not, and we've had no indication of that, Deputy Director Jing, nor is that likely. President Wright seems willing to absorb a variety of blows—the spacecraft, the killing of Major Breen, the death of the Lee family, and the kidnapping of Williams."

"It is private penance for the attack on our missile center. Like Kennedy's early-term Bay of Pigs fiasco, this looms as a major foreign affairs disaster. The question we must answer is whether it is an instinctual political move on Wright's part or whether it is cowardice, a fear of retribution."

"It's possible even he doesn't know," Hao said.

"I believe that. Let's learn more."

"How?"

Jing considered the question. He also looked ahead at the potential for advancement. If he could craft a careful, accurate psychological predictor of John Wright, then his document would become a roadmap for Beijing in the South China Seas, in the Koreas, throughout the Far East.

The Jing Doctrine.

This was the moment, the opportunity, and what had kept him up was how to seize it. A misfired assassination had provided the means.

He poked through his notes, which considered the internal forces that historically push and pull American leaders. In any administration there would be hawks, especially on the Joint Chiefs of Staff, urging a response other than the peace and placation policy on which Chinese aggression depended. The failure of the bomber might embolden them to push harder. On the other hand, there were doves like national security advisor January Dow who—and he understood this, was not so different himself—was young and ambitious. She had one eye on her job as national security advisor and another on advancement. Perhaps secretary of state and, at some future date, the vice presidency or presidency.

"I believe we have a way to go before Wright pushes back," Jing said. "We have an asset that can help us determine that."

"Williams?"

"Yes," Jing said. "At this moment, the last impression President Wright must have of this situation is a win, not a loss. This Captain Mann not only survived, she killed the bomber. We have to rearrange the board and see how he reacts."

"By disposing of Williams? We may be doing him a favor at this point."

"You're forgetting," Jing said. "This is not about Admiral Williams. It's about Wright and his team's reaction."

The deputy director had isolated and emphasized a word on his tablet: "contact"!

"I want you to request a videoconference with the Oval Office in my name," Jing said.

"You want to speak with the president?" Hao clarified.

"That would all be posturing, pointless. No, I want you to give them a chance to speak directly with Chase Williams. Tell them that. Arrange it in the conference studio, as if Williams is a guest and not a prisoner. One armed guard, out of view."

"He will try to escape. It's suicide by sentry."

"Perhaps. It's of no importance to us one way or the other. However, it will be to the administration. What I want you to do is tell Williams, right before he goes on, that he will be spending the rest of his life in Qincheng Prison. Tell him it's the one General Chang was visiting when he was assaulted by the American invader. If Williams chooses to die during the video call, then Wright's latest move is a loss. But there is another possibility."

"What's that?"

Jing said, "It's the one I am most interested in. Arrange it as soon as possible."

"I'll see to it," Hao said.

Jing ended the call and sat a moment listening to the purr of the great engines. He regretted the lost opportunity at Fort

Belvoir, but there was still time to find the others and, for the moment, he savored this inspiration.

War was not a short-term project, nor was it foolproof. But so far, this one had worked out better than he had dared to hope. He lay back and savored a final thought before going back to sleep: a problem *is* possibilities.

CHAPTER TWENTY-THREE

Embassy of the People's Republic of China,
Washington, D.C.
March 23, 6:07 P.M.

Williams was led blindfolded and at gunpoint to the bathroom. He was accompanied all the way by someone who either did not understand English or had been instructed not to talk to him or both.

"You don't have to worry," Williams had said as he was unstrapped and escorted from the room. "I'm not steady enough to bolt for the door."

That was all he had said. His clothes were cold and damp from whatever drug-induced perspiration they had absorbed. He was hungry now, not having eaten since—

Was that this morning? he wondered. *A day ago? Longer?*

Time and orientation were not the only elusive qualities. The only sounds he heard were those that he himself made. The carpet was deep and the wood paneling—he had brushed a hand against it—was solid. He wondered if this was a special wing at the embassy reserved for guests of the People's Republic of China.

Touching the wall had not been intentional. The admiral was still unsteady, recalling the first time he had been on the deck of a battleship during a severe storm. That had been forty years ago. He marveled at how the body remembered sensations and feelings with such clarity.

The young body and the child's mind, he thought. The forces that shape the direction of a life.

When he was returned to the room, Williams was not tied to the bed.

"You want me to pace?" he wondered aloud after the door was shut and locked.

It was dark and he had to feel for a light switch. It was hardly worth the minimal effort. In addition to the bed there was an empty nightstand. The floor was tile—atop concrete, from the cool, solid feel of it. There was a camera above the door, out of reach. He tugged at the edge of the bed, bolted to the floor. There were no linens, just a bare pillow and mattress; the only way to blind the thing was with an article of clothing.

"Which is probably why you keep the temperature at, what, fifty-five degrees?"

Too cold to go bare-chested or pantless. He just now noticed that the jacket he had been wearing that morning was gone. The Chinese had a foreign sense of humor: It had probably been given to one of the drivers as a shimmy. It was a way of letting everyone know, even the lowest ranking member of the staff, that the American admiral had lost face. Williams' highest reach now was to put a shine on a Chinese automobile.

The room had a window, but it was shuttered from the outside and there were metal slats on the inside. He was no less a prisoner than if they had been bars; somehow, though, narrow, flat, gunmetal-gray panels seemed less stark.

"Chinese design sense," he said. "A statement, like prison-plus."

Apart from the spartan decor there was another grim reminder of his status: Williams was already talking to himself. He had been to enough debriefs to know what that meant. He was psychologically preparing for a long stay.

"But will it be?"

His tactical brain kicked in, then. Still woozy, he sat heavily on the bed.

"They want me for something," Williams said. "I'm either a hostage or they're planning a deeper interrogation."

Stop talking, he told himself. The camera system probably has ears as well. And ears on the other end. And it's probably being recorded. *Set an example,* he thought.

He lay back. The mattress was also damp with his cold sweat. His body heat would warm it soon enough, like that flight suit when he had flown in the back seat of an EA-18G Growler. Flying at nearly Mach 2, fifty thousand feet up, would wring sweat out of any first-time passenger.

Enough about you, Williams thought. But there was a problem with that. Williams' mind had nowhere to go that was not bleak. He thought about the team and about Major

Breen, about the video Hao had showed him. He mourned the lawyer who became a combat casualty, but he also hurt for Captain Mann who would have had to okay his going to the park. And then there were Lieutenant Lee and Lance Corporal Rivette: they would not let pain sit on them. They would act, probably whether they had permission or not. Grace might hesitate, but Rivette was raised on the street and all his military training would not have overwritten those instincts.

Further reflection was interrupted by the arrival of Dylan Hao. The man arrived with a guard but entered the room alone. He shut the door and folded his arms.

"We are at a turning point in our association," he said.

"Which of us is getting crunched?" Williams asked.

"I think you know the answer to that," Hao replied.

Williams did. But hearing it still hit with the force of a jailor telling an inmate on death row, *It's time.* The admiral did not think they were going to kill him. He had faced death a number of times in his career, most of those on the handful of missions with Black Wasp. That was not his deepest fear.

Whatever it is, face it with dignity, he reminded himself. The Chinese were experts at psychological warfare, but whatever they did, he would try to hold on to that—and to his God. When there was absolutely nothing left, there was always that.

"Like Hope at the bottom of Pandora's box," Williams said, rising slowly.

"Pardon me?"

"Just something I read as a kid," the admiral said. "One of those things that stays with you."

Hao rapped on the door once with the back of his knuckles then opened it. The guard outside stepped back so they could exit. The grim-faced service member was People's Liberation Army Navy Marine Corps, by both his uniform and the weapon he held before him: a 95 Shì Zìdòng—a Type 95 Automatic Rifle. The young man's robot-eyes, steady and dead, suggested he would fire without hesitation.

Hao led the way, the Marine behind, as they walked down the corridor. Williams had turned twice on his way to the bathroom; he surmised they were headed somewhere else.

"The crunch, as you said, is this," Hao spoke as though that earlier conversation were still ongoing. "You are being taken to a conference room where you will place a video call to the president."

"He's expecting my call?"

"No," Hao said.

"What makes you think he'll take it?" Williams asked. He was about to say, *President Wright delegates second-tier stuff to his chief of staff,* but stopped himself. He did not want to give this slippery son of a bitch any additional information.

"The call will be placed in the name of Wang Jing, the official to whom Dr. Dàyóu and his family will be turned over"—Hao looked at his phone—"a little after midnight, some six hours from now."

"Okay. And when the president takes the call?"

"I wish the president to know that you are neither drugged or under duress, so I will furnish the topic at that time," Hao said.

Williams was about to ask, *Is it about my team? Is it about our last mission?* Instead, he balled his fists and dropped them stiffly at his sides as if they were pendulous weights pulling his mouth shut. *Do not speak. Do not implore. And if you don't like what Hao says, do not say anything to the president.*

But despite that bravado, it was an uncertain man who made his way down a moody corridor that, nonetheless, had the tenor and appearance of the proverbial last mile . . .

CHAPTER TWENTY-FOUR

Jaz Rivette looked up from the computer screen.

"Yeah, it's like you said," the lance corporal told Jay Paul. "The part of your plan that's actually a plan is pretty simple."

In a way, Rivette was relieved. Major Breen had been Black Wasp's go-to officer for tactics and logistics. His schemes, whether for training or on missions, were always somewhat detailed, even if events never quite played out the way he had explained them. Rivette and Lieutenant Lee were always the first to admit the left turns were usually their fault.

As in China.

They were still on the bar stools, Rivette with his grip at his feet. It was beginning to get dark outside and they were illuminated. Though the shades had been drawn, their silhouettes made good targets. If someone came after them, he wanted to be ready. To his right, Grace was seated so she could look at Paul, the computer, and the window. A streetlamp had come on outside; shapes there cast shadows too. She tried not to let passersby and bicyclists distract her.

Paul took down the schematic of the embassy, which had been furnished to Trigram by one of the members of the architectural teams. He was seated to the left of Rivette, closest to the window. He did not seem concerned about a surprise attack.

"I will take you to the site in the van," Paul continued to discuss the mission. "When you leave the embassy, I will be waiting for you."

"Just to be clear, whatever happens inside is our call?" Grace said.

"That's right," Paul said.

"We do what we decide to do to Kebzabo and then you give us a lift back here," Rivette said.

"Also right."

Grace's expression did not reflect the deep concern she felt. "I haven't been around the intelligence community very much, but isn't that uncommon?"

"Which part?"

"Agents helping people they barely know and not expecting a quid pro quo. Helping for the sake of what you said—justice?"

"You are hardly people we don't know," Paul corrected. "You work for Chase Williams, and Mr. Williams and Mr. Berry go back a way."

"Then you're saying this *is* personal?" Grace pressed.

"In a way that relates to what I just said," Paul told her. "Admiral Williams."

"Listen, mumble gums, you lost me back at the blueprint there." Rivette cocked his head at the laptop. "Can you just cut to the bone here?"

"Sorry, I thought you were a step ahead of me."

"We're not even on the same street," Rivette said.

"Hold up, Jaz," Grace said. Like most operatives and politicians, Jay Paul was accustomed to speaking around topics. Not committing himself so that if there was a slipup, he had plausible deniability. "You want to use the assassin to help us get Chase Williams out."

"In a manner of speaking," Paul said.

"Not as a hostage, because he does not have that kind of value to Beijing," the lieutenant went on carefully, methodically, as though she were crossing Potomac ice. "Even if Kebzabo pinned Major Breen's murder on them, there's nothing anyone in our government could do about it."

"Correct."

"You want him to go in and blow somebody away?" Rivette said with disbelief. "He'd never do it. He wouldn't get out alive."

"Also true," Paul said. "No, Joseph Kebzabo has just one use to us. I'll tell you about it as we drive."

"Why?" Rivette asked.

"Because the day staff goes to their residences in the compound at seven," Paul told them. "They're tired, eager to go. You stand a better chance of being waved in just before the night people arrive with nothing to do."

"Wait, what about the documents?" Rivette asked.

Paul pointed to a message on his computer as he slid off the stool. "In the van. Delivered six minutes ago by R.T."

"Who?" Rivette asked.

"Red Toyota, one of our guys."

• • •

Paul went to the van first and checked the documents. While he was sitting there, he surveilled the street by eye and video camera, making sure the house was not being watched. When that was done, he motioned for the others to join him. The back was an open compartment and the Black Wasps sat in canvas slings located close to the front seat. The fold-down seats were almost identical to those in any number of military transports in which they had traveled.

By convenience rather than design, it was nonetheless a comforting, familiar touch.

Rivette looked at his documents. "Dig it. My Chadian name is Innocent Olivier."

"Good call," Grace said.

"Why so?"

"Because you speak passable French if you have to. If you were Hassan or Abakar, you'd be expected to know some Arabic dialect."

Rivette was glad someone was thinking as he quickly memorized some of the details. He checked pronunciations and locations on his phone as the vehicle headed back toward Massachusetts Avenue NW. There was the usual midweek rush-hour traffic—automobile, wheeled, and on foot—and the trip was slow by circumstance and design. Grace was not surprised to find their driver as fastidious behind the wheel as he was with his appearance. Paul did not want to break any rules, or fenders, that would result in an investigation of Rivette's backpack. The gun was on top of a tablet to prevent it from leaving a telltale impression in the bag.

As they drove, Paul explained the rest of the mission. Grace was both curious and suspicious about that. It was a part he had intentionally concealed back at the house.

"What Matt Berry wants is that, alive or dead, Kebzabo is removed from the embassy and brought to the van."

Seated on opposite sides of the van, the Black Wasps looked at each other. The abduction did not entirely surprise Grace; the "or dead" part did.

"I'm not seeing the bigger picture behind that," Grace admitted.

"I'm afraid I can't share any more," Paul told her.

"Why, who're we gonna—" Rivette began, then stopped. He remembered what Captain Mann had told them about the Chinese having a killer truth serum. If the Chinese had it, then their minions from Chad had it too.

"All right," Grace said. "But going in and coming out with a body, alive or dead, is going to come with a high price. Even if we get out, there will be video. We'll be exposed."

"Not necessarily," Paul said. "All the cameras at the

embassy are wireless. No cords to be cut, theoretically more secure. R.T., the man who dropped off your papers—which I'll give you in a moment, they look fine—that man has a 16-band 5g jammer in his red Toyota. He's already parked around the corner ready to pull the plug, which will also kill cell phones, GPS, even LoJack, and all the other go-to tools of embassy security."

"LoJack," Rivette said. "I don't see us stopping to steal a vehicle."

"One never knows," Paul said.

"What about metal detectors?" Rivette asked.

"There's no security station as such. The sensors are built into the front door. They will go on the fritz along with everything else."

"No hand check of the bag?"

"There's nothing about that in the security manual," Paul said.

"Which you have."

"We have the entire set from all local embassies," Paul said.

Grace was beginning to realize that Trigram was not quite the boutique she had imagined but a serious intelligence operation, as well connected as any she had encountered since becoming a Black Wasp. All the cautions she had heard on podcasts, read in newspapers, about the "deep state." It was obviously much more than just a public sector concern.

"You'll be there, you said. Right?" Rivette went on. "I

don't want to come out with a body and then have to stop and steal somebody's Jag, y'know?"

"I'll be there," Paul said. "I want this as much as you do."

"Why?" Grace asked. "Did you know Admiral Williams?"

"Barely," Paul said. "The man behind this, Dylan Hao, was someone Berry trusted. We want him burned."

"Do you ever do the burning yourself?" Grace asked.

"If you mean the firm, no," Paul said. "If you mean me, also no. We have to maintain good relationships with our clients. They have to feel safe. That means no muscle from our side."

"Another question," Rivette said. "We get caught, they use drugs, your operation is compromised."

"That's why I don't take selfies with agents," Paul deadpanned.

It took a moment for Rivette to realize that he was joking.

"If that happens, all they'll get is a clean safe house," Paul said. "They already know about Matt Berry, Trigram. We're untouchable. Matt and the top people—they're like J. Edgar Hoover used to be. They know too much about everyone."

"Except Hao," Grace said.

"And look what's raining down on him," Paul said. "It's nearly time. We'll talk more on the other side."

Rivette shook his head. "Ball of confusion," he remarked as he opened his backpack to put his documents inside.

"You'll want those in a pocket," Grace said. "The gun? Cameras before we go in?"

"Right," Rivette said. He put the papers in his pants pocket. "They'll look more used this way."

"You're getting the feel for this," Paul said. "In our work an assignment is more than weapons, it's also attention to detail."

"And the words are nicer," Rivette said. "We go out, it's a mission."

"You go out, there's killing," Paul said. He stepped aside to place a call.

It was not a critical remark, but it felt like one. The nuances of this world as opposed to the bubble of Op-Center, of his old life in the street, were unfamiliar to Rivette.

"I think I see what Major Breen was talking about all that time, the stuff about codes of conduct and all that," Rivette said. Mentioning Breen, his voice was both respectful and mournful. "You go into something with no restrictions, you could find yourself shooting up God-knows-what."

"I did that in China," she said. "I crossed a line. That's what brought all of this on."

"I read the report you wrote and I don't think so. You tried to do the right thing."

She shook her head. "Maybe with Dr. Dàyóu, but I tore into that general because I lost it, Jaz. Because of what he'd done to Dàyóu's son."

"Payback," Rivette said. "He earned it."

"What about Kebzabo? What about the guy who took the admiral?"

"I don't know. We won't know till we get there."

"I know now," she said. "All of my Taoist training feels

under the wheels of a van in New York. I want to kill everyone who had a hand in all of this."

"Is that just you talking or is that really your plan?"

Grace did not answer. In just a few minutes, she would find out.

And there was another concern too, different but no less significant. No one in the Oval Office would have any doubt about who had pulled this off. When this was done—and it would be, must be done, if only for the admiral—Grace wondered what kind of future she and Jaz Rivette would have, if any.

CHAPTER TWENTY-FIVE

Embassy of the People's Republic of China,
Washington, D.C.
March 23, 6:29 P.M.

There were no cell phones and earbuds for these boys, Williams thought as he reached his destination. Terrorists and anarchists had co-opted mobile devices. China would not afford to have itself lumped in with the common herd.

The room was a full broadcast studio with a professional camera and an overhead microphone and lights. There was a black table with a monitor so he could see other parties remotely.

Williams was shown to a comfortable chair in front of the camera. Hao sat beside him, to the right, out of view. The screen was dark. Almost obscenely, there was a water bottle to Williams' left—as if this were a board meeting. The guard with the gun was by the door, on the inside, roughly ten feet away.

The wooziness caused by the scopolamine was largely gone; this Oz, this Wonderland was exactly what it appeared to be: gross and surreal. Williams wondered if the guard would actually shoot up the studio if he tried to walk out. Williams wondered if that was the *plan*.

"Would you like to preview your appearance?" Hao asked. He pointed at the dark monitor. "I can arrange it."

Williams was disgusted. His predecessor at Op-Center, Paul Hood, had once written a memo to his staff about the "Stewards of Indifference," government workers who saw people as pawns and statistics rather than human beings. People were dying and Hao was being glib. It went deeper than the problem Paul Hood had indicated. Politicians as a rule did not respect sacrifice. When it was asked of them, when they were "it" in the geopolitical game of spin the bottle, they ducked or ran. Only soldiers who had seen bodies torn and destroyed honored that in all sides of a conflict.

Williams wondered if John Wright was a ducker.

Suddenly, to his right, there was a new obscenity. Hao had barked out a laugh. Something he had seen on the phone amused him.

"I'm informed that the conference will begin in one minute," Hao said.

Williams did not bite, if that was the intent. He did not ask what had just happened, but he was alert for some kind of ambush.

"There is no need to be cautious about what you say," Hao advised. "You told us that Black Wasp reports directly to the president and that he and the chief of staff are the only ones aware of that relationship."

"You trying to shame me?" Williams could not help asking.

"Not at all," Hao told him. "I'm letting you know you need not hold back. A man's farewell to the last Americans he will ever see should be free and open. You are on Chinese soil here and, tomorrow, you will be on Chinese soil again— Qincheng Prison."

Williams had been expecting to be part of some warning, a caution perhaps, or be forced at gunpoint to express regret or accepting humiliation, the traditional substance and stuffing of hostage videos. He had been prepared to tell Hao to go to hell—not this. It hit him like a point-blank bullet delivered with studied, casual composure.

The admiral struggled not to react, not to jump at Hao or throw the water bottle at the camera. He was not afraid of being shot. That would be a mercy. He was afraid of giving Hao the satisfaction of an emotional rage.

The screen before him winked on. There was only one face looking back at his, framed from the neck up. It belonged to Angie Brunner, not the president.

That was the game, Williams realized. To place a value on his head, to see if the admiral was important enough to the president to show up for the call. Wright was curious, of course. That's why he accepted a videoconference. So Angie Brunner could be his ears.

That was probably why Hao had laughed. He must have known the chief of staff would be the only one on the call.

In Hollywood, Angie Brunner had delivered career

deathblows with calculated indifference. And her expression now was neutral. But she did not have that chin-out assurance he had seen in all their previous face-to-faces.

It occurred to Williams, as it must have, suddenly, to Angie, that as he was studying her she was evaluating him. The chin came up a little—for his benefit as much as hers.

"How are you?" Angie asked.

It was not a real question; it was just something to say. She already knew the answer. The president had cut him loose. He was a seaman without anchor. There was a phrase the admiral had learned in meetings, especially where important tactics and policies had to be decided. He used it now.

"Give me a moment," Williams replied.

Hao's pronouncement about Qincheng hung in the air like tear gas, stinking and disorienting. But Williams found a safe harbor, not in Angie's uplifted face—in her eyes. They were compassionate and feminine and gender-role guidelines be damned, they steadied him.

"I have a message for the president," Williams said evenly, then stood and stepped back so she could see the upper part of his body.

Hao shot to his feet when Williams rose, knocking over his chair; the guard at the door squatted slightly and tensed, bracing himself if he had to fire.

Williams ignored them as he raised his right arm and saluted. He remained at attention and watched as Angie's composure broke around the mouth.

Hao was not chuckling anymore. He was not smiling.

Whatever he had hoped to learn or achieve, this part at least—the end of Chase Williams—had not happened. Whatever happened next, the exchange with Angie and the blow to Hao would give him strength.

The double agent growled instructions to the sentry in Chinese. Williams guessed, correctly, that he was to be taken back to his little prison. Hao remained behind and the admiral went willingly.

Yes, he would try to make a break at some point. He had no intention of going to Qincheng. But, for now, he was content to have dead-ended his captor.

CHAPTER TWENTY-SIX

Embassy of Chad, Washington, D.C.
March 23, 6:56 P.M.

In China, on their previous mission, Grace Lee had spent a considerable amount of time watching the Taiyuan Satellite Launch Center. There had been diagrams before that, and National Reconnaissance Office photographs. But pictures never truly capture the nature of a place. Even after she had watched the facility from the woods, it was different when she went in. She was forced to interact with physical obstacles and opposition military personnel. It was a sharply different experience from studying and watching.

The Embassy of Chad was the same. It had been a useful exercise to case the building earlier, and then to go over the architect's schematics with Jay Paul. For one thing, everything looked different in the dwindling light of dusk. For another, as soon as she and Rivette left the van and made their way to the gate, the experience itself was heightened along with their adrenaline levels.

"It's like that island we went to—but in slow motion," Rivette said.

She knew what he meant. The island was one of the Prince Edward Islands, closer to Antarctica than it was to South Africa, which claimed the land. The time was the previous November. The two had been air-dropped to liberate a remote outpost and hit that ground running.

The two were once again shoulder to shoulder, but this time they were walking from Massachusetts Avenue NW to the main entrance on S Street SW.

"At least it's warmer here than at the South freakin' Pole," he said when the embassy was a block ahead. "Shouldn't you be not coming with me about now?"

Grace did not answer immediately. Rivette regarded her. Her Shaolin kung fu animal was a leopard. She had that air about her now, watchful and sinuous. He stopped.

"This close to a target you got that look. What'd we miss?"

"Joseph knew what the major looked like. Someone knew where to find Captain Mann. If the admiral talked, and the Chinese hacked our files, chances are pretty good they know what we look like—or at least will be watching for a young Black man and an Asian woman with 'that look.'"

"Damn. Shouldn't Paul have picked up on that?" Rivette said, glancing back at her where the van was parked. "Or maybe he's using us for some kind of deep-state fast shuffle?"

"He may not know all the details," Grace said. "I don't think Berry shares everything with anyone."

"So what do you suggest?"

"We want Kebzabo so we proceed. But I'm going in with you."

"You don't have credentials. I still think I should get in and find the dog-walker entrance—"

"Jaz, they may not wait long enough to check your ID. For all we know you're on some kind of front-door watch list."

"Like a friggin' L.A. bistro," Rivette complained. "All right."

They resumed their approach.

"Look," Grace said, pointing along the street where they had been walking earlier.

Rivette followed her finger. The red Toyota was in place on the street where they had been walking earlier. He felt better knowing that Jay Paul had at least been reliable on that count.

"I was worried for a second there, y'know?" Rivette said. "All that intrigue talk, maybe Berry or Paul selling us out for favors from Chad."

"China, not Chad," Grace corrected him. "It occurred to me, too, but I don't think so. Remember, the admiral trusts Berry."

"And look what happened," Rivette said. "The agent was double."

"Fair," Grace agreed.

"Though, hey—" Rivette said. "How is Red Toyota going to know when to cut the wireless? He can't see the door from there."

"Paul can, from the van. He'll signal R.T."

"Efficient or a control freak?" the lance corporal wondered.

"It's their chain of command," Grace said.

It was strange, Rivette thought, how in the heart of civilization they could be in greater danger than in the so-called wilds of South Africa or the Middle East. Yet here they were.

The gate loomed. There was an intercom and camera at the door. The camera light was still on.

"Doesn't mean Toyota-guy won't kill it once we're inside," Grace whispered.

Rivette nodded and held up the document Paul had given him.

"State your business," said a woman's voice with a coarse French accent.

"Je m'appelle Innocent Olivier," he said. *"Je suis étudiant dans le Université de Moundou, dans les sciences sociales. Nous chercons l'informations sur Washington."* He half turned to Grace, who was slightly behind him. "I mean, I said we wanted information."

"Nice."

The rough voice returned. *"Entrez-vous."*

The cast-iron gate door clicked. Rivette pushed it open and held it for Grace. It slammed shut loudly behind them. Grace lingered there a moment and Rivette held up. The lieutenant pretended to see someone she knew and waved. In reality she was testing the lock. It did not budge. A visitor had to be buzzed out and buzzed in.

They resumed walking toward the beige structure with

its two glass doors and charcoal-gray frame. Inside was dark, a combination of smoky glass and dim lighting.

"Bottleneck," Grace said softly.

"Where?"

"We've got to come out this way to open the gate. That means I've got to find out where the button is."

"Roger that."

The glass door was not locked. That was a safety measure, the same as on many military bases: if there were a fire or bomb inside the compound, workers would be able to get outside any and all structures.

Moment of truth, Rivette thought as they were about to go through the doorframe metal detector. If it were not wireless, if R.T. had failed to jam the signal—

There were no alarms. At least not audible. They entered, Rivette going first with his papers and a big smile. He had mastered the art of insincere sincerity when dealing with gang members back on the streets of San Pedro. The receptionist did not register concern, so it was unlikely any lights had gone off at the desk.

Rivette approached the reception desk that sat in the middle of the room, fashionably spartan with the same beige block as on the outside. The receptionist was a big woman with powerful hands. She wore a black suit and her hair was tightly pulled behind her. She tapped an earbud in her right ear. Another good sign. It, too, would have gone out. The woman did not seem to notice that the laptop on her desk would have lost its connection; she was playing solitaire.

There was a small room behind her that looked like it was transplanted from a country club, with cane-back dark wood armchairs, small tables made of redwood log, and a bar that had change-of-staff workers filling most of the dozen seats.

As the Black Wasps approached, the woman's night staff replacement appeared in the doorway of the lounge. He was a tall, bony man who was one of the workers Rivette had seen at the bar. There was a faint smell of Scotch about him. The lance corporal's quick cell phone research had told him that the majority of Chadians did not drink. That was in Chad, though. The late shift here must not be too exciting.

Not usually, at least, Rivette thought. He walked up to the desk. *"Bonjour,"* he said pleasantly.

"Bonjour," the sober-eyed woman replied.

"Mon ami, de Chine, ne parle pas la langue," he said. He turned to Grace. "I told her you didn't speak the language."

"I got that. She's probably used to seeing Chinese here."

While Rivette explained the reason they were here, Grace had her eyes on the lounge. There were nineteen people in the room. She wondered how many of those were needed for diplomatic duties and how many were there working for China. Before they had arrived at Prince Edward Island, where they would be facing the Chinese Navy, Williams had said that she and Rivette should also watch out for the markings of personnel from Albania, Bhutan, Chad, and, of course, North Korea, small nations that were among the proxies for Chinese interests on the global stage. He had remarked that those were the real hornet's nests of the world—and she understood why Op-Center's strike force was given the name Black Wasp.

Grace wondered if cabin fever set in here, since the surrogates had to be on call 24/7. She edged a little closer to the door, drawing the critical eye of the bony man. She smiled up at him and he glowered back. But she could not see the entire bar and she needed to. There was one person above all who would probably need to unwind today. When the nearest side of the bar came into view, there he was, dressed casually, a big man with a familiar back-of-the-head.

Rivette stepped over to her as the receptionists swapped places. "Ms. Yaya, here, says that there's a man at the bar who can help me. She'll introduce us."

"Our boy is at the bar," Grace said softly.

If they had been ID'd, this was going to get messy very quickly. But messy did not mean sloppy and the lieutenant was already considering options.

"Your tablet—in the bag?" Grace said. "You'll need that."

"Right. My tablet."

Rivette knelt and unzipped the bag. He removed the tablet from under the gun and tucked it under his arm. He held the straps of the bag bundled in his right hand. The receptionist—a head taller than Rivette—loomed behind them.

"*Allons-y*," the woman said, not pleasantly, in a way that informed both Grace and Rivette that the hunt had just been flipped.

Rivette was considering options. There did not seem to

be any. Joseph Kebzabo was too big to carry; he was going to have to leave in good working condition.

They were just a few steps from the end of the bar and their target. The assassin was dressed in a sweatshirt and sweatpants.

His day-off clothes, Rivette thought. *Called in sick. Had someone to murder.*

The assassin turned toward them, his expression disapproving. He did not appear to be armed.

"Monsieur Kebzabo," the woman said. *"Les voici."*

The assassin nodded.

"Been made," Rivette said from the side of his mouth.

"Noticed," Grace replied, "My lead."

The lance corporal had intended to follow Black Wasp protocol, which was to wait for the lieutenant to give an order or make the first move. The fact that she mentioned it told him that she was going to make first contact with the target.

"Chinese? English?" Grace asked the man.

Kebzabo looked like a man who was on guard for a trap. After a moment he replied, "English."

There was a stronger smell of alcohol on his breath. He had been drinking for quite some time.

"Do you know who we are?" Grace asked.

Again, he hesitated. He nodded once.

"Do you know who *I* am?" she asked. "Have you any idea what I am worth to the Chinese?"

Kebzabo could not suppress a little smile. He nodded again.

Rivette shot her a what-the-hell-are-you-doing look. She ignored him.

"I'm here to make a deal with you," she said. "The Chinese are holding my commander. I want to trade places with him and I'd like you to serve as a go-between."

Kebzabo was clearly interested. Rivette was equally clearly not.

"This is nuts," the lance corporal said.

"Quiet!" Grace snapped. Her eyes were on those of the killer. "You understand? You knock on the door, explain what I want to do, and it's a bloodless exchange. Everyone wins."

"Everyone wins," Kebzabo repeated. "What if they don't agree?"

"Then our business, yours and mine, is done."

Kebzabo was still guarded. His gaze shifted to Rivette. "What about him? He is wanted too."

"Don't be greedy," Grace warned. "You get me, that's all."

Rivette did not agree with the lieutenant's offer. He wanted to say, *I go where you go,* but kept quiet. This was the lieutenant's play.

"Yes or no," Grace pressed. "Are we agreed?"

Kebzabo nodded once. "When do we go? How?"

"Now. In my vehicle. My companion will drive."

Kebzabo regarded Rivette. There was mistrust in the eyes of both men. "I am not comfortable with that," the assassin said.

"Then how about this?" Grace asked. "There is an Osprey .45 with a silencer in that backpack. Lance Corporal, give him the bag."

Rivette's dislike of the plan, whatever it was, grew exponentially. But the lieutenant still had "that look" and, with a sharp, unhappy exhalation, he handed over the bag.

Kebzabo put his big fingers inside. Rivette wished he had thought to put a mousetrap in there, something, anything to make him feel less helpless. He did not look at Grace not because he was angry with her but because he was angry with himself. He should have figured she would do something loyal and irrational.

Kebzabo withdrew the gun. He checked the clip, held the weapon, savoring the weight and balance.

"Let's go," the assassin said.

The big man straightened his back before climbing from the stool on which he had been sitting for quite some time. There was a hint of unsteadiness in his posture—and perhaps, in his judgment.

And then Rivette thought back to what Grace had just said.

Now. In my vehicle. My companion will drive.

The lounge had tumbled into a deep, watchful silence. Tipsy, confident because he was holding a sexy gun, Kebzabo was actually going to walk to wherever Grace led him. With a dismissive flick of the wrist, he tossed the backpack back to Rivette. In his liquored and probably exhausted brain, he was going to be a hero twice today. Three times, since he probably intended to use the gun to force Rivette to surrender as well.

"*Si quelqu'un devait aller avec vous?*" the receptionist asked.

Kebzabo pointed the gun toward the ceiling. He was sober enough to know not to wave it at anyone.

"*Non,*" he assured her. "*J'irai bien.*"

Rivette leaned toward Grace. "He says we won't be any trouble. You *do* realize that he can shoot us dead and all he'd get is a ticket back to Chad. Which he'd probably welcome at this point."

"I realize that."

Grace was not cavalier about the assassin or their situation. Unarmed, neither was Rivette. But she was already thinking ahead, concerned about what Jay Paul's reaction would be when he saw them coming toward the van with Kebzabo behind them. The plan had been in the back of the lieutenant's mind until she saw the odds against getting out with Kebzabo. She had not mentioned it to either of her partners. Black Wasp did not share everything with people they did not know. And she had wanted Rivette's reaction to be authentic, which it was. That helped make it real to the killer.

The three started toward the door with Kebzabo several paces behind. There was no way to alert Paul. As far as Grace could figure it, she had just one course of action.

"When we get outside we'll cut to the other side of the street," Grace said quietly. "That'll give Paul some breathing room. We don't want him bolting."

"Gotcha."

"*Tais-toi!*" Kebzabo ordered.

Grace did not need a translation to know she had been told to shut up.

She started to cross in the middle of the street, Rivette following her lead. Traffic was lighter than before. Paul would be able to see them now.

Grace had no idea what the buildings were on the other side, only that there were parked cars and no trees in front of them. She had to act before Paul had too much time to think.

"Between the Mercedes and the BMW, you go first."

It was a tight fit, and Kebzabo did not object when Rivette maneuvered between the fenders, followed by Grace. As she moved through, she placed her right palm on the trunk of the BMW, her left palm on the hood of the Mercedes. In an instant she had raised herself from the ground as if she were doing a handstand; instead, she kicked back, hard. The bottoms of her feet landed side by side against Kebzabo's chin, knocking him onto his back. Rivette swung around the BMW in case the .45 went off. It did not. Kebzabo was a seasoned gunman who knew to keep the safety on.

A Jaguar swerved to avoid hitting the man and then drove on. The occupant was most likely already calling 911. Grace did not have time to care. As soon as Kebzabo fell, Grace had dismounted, dropped to one knee beside him, and grabbed the hand with the gun. She twisted hard, having dropped her elbows to shorten the turn radius. The wrist snapped, the gun came free, and Kebzabo shrieked with pain. Even as he cried out, Grace's tight leopard paw strike to the soft tissue at the base of his throat caused a gurgle that drowned the cry.

As the assassin lay gagging, trying to get his elbows under him, Rivette recovered the gun and pointed it down.

"Don't do anything stupid, like try to get up," Rivette warned.

Grace rose, and before she had a chance to look toward the van, it rolled up beside them. The lieutenant yanked the side door open and Rivette jumped inside. They pulled on Kebzabo, who willingly got to his feet. By the gorilla-like swing of his shoulders he clearly intended to fight back. Grace doubled him over with a jiujitsu punch to the gut. The lieutenant did not typically resort to the hard-hitting Japanese styles of combat, but this was the man who had executed Major Breen. The hit felt good and Rivette approved.

"Sometimes you just want to fold a big assassin in half so your partner can haul him into a van." The lance corporal smirked.

Grace jumped in behind him and seconds later they were driving back along Massachusetts Avenue NW.

"That was a fine play," Paul said. "You had me guessing. When we get back to the house, I want to hear how you arranged it."

"What are you going to do with him?" Grace asked.

"Yeah, I'm thinking—we got any rope around?"

Paul flipped open the storage compartment beside the seat. Instead of rope he produced a Smith & Wesson .38 with a hand-crafted silencer. He half turned in the seat, aimed, and put a bullet into the top of Joseph Kebzabo's head. Everyone in the back jumped—Grace and Rivette when they heard the pop, Kebzabo as the bullet emerged from his chin.

"We won't need any rope," Paul said. "As for what we're going to do with him, he's going to pay his overlords a visit."

CHAPTER TWENTY-SEVEN

Embassy of the People's Republic of China,
Washington, D.C.
March 23, 7:20 P.M.

Dylan Hao remained in the very quiet, still, soundproofed audiovisual conference center long after Williams had been returned to his room. He had dismissed the guard and sat in the same chair the hostage had been in and looked at the black, dead monitor.

In his trade, Hao would look at a computer screen, a person, a new day, everything, and see possibilities. It was another opportunity to challenge himself, to find a way of serving the nation he loved, the country he hoped would subsume the world in his lifetime. From earliest childhood on a small dairy farm in Shanghai, he had listened to his grandparents speak reverently of the Chángzhēng, the Long March—the temporary rout and flight of the Red Army of the Chinese Communist Party. The retreat had lasted from 1934 to 1935 under the direction of the heroic new Chairman of the Politburo Mao Zedong—if a struggling young army in rebellion could be said to have a government. Mao rallied and, in 1949, ousted Chiang Kai-shek who had ruled the nation since 1929.

Chiang went to Formosa, which became the benighted Taiwan where Hao was sent for his education. It was not just for schooling Hao had gone. It was to serve his nation by undermining the leadership in Taipei by pretending to be a loyalist. That brought him to the United States where, posing as a Taiwanese patriot, he served the cause of reunification and beyond.

That does not come to an end in this room, he thought. *Not because of an American hostage, unarmed, who saluted a functionary who was not his president.*

The Chinese agent phoned the commissary to have a pot of coffee sent over. He could not afford to hypothesize in the negative. He needed a plan. That was another reason to leave Wang Jing out of this. If Jing had not been so insistent on Williams ending his days in Qincheng Prison, the solution would have been easy. Hao would have instructed the guard to shoot the hostage as the chief of staff watched. It would have been a great coup for Hao: a second member of the Black Wasp team would have died today. President Wright, who did not show up for the conference, who wanted to be rid of the problem of Dr. Dàyóu, would have done nothing, said nothing. And Wang Jing would have had blood.

Instead, Hao had a problem. Two, in fact. Williams had saved face. The man had mocked his captivity and dishonored his captors. The other problem was that he did not have direct access to any other member of the Black Wasp team. He had left Williams' government phone behind, suspecting it would be tracked. He needed another—but that was for later. He had this other problem now.

The coffee arrived. Hao poured a deep cup, black. There was a time when even a still mug of coffee held a future that was his to write.

It's not as though you were in command of this operation, he thought. Technically, Hao was in charge of the execution of Jing's wishes, the deputy director's uncomplicated vision of cause and effect. There had been an attack the month before and this was the counterattack.

But then, Hao had read General Chang's report on the explosion of the *Qi*-19 hypersonic delivery system. Dr. Dàyóu had not been in charge at the Taiyuan Satellite Launch Center. General Chang had that honor and that responsibility. Nonetheless, it was the chief engineer who bore the blame. Hao would not allow that to happen here.

Attack and counterattack, Hao thought.

Williams had saluted. He was an enemy combatant, unrepentant, and in custody. What would, what could Jing say to the execution of such a man?

Wouldn't you rather tell him that than the message of stalwart defiance the woman would carry back to the president?

Hao was considering that when the door of the conference room swung in. It was an embassy worker, someone he did not know. The man looked panicked.

"Sir, come quickly!" the older man insisted.

This was the kind of blank screen of potentialities that Hao did not enjoy. Something had happened. He was responding rather than initiating.

Hao walked briskly after the man, overtaking him and following where he pointed, down a lengthy corridor toward the front of the central building.

Hao's long march, he could not help thinking. *It is up to you, not Jing, how this ends.*

There was a crowd at the door. Hao shouldered his way through. A marine guard stood outside, his hand raised toward the group to keep them back, like a traffic warden. Hao stepped outside. He could not imagine what had stirred in everyone such agitation.

"What is it?" he demanded.

"At the gate, sir," the officer replied.

Hao strode past the man. The two gate guards were side by side in the center of the entrance instead of at opposite ends. They were standing back, their Type 95 automatic rifles raised toward the street.

It was not just excitement; these men were on alert. Yet there had been no embassy-wide alarm or his phone would have beeped. Hao hurried his pace, the lights throwing his shadow ahead of him, the darkening street coming nearer—

What looked like a sack of laundry was crumpled against the base of the bars. As Hao neared, he saw the contours of a body, the bare, bald head—the raw, red wound in the center of it.

He stopped hard. That was Joseph Kebzabo lying dead on the street.

Hao called out. "What happened?" He did not want to approach the two armed guards from behind, with their backs turned. He did not think they had ever seen combat, let alone a dead man.

Both men looked back. One turned, lowered his weapon. The other resumed his defensive stance.

"Sir, he was thrown from a van," the guard said. "The vehicle did not even stop, it just sped away."

Hao nodded, the man turned back, and the agent crouched and stared at the body. He did not care for further details. It did not matter. He did not care about Kebzabo. The assassin had been sloppy, had slipped up. That's why Beijing used Chadians: they were expendable.

Hao stood and walked back toward the door, back to the faces that seemed to be floating behind the dark glass. The embassy would have to report the incident, but he would instruct the witnesses not to describe the van. That would prompt an investigation that would reveal too many moving parts that neither Jing nor the ambassador would want exposed.

This was almost certainly Black Wasp and he had to give them credit for investigation, execution, and hubris. That fact was actually liberating. Hao would be justified acting on his own initiative to respond at once to the affront.

The American president had written off Chase Williams. It would fall upon the leader of Black Wasp to pay for this.

CHAPTER TWENTY-EIGHT

P Street NW, Washington, D.C.
March 23, 7:45 P.M.

The denouement had been as clean as the opening. After depositing the remains of Joseph Kebzabo in the gutter, Jay Paul drove back toward P Street. He parked on Twelfth Street NW off O Street. There, he quickly wiped the fingerprints from the few things they had touched. Then he walked the group back to the safe house. They would recover the van in a few days, claiming it had been stolen from in front of a house they had been visiting.

There, the matter would likely end.

It had before.

The group walked in silence, Grace in thought, Paul watching for observers, Rivette texting with Little Guillermo.

"I feel like I'm back in San Pedro, sending messages to the Pacific Island Gang," he said as they reached their destination.

"Is that the only similarity?" Grace asked.

"For me, yeah. I was ten."

Once they were inside, the lance corporal sat, then stood, then paced. He was boiling off energy he had not spent on this mission.

"But since you mentioned it," he picked up the conversation from outside, "I was about as useful as I was then. I did not even discharge my weapon."

Jay Paul had gone into the kitchen to make just-add-water ramen noodles. The kettle was still steaming on the range as he slit the cellophane wrapper with a knife and peeled back the foil top. Grace had selected an armchair in a corner of the living room, away from the windows. She was sunk deep and was even deeper in thought.

"There was a gang with the acronym of P.I.G.?" Paul asked with amusement.

It took a moment for Rivette to figure out what he was talking about. "The Pacific Island Gang? Yeah. We just got back from what we did and that is what you're thinking about?"

"That and my noodles," Paul said. "Why? You've been on missions, you've killed. What's on your mind?"

"I'm trying to understand what happened out there and where we're going," Rivette said, gesturing broadly at the world beyond the safe house. "We pretty much screwed the pooch on our military future, as expected. But now it's real. We busted into an embassy and beat up one of their guys."

"A righteous cause."

"I do not think Major Breen would have called it that."

"He had an active conscience," Grace said.

"He said he loved the law and wanted to go back to it one day," Rivette said. "He didn't figure Black Wasp was a rest-of-his-life thing."

"Yet that's what it ended up being," Paul said as he started eating.

Grace fired a disapproving look.

"I'm stating a fact and a reality," Paul said. "In this line of work, boots on the ground, you can only plan—you can only *think*—about five minutes ahead, if that. That's why I buy five-minute ramen."

"I'm not planning or thinking, I'm just missing a comrade whose guidance—and this was my only point—was important to me. Wrong or not, I could use it now. I don't see where we go from here, Grace and me."

"Matt Berry has some ideas," Paul said. "He'll tell you about them when he gets here."

Grace snickered humorlessly. "I should have expected that."

"What?" Paul asked.

"An angle," she answered. "Maybe two or three or more."

"Like what?" Rivette asked.

"For one," Grace said. "He was betrayed by his inside man. He will want that man's head."

Rivette frowned. "Do you mean that—"

"Figuratively, Jaz, yes. Though right now nothing would surprise me." Her eyes drifted toward Jay Paul. "Executing Kebzabo was Fort Sumter, the opening salvo of Trigram's war."

Paul sucked up a long noodle. "You're selling Matt short. It was also payback for Major Breen. And there's something else, which he'll tell you about face-to-face."

"I thought folks like us can't plan," Rivette reminded him.

"I said people with 'boots on the ground,' not at the operational level. He has a vison."

"When will he be here to share it?" Grace asked.

"Why? Do you have somewhere to be?"

That was the second breezy comment Paul had made and Grace didn't like it. She rose from the chair like a snake, one of her favorite kung fu forms. Rivette stepped back.

"You better do less talking," she said.

"Sorry?"

"I don't like your tone. You proved you could execute a killer we hauled in for you. Don't let that go to your head."

"Lieutenant, you don't know me well enough to call me out—"

"Are you saying you weren't being a power-boosted asshole?"

Paul sat back as though trying to decide whether to ignore her or throw the knife.

Rivette said, "Mr. Paul, chill. Her folks—"

"Don't apologize for me, Jaz," Grace snapped. "This has nothing to do with what happened to me today, or to you, or to Mr. Paul. The admiral is a captive. Our commander has gone radio silent, probably to protect our whereabouts. This job isn't near finished enough for flippancy. Or waiting. We shouldn't be waiting for Matt Berry to arrive before considering how the

Chinese are going to respond, because they will. If there's a people I know, they're it."

Rivette took the lead. "You're not wrong," he said. "How will they respond? How would you respond?"

"Immediately and in kind," she said. "They have only one asset in their possession right now and I'm sitting here thinking about what we can do for him."

"Admiral Williams," Paul said. "Just so you know, Matt Berry has been working on that."

"Nice to know. Can you tell us how?" Rivette asked.

"He has been working on the West Wing, trying to convince them to make the admiral's release a condition of the Dàyóu family handover."

"With what leverage?" Grace asked.

"Trigram works closely with our intelligence agencies," Paul said. "They want to continue having first look at relevant information."

Grace shook her head.

"It's not what you might think, Lieutenant," Paul said. "We sell to our allies and we sell Russia against China, Spain against separatists, that sort of thing."

"You don't sell out," Rivette said, still feeling like a peacekeeper.

"We may not have that long," Grace said. "These Chinese, especially the military personnel, are not a contemplative breed. A situation is presented, they act. I was the standard-bearer of that idea when I was over there last month. If I hadn't been, Major Breen and my parents would still be alive.

You act or the moment passes you by for all the reasons you've outlined. There's always another buyer, always another voice wanting to be heard."

Rivette was not accustomed to hearing the lieutenant speak so personally. She usually spoke with the full authority of her training, the weight of her Taoist background. He had nothing to offer in support.

Paul had stopped eating while they spoke. "Look, that was an insensitive statement before and I'm sorry," he said before returning to his noodles.

Grace returned to her seat. Rivette went over and asked her if she wanted something. She did not drink alcohol and he suggested tea.

"Sure. Thanks, Jaz."

The lance corporal glanced over at Paul. "That was cold, back in the van," he said softly.

"It was that."

"But I felt kinda the way I did when the admiral killed that terrorist. 'You murdered, you die.' I just want to say, regarding what you just said, that general you took apart in China—he was a bad man. You did the right thing for the world and the Dàyóu family."

"You may be right," Grace said. "I only wish that's why I did it. I lost it, Jaz. And all of this is the result."

"What's it you always say—the universe does things for a reason?"

She nodded and fell back into a reflection. "The universe knows all; you do not."

"Don't think so hard," he said.

"I'm not," she assured him. "I'm . . . accepting."

"I like that," Rivette said, giving her shoulder a little squeeze before heading into the kitchen. Grace sat in the semidarkness of the corner wanting to scream and rage and beg her parents' forgiveness. But the first two would do no good and the third—

"I miss you already," she said under her breath. "God, I'm so sorry."

Rivette was just bringing Grace her tea when there was a beep at the door. He was on his way to the backpack and his firearm when Paul told him it was just Berry activating the keypad lock. Berry pointed to a security camera linked to his computer. A moment later Matt Berry entered, quickly and firmly closing the door behind him. He did not appear to be wary of anything in particular. Grace suspected that was how he always entered the safe house—or the Oval Office, back in the day—assuming adversaries were somewhere nearby.

He acknowledged the three by inclining his forehead to the group, then removed his trench coat and hung it on a hook by the door then doffed his baseball cap and tossed it where several others sat on the handles of umbrellas in an antique iron stand. He was carrying a shoulder bag and looked the same as he had that morning: an expression that suggested interest but not engagement. It was impossible to tell what was going on in his mind. Paul came in from the kitchen with eager eyes; even he did not seem to know how Berry's after-noon had gone.

"It's no-go with Wright, Jay," Berry said without preamble. "The Chinese put him on a video call that was supposed to be with the president. Wright delegated that crap job to his chief of staff. I didn't get to talk to Angie Brunner directly, but I'm told that whatever Williams was supposed to say, he didn't. He just stood and saluted."

"My man," Rivette said.

"January Dow called me on behalf of the president," Berry continued. "He brought her in on this and because, in her words, 'he has had a bellyful of Op-Center.' Meaning that she has had a bellyful, but that doesn't change the result. She was the one who 'won his ear,' as they say in the trade. The call to me was her victory lap."

Paul accepted the news the same way he had shot Keb-zabo: with dead-eyed dispassion.

Berry stopped between Grace and Rivette. "I'm sorry. The national security advisor is a coldhearted realist."

"Nicer way of saying the word I'm thinking of," Rivette said disgustedly.

"Major Breen died in the line of duty and this woman has had enough of us?" Grace said in an edgy whisper.

"Did she know about the gift we gave the Chinese?" Paul asked.

"If so, they may not have made the connection to the killing in the park."

"The murder of Major Breen," Grace corrected. "I've had a bellyful of polite language today."

"So have I." Berry strolled to where she was sitting. He put his bag on the floor. "My world is overstuffed with it. I told you intelligence is the coin. Delicacy is the shipping charge. But in my world, not theirs—in the world of national and international security, not diplomacy, the tax is what you saw today. Cosa Nostra tactics. Death for death, and the quicker the better. Turn the other side's satisfaction into quick, unexpected disorientation. That's how and when they make mistakes."

"Thank you for the 101," Grace said. She stood. "I've been trained to fight and to kill, if necessary. In my world, that tradition goes back thousands of years. You've been doing it here for—what, three hundred? Four hundred? When I was in China, I was flooded with that. I overreached."

"Are you saying you've had a bellyful?" Berry asked. His tone, and now his expression, were challenging. "What would you do if Bruce Chan were in this room?"

She shook her head, indicating she did not know the name.

"He's the man who drove the van into your parents' building and knocked them around like they were big, curbside bags of trash," Berry said.

The shock of the event returned, constricting Grace's chest. And then the words Berry had used hit her. Her eyes shifted to his and dug in.

Berry did not flinch as he got in front of her outrage.

"Sorry, Lieutenant, but I won't dress it up with pretty language or euphemisms," he went on. "He stole the van from a construction site—I have that video—and crushed them. When I wasn't trying to rouse the Oval Office to something resembling a backbone, I was reviewing the day's imaging from the Peterson Space Force Base Northeast Continental Region Excelsior satellite. I was trying to match the construction site video to surveillance up and down the island of Manhattan and the other four boroughs. I found him in Columbus Park. Bruce Chan, a local hire. He took a subway to Flushing to confuse pursuit then came back. You want his address?"

The other two people in the room had not moved, and Rivette had barely breathed.

Grace's stance had been defiant until then. It seemed to deflate and she turned away.

"I'm sorry, Lieutenant," Berry said. "This is a rotten business. The language is like snuff, a pinch up the nose to cover the stench."

She stood facing away. Rivette was not sure what she would do next; he had seen her explosive roundhouse kicks to the jaw. They were devastating and always ended with a loud snap. To his credit, Berry did not back away.

"Thank you for your efforts on my behalf and for the admiral," she said. "The sentiments—they stand, but I apologize for my manner."

"It's been a shit day," Berry said and went to the liquor cabinet in the kitchen.

"Getting back to Dow, would it have changed anything if

they knew the man we terminated—that I shot in the head"—
he corrected himself for Grace—"was the assassin who blew
Breen away?"

"Stop that," Grace said firmly.

Berry motioned for Paul to tone it down. "If I revealed
that, she'd want to know how I knew. Dicey position for us,
then."

"What about the admiral's position?" Rivette asked. "That
sucks too."

Berry poured himself a brandy. He raised it to the lance
corporal. "Here's to youth and idealism." He took a sip and
returned to the living room. "I don't need to be reminded of
Chase's position."

"You maybe do," Rivette disagreed.

"Not by you," Berry said. "I'm the one who got taken in by
Dylan Hao, I'm the one who sent the admiral to meet him, *I'm*
the one who did that. But if I stay put on the reality of what
sucks or doesn't suck most, we won't find a solution. Right
now, Lance Corporal Jaz Rivette, that means the four people
in this room must remain free and mobile. Giving someone
like Dow information—that limits what we can do. We'd be
taking on another adversary."

Rivette considered the twisted reality of fighting people
who were supposed to be on the same side.

"Okay, I'm sorry too," the young man said, echoing his
partner. "You have a plan?"

"I do," Berry said after a second sip. "We wait."

The twin faces of unashamed idealism turned on him with open disapproval.

"For what?" Rivette asked.

"For China to show what they do when they're recklessly disoriented," Berry replied.

"You mean like putting a bullet in *his* head and dumping him at the White House?" Rivette asked.

"It's possible," Berry agreed, "but I'll tell you this." He reinforced himself by draining the glass and went to pour himself another. "Of all the scenarios Jay and I could rattle off right now, that one is far and away the kindest."

CHAPTER TWENTY-NINE

Embassy of the People's Republic of China,
Washington, D.C.
March 23, 8:00 P.M.

Dylan Hao went directly from the front entrance of the embassy back to the video conference room and, through it, to the area where Chase Williams was being held. Along the way he received a terse text message from Wang Jing:

> Your targets went to the Chad Embassy
> and left with the assassin. I am informed you
> have his body now.

The agent was surprised and enraged by the efficiency of the American team. This act must cost them.

It must.

Hao snagged the guard who had been in the room with them. The man had returned to his post at the ambassador's entrance in the East Wing. Ambassador Qiang had gone to a reception at the Russian embassy, a necessary diplomatic duty and a means of establishing plausible deniability for the run-up actions to the turnover of the Dàyóu family.

The agent disliked failure. He disliked it more than Wang Jing. He disliked it even more when a careful plan was derailed by an obstinate American whom he thought he had broken. That man and the woman who had caused so much damage in China.

"Bring him!" Hao ordered as he unlocked the chamber door and threw it open.

Williams was sitting on the floor in a corner. He was trying to imagine what life would be like in the prison cell he would soon occupy—without the amenities of quiet, warmth, and relative peace.

The guard stepped over and used the rifle to gesture for Williams to stand.

"What if I don't?" he asked Hao. "Will you have him shoot me where I sit?"

Hao covered the room in three large strides. He kicked the captive in the temple with the heel of his shoe. Williams' skull slapped hard against the wall on the other side.

"You may walk or you will be dragged, it is up to you," Hao said.

Williams decided quickly—painfully—that dignity would be preferable to further defiance. He pushed off the floor and slid his back up the wall. He rested there for a moment while his head cleared.

The guard motioned again with the Type 95. Dizzy but upright, with still-lingering effects from the drug, Williams half walked, half slouched toward the door. Hao cut in front of him and led the way back to the videoconference room.

Hao pointed to the chair in which Williams had been seated before. He said something to the guard—along the lines of "I'll be right back," Williams surmised—as Hao left and the guard remained, standing behind the chair.

"Who am I going to talk to now?" he wondered aloud, knowing that his companion would not understand. Williams looked around at the other equipment, which included a modem and an ethernet cable. "That's for the conferencing—but the light's off." A red light on the camera flashed to life. "We're making a video. That's my guess."

From Hao's manner, Williams guessed he had either been chewed out for the admiral's noncompliance or—

Did something happen I don't know about? Williams wondered. Did Angie do something? Black Wasp? Wright?

The guard was nearby. Did Hao want him to try to take the gun away and get shot dead in the process?

Unlikely. Chances of success were not good, especially with the aftereffects of the drug and the kick in the head. And the guard was out of camera range.

Williams stopped talking. He stopped thinking. He had been trying to keep his spirits up, but it was not working. He sat, breathing deep as he did in any crisis, trying to be ready for anything.

Hao charged back into the room, unclipping the blackjack from his belt and stopping just out of camera range.

"Feel free to cry out," Hao said. "We're not recording sound."

The agent drew back his arm and snapped his wrist forward. The hard rubber club broke Williams' nose on contact. The admiral tasted blood even as his head snapped back. Williams' hands came up reflexively as he saw Hao prepare to swing again, this time at his throat. The hard rubber drove his right hand back against his face, stinging the palm mercilessly. Williams had to snap his jaw shut to keep from squealing. The hand fell and the blackjack struck again, this time in his chin. His head fell forward and pulled him with it.

Hao shouted an order and the guard dragged Williams up, dropped him in the seat. Hao shouted again and the guard grabbed the prisoner's collar in back and held him steady. This time the rubber struck Williams in the breastbone. Air blew from his mouth, spraying the blood from his nose, causing Williams to suck it back painfully.

"We don't want you to lose any teeth," Hao said, setting the blackjack on the table with the monitor. "Every space between them must bleed."

Hao punched Williams in the mouth. The admiral's jaw flopped open, blood ran over his lips, and then his head lolled this way and that. He was lost in a nightmare limbo of pain and confusion, his ears ringing, lungs wheezing, eyes seeing nothing but blurry movement.

And then, through the blur, he heard Hao speak.

"Salute now, Admiral."

CHAPTER THIRTY

The White House, Washington, D.C.
March 23, 8:29 P.M.

"There's a communication from the Chinese, sir."

Angie Brunner looked up from the text sent by the White House director of external communications. She was seated with President Wright and January Dow in the Oval office. Dinner had been sent over, but the sandwiches had barely been touched.

"Let's have it," Wright said. "January, after we see this—which may be about the body they found—I'll talk to Ambassador Cherif more about whatever the hell happened at Chad's embassy."

"A young Black man and a young Asian woman came in, said something about Chase Williams, and then left with a security officer," January said. "That officer may well be the man who turned up dead at the Chinese embassy."

"Maybe," Angie said. "And if it's true they had to have done that for a reason."

"Murdering a foreign national?" January said. "Yeah, Angie. They're out of control."

Wright contributed nothing to the ongoing debate as he picked up his tablet to read the Chinese message. He appreciated both points of view but, at the moment, his trust was on the steely skepticism of his national security advisor.

The file had been cleared as virus-free and the president opened it. The policy was for the president to view all messages directed at him from recognized political entities, or to delegate who was to open them. Typically, that was his executive secretary—who had gone home two hours earlier—or January Dow. Because of the looming Dàyóu handover, Wright himself had let the staff know that he wanted to see every communication from China ASAP.

The president clicked play. The video showed Chase Williams, still but not relaxed, from the chest up. And then a shadow moved into the frame and the admiral's head went back.

"For the love of God," Wright said as he watched the video play.

Dow and Angie took that as a cue to use their own devices to access the video. They were a few steps behind in their viewing. Dow scowled but Angie reacted with open horror.

This was real, not a motion picture like the kind her studio used to make. The chief of staff could not speak. When it was over she punched off her tablet as though it were itself a danger. Dow set it on the coffee table that separated the women.

"Why didn't they kill him?" Angie asked.

"In case they need him again," January said. "The time stamp shows it was made after the body was left. It was obviously a response to that, to Black Wasp's visit to the Chad embassy that ended with a bullet in the head of the man they left with. Like everything else the Chinese have done since Lieutenant Lee attacked the Taiyuan Satellite Launch Center, this was a response to something."

Angie disagreed with January's assessment of what happened at Taiyuan, but this was not the time to litigate that disagreement.

"Mr. President, we have to get Admiral Williams out," the chief of staff said.

"How?" January challenged her. "Black Wasp? What do we have to trade? We're already committed to giving them back their citizens."

"We cancel that unless Chase Williams is returned," Angie said.

"No," Wright said. "That's not on the table."

"Then we have nothing!" Angie said.

"They want Grace Lee," January said to Angie. "That's clear from what happened to her family. You want to trade her for the admiral?"

"I'm not giving them a prisoner upgrade," Wright said.

The president pushed his laptop aside and folded his hands. He was not a man of deep faith and Angie did not think he was praying.

"Sir, put aside this situation for a moment," Angie said.

"The admiral knows more about our naval defenses than anyone who is not titled secretary of the navy. If Beijing keeps him, our security will be severely compromised."

"They did not need a hostage to target and destroy *Phoenix One*," January said. "Those old paradigms, the movie script nonsense—that's all over. They can hack any system to get whatever information they need."

The national security advisor had just called Williams not just obsolete but entirely expendable. Angie wanted to throw her coffee mug at the woman.

"I'm going to call the Chadian ambassador, though I have a feeling he's going to confirm what January just described," Wright said.

"If that's true, there was a reason," Angie said with fresh resolve. "The Chinese did not call the Metro police, did not admit officers who showed up when the murder was reported, seem disinclined to be part of any investigation. There is a binding tie in all of this. The renegade actions of Black Wasp."

Wright told the director of external communications to call Ambassador Cherif and told January Dow to stay. That was a signal for Angie Brunner not to stay. The exchange was going forward, Williams be damned, and the chief of staff was not a required voice in that process.

"Mr. President, may I speak with you a moment?" Angie asked.

"January, would you excuse us. Please."

"Certainly, sir," the national security advisor said with an official voice unmarked by resentment.

Why not? Angie thought. *January had nothing to be bitter about.* The national security advisor had just won—twice. First by making her influence strongly felt, then by Angie having to ask for alone time with her boss. That last one was a first.

The door shut gently behind January in a fitting if uncommon show of temperance from the woman. For a moment it felt like old times on the campaign trail, just Angie and Wright and a problem.

"Mr. President, I have the ambassador," the voice of the D-Ex came from the computer.

"Ask him to hold just a moment," Wright said. His tired eyes fixed on Angie. "I know you don't like this—"

"It's not just *this*," she said with old, familiar bluntness. "What we do here will resonate in the nation and in your administration for years."

"You don't think I know that?" he said. The president was also letting down the façade of commander in chief.

"It's kind of sick, actually," she said with a snicker. "I think I know this feeling better than you do. You didn't have external enemies in Pennsylvania. The knives were all in the statehouse. You weren't at war with fifty states. At the studio, I was at war, constantly. Not like this, not life and death, but the approach was the same. I had to gamble big, not compromise."

"And what does that look like here?" the president asked. "I've got white papers and recommendations and God knows what else playing out this approach or that. I read them all, you know that, and precisely for the reason you just said. January is making an internal power play, don't you think I see that? But my sense of this thing is to make a tactical retreat. Step back, regroup, and pursue a course that does not include trigger events like a Black Wasp taking on authority it does not possess to attack a foreign power."

"It was initiative," Angie said. "Opportunistic and bold. And though we are returning the asset to China, we gleaned a great deal of intelligence about a deadly missile program that has these shores in its sights."

"At what cost?" the president asked. "It's too high already." His expression softened. "Remember Little Rock?"

Angie's shoulders sagged. She was spent and now she was confused. "Sir?"

"The campaign, a little over a year ago. Polls were good in your home state of Texas and across the South. Arkansas was a problem until we hit Douglas MacArthur's hometown."

"'I shall return,'" you said. "'As nominee Wright and then as President Wright.' The internet mocked that, Little Rock loved it, and you carried the state. Sir—John—it took two and a half years for MacArthur to return." Angie smiled faintly. "I know. I greenlit the movie. A lot of people died while the general waited."

"A lot of people lived because he fulfilled his promise," the president said. "A temporary setback. Then forward, hard."

Angie knew the talk was over, the argument lost. She stood. "Your call," she reminded him.

"Thank you. As soon as January is back," he said.

Angie understood. It would be bad politics to start without

her. The national security advisor would take it as a slight and she would redouble her already considerable efforts to push Angie aside.

The chief of staff walked briskly for the exit. She did not acknowledge January as the two passed in the doorway, the women oblivious to each other like shoppers in a revolving door. It was new for Angie, ignoring and being ignored. In Hollywood, people on the way up or wanting to be on that escalator made eye contact. They looked eagerly, fawningly at celebrities or executives. The latter were instantly recognizable because they did not need to connect with anyone around them.

Technically, Angie and January were equal. Historically, Angie should have the edge because of her two-year association with Wright. This situation not only blunted that edge, it gave January the win. It was not just Angie's ego that was bruised, though it was. It was her concern that this move so early in his term would establish Wright as weak, not sensible. That image would be difficult if not impossible to overcome without a complementary show of power.

Angie reached her office. She was not ignoring the looks of West Wing workers, she was oblivious to them. Her mind was like a Texas twister. Just a few weeks ago Op-Center had what they were calling a big win too. They were privately celebrated by the president with January Dow and the rest of the intelligence community impressed and wondering who had delivered the miracle of Dr. Dàyóu.

Now the members of Black Wasp were dead, imprisoned, or—

Draping the streets of Washington with bold deeds and a dead man, she thought with a sudden sense of pride.

She tapped her fingers on the desk. Her computer showed unread emails piled three numerals high. The file of voicemail messages would take the rest of the night to listen to if she bothered. None of that mattered at the moment. What the president had detailed was provincial, wrong, and it would backfire. He had to be made to see that and she had less than four hours before the handoff.

She needed input, and not from her staff of insiders and people who wanted to move upward in the West Wing, in the State Department, anywhere that brought them closer to the top.

Reacting with the instincts that had guided her life and career—not with calculation, the way they did things here—Angie grabbed her phone and placed a call.

CHAPTER THIRTY-ONE

Fort Belvoir, Springfield, Virginia
March 23, 8:45 P.M.

It was frustrating for Ann Ellen Mann to be out of the loop.

In Afghanistan she had been in the belly of the beast 24/7, seeing and hearing everything. In Philadelphia, everyone on the base reported to her. Even retired naval support activity personnel like Captain Richard "Atlas" Hamill came calling with news he had heard about other bases, other colleagues.

Here, now, in the Black Wasp residence, she felt like she was in solitary confinement. In the "cooler," cut off and uninformed. She knew only what she saw on the news or on Twitter or Gettr, and almost every scrap of that was unreliable or contradictory.

There were no messages from Black Wasp, and that concerned her. She had resisted contacting them because she did not know if her devices were now being monitored. The signal could be triangulated, the team found.

It was a sad day to have reached a point where she did

not, *could not*, trust her own people. But even the dinner that the Officers' Club had been instructed to send over was something she had ordered a week before, on-site. Records were kept, details known.

The captain had barely moved from the kitchen table for the better part of five hours, save for when she shot a man to death. That did not just feel like a different day, it seemed as if it had happened to someone else. More than that, whatever posttraumatic stress had come home with her from Kabul now had a seat at the table in Fort Belvoir. She had thought about that when she had been seconded to Op-Center, going out on missions again. Mann had just not expected that to come with the suddenness of a Taliban or ISIS ambush.

She did not feel sorry for herself; that had come and gone enough in her life and she was done with it. What she felt was useless. Just this morning, that did not seem possible.

And then her phone chimed. The caller ID dispelled the feeling of helplessness.

"This is Captain Mann," she said.

"We have to talk," Angie said, launching headlong into what she had to say. "In confidence, please. I don't know you well but I'm trusting you."

"Thank you and of course."

The chief of staff brought the captain up to date, sparing none of the facts but sharing none of her personal concerns. The fact that she had broken the chain of command to call was evidence she had them; Mann did not take lightly the position the caller was putting herself in.

"However this thing blew up, I admire and respect Chase Williams," Angie said. "I also don't think that a white flag play is the right one. Not completely."

"I agree," Mann said firmly.

"I thought you might. My question is what do you suggest? This is like nothing the president and I have faced and he's letting January Dow call the shots."

Captain Mann barely knew the national security advisor, but Chase Williams did not like or trust her.

"What about the Joint Chiefs, the vice president—"

"When they heard the details about Black Wasp's mission and the lines they crossed, the cut and ran from anything and everything Op-Center. That includes Chase Williams, who I thought they considered one of their own."

"That's what happens when generals become politicians," Mann said. "The problem is, we don't know what Black Wasp is planning. After that theatrical maneuver at the Chinese embassy—which frankly doesn't sound like Lieutenant Lee or Lance Corporal Rivette—I'm suspecting they are not on their own."

"Who would they be with?"

"I'm thinking Matt Berry."

"That . . . figures," Angie said, annoyed at having overlooked the obvious.

"From what I've read in the files and heard from the admiral, Mr. Berry doesn't like to color in the lines."

"No. Do you think Black Wasp is with him?"

"I don't know. I wouldn't say on a line your people can listen in on there or for that matter here," she said.

Once again, Angie forgot this was a different kind of industry town from the one she was used to. They would not be able to discuss a plan even if she wanted to.

"Captain, do you have transportation?"

"I do."

"I'm going to have the guards pulled off your residence," Angie said. "I imagine cabin fever is getting as bad there as it is here."

"I could use some getting out, yes."

"Thank you, Captain. Those are words I used a lot in my previous life. I don't think I ever meant them till now."

The chief of staff hung up and Captain Mann felt buoyancy return to her spirit. The black stains of the day were still front and center, but at least now she could do something about the forces behind them.

She would wait until she was away from the base before texting Lieutenant Lee. She wanted a head start. If anyone was listening in or tracking her phone, she could always lead them in a wrong direction or leave the phone where finding it would do no one any good and instruct Grace to do the same.

Intrigue against her own government. That, too, was something she did not see coming.

Mann considered briefly whether to change from her uniform to civilian clothes. She opted against it, feeling that a military vehicle in city streets might draw attention; with a civilian driver it was sure to. She grabbed her black, light-weight puffer jacket from the closet. That would be sufficient to hide her affiliation if that became necessary.

As she prepared to go, Mann received a call. She had plopped the phone on the bed; it was one of the last numbers she expected to see: Chase Williams' private phone on her personal phone. She grabbed her cell.

"Chase?"

The voice answered, "No."

Mann was surprised, then angry, then wary. She did not respond. This was someone else's call, their hunt.

"My name is Dylan Hao," the caller said. "Do you know it?"

"Yes."

"Good. I am going to tell you where Chase Williams is being held. He will be there for another three hours."

"Is he with you?"

"Nearby," Hao said.

"Let me speak with him."

"I cannot do that," Hao said. "*He* cannot do that. If you want to see him, come to the Chinese embassy."

Mann thought of the beating Angie had described. If the captain could reach through the phone, there would be one less international spy.

"The Chinese embassy came to me a short while ago," she said. "We don't seem to get along."

"This will be different, I assure you," Hao said.

"Your promises aren't worth much, Mr. Hao. And why would you do this for me or for Chase?"

"We are not heartless."

"Then turn him loose."

"We are not reckless," Hao replied.

"It's a good policy. I think I'll do the same. There was one attempt on my life today."

"Not on *your* life," Hao said. "We have no quarrel with you."

No, you only want to murder every other member of my team, she thought.

Mann did not for a moment believe this was a beau geste on Hao's part. What did he really want? She had not been part of the team during the China incursion. He could only know about her involvement with Op-Center if Williams had been drugged and told them.

The captain ruled out the possibility that she would be used as bait. They already had Williams. *What,* then?

Major Breen had once talked to her about the trials he had been involved with. He always started by taking a look at the parts that comprised the matter at hand. Weapons, motive, location, participants. What did she have?

Hao had contacted her. He had called on *her* phone, not the government phone. That number had to have come from Williams' personal cell; Hao had tossed the admiral's government phone in the trash.

Before I was offered command of Black Wasp, Williams had

called me from his personal cell, she remembered. That was after they first worked together in Philadelphia.

The Chinese called her private number because they had Williams' phone and she was the only Black Wasp on it.

Why bring me to the embassy? He must believe I'd come if for no other reason than to see where Chase is being held, use that to plot a flash-strike rescue.

In short, bring Black Wasp to them.

There was another possibility. Mann would likely be carrying her government phone. The Chinese would insist that she leave it behind at the main entrance or before she saw Williams under some pretense—to prevent tracking, clandestine photos, voice recordings. That would give them the opportunity to clone it. They would then have the ability to locate and track the other Black Wasps days or even weeks from now.

"Thank you for the offer, Mr. Hao," Mann said, "but I must decline."

"Captain, unless you want to become a casualty of this—"

She terminated the call and looked out the window. The guard in the back had departed. She checked out front. The sentry there had also left. Putting her weapon in the pocket of her civilian jacket, which she would keep beside her, she stuffed both phones in the other pocket then grabbed the bag she had brought to the Black Wasp drill that morning. The officer left the lights on, slipped into the night, and went to the Infantry Squad Vehicle in the driveway.

CHAPTER THIRTY-TWO

Embassy of the People's Republic of China,
Washington, D.C.
March 23, 8:59 P.M.

The call to Wang Jing was overdue and brief. Hao placed it in the same room, on the same equipment where he had suffered three setbacks, one after the other after the other.

He did not portray them as such to Jing. With luck and deft deception—Hao's craft, of course—the deputy director would never know the truth. He would deplane at 11:20 P.M., be met by the American contingent, and collect the Dàyóus. Hao would be there as well, with Chase Williams, after which they would all board the aircraft and go home.

Home.

Hao was not even sure what that word meant anymore. It used to be territory, yet he had been away from that soil, those sights, for so long home had simply become a concept, a genetic familiarity with people and a deep, longing affection—but for memories. He looked at WorldView videos from Beijing, Shanghai, other cities. He did not recognize many of the streets, buildings, and bridges—or even the streetlights. Those cameras were not sensitive enough to tell him whether the air still had a smoggy tester of sickly yellow. Bicyclists and pedestrians wore face masks, but they had always worn face masks. Did each breath still have a familiar sulfurous taste? The people he had known years ago—he had not communicated with them since coming to America. It had not been permitted. He had tracked some of them on social media. They had new husbands, wives, children, positions. Would they have anything in common, still, especially if he could not discuss the work he had been doing?

Home. Either you carry it with you or it is not with you at all, he thought.

And then, Hao wondered, what would he himself do next? If he could shade the truth he would rise. If not—

His thoughts turned back to Chase Williams, and they became dark. He watched the embassy video for the fifth time. The man had been bravely stubborn at first. After that he had been senseless. That was not good enough. There was no suffering in that.

And then there was the woman, Captain Mann. He had misjudged her too. A non-combatant commander with a limp, according to what Williams had told him, she had nonetheless thwarted the attempt to kill the Black Wasps and satisfy Jing's command to flatten their home base. Then she had failed to accept an offer to come and see her leader. She would have come and gone, been photographed on the embassy video. In

Hao's hands that footage would have been evidence of trea-
sonous complicity in the destruction of Op-Center. All he
had needed was the woman walking into the embassy and out
again a few minutes later.

*Just that. Come and see your admiral for the last time, give
him comfort.*

"You could not have suspected that," Hao muttered. "You
were an interpreter put in charge of logistics in a minor naval
facility."

Williams had said, as part of his drugged regurgitation
of data, that she had wept for some captain, "Atlas" Hamill,
when he was murdered. *She should have come.*

Bolting to his feet, Hao went back to Williams' room.
There was no guard; the door was locked and the prisoner
was too weak and broken to go anywhere. Hao's finger trem-
bled with anger and his brain searched for a next move as he
punched the code on the keypad. He pushed the door open
and shut in one fluid move, then stood in the darkness listening for Williams' strained breathing. He wanted to savor that,
at least, but he did not hear it. He felt for the light switch—

An elbow closed around his throat from behind. It was
a momentarily powerful grip that weakened as Hao pulled at
the long, thick arm. The agent was able to step away and the
attacker fell upon him again—literally fell, losing his balance
and grabbing at the man's shirt.

Hao shoved the figure back. Chase Williams fell against
and over an armchair and landed on the floor. His shirt was

bloody and soaked with perspiration, his arms were bent at the elbow as if they had something to do, his fingers were curled, grasping and useless.

There was no expression on the man's bruised, red-streaked face.

Now Hao heard the crackling rale that rose from the man's chest as it struggled for breath. He looked down and smiled at his prisoner.

"I am impressed, Admiral," Hao said. He looked behind him, saw the ruddy smear on the wall, then turned back. "I'm glad we didn't tie you down. This was worth witnessing. You barely had the strength, but you had the will to haul yourself from bed, prop yourself at the door, and wait for me. You had no hope of escaping in this condition, in this situation, but you had one final show of defiance in you."

Hao walked over and squatted.

"You want to grab me again? Go ahead. I want to see that fire before it dies."

Williams' arms fell back on the floor, wide and spent.

Hao lingered, grinning. "It is enough just to breathe now, yes?" He rose slowly, still looking down. "Stay there. Rest. I underestimated you and Captain Mann and the rest of Black Wasp. I cannot tell that to my superior, but you have given me an inspiration. The very fortitude of your team will be its undoing. And the best part of it is—you will be there to witness it."

Newly inspired, Hao returned to the conference room to inform Wang Jing that all was going according to plan, that

the beating of Williams had ensured the continued cooperation of President Wright, and he would have a special surprise
for him at the airport.

And a job for the armed squad traveling with him.

CHAPTER THIRTY-THREE

Lafayette Square, Washington, D.C.
March 23, 9:10 P.M.

There was a notorious cellular dead spot in Washington, D.C., one where converging microwaves and electronic blockers and other forms of electrosmog made even the delivery of text messages impossible.

It was Lafayette Park in Lafayette Square, athwart the White House. That was where Ann Ellen Mann headed. There was no joy in this day, but it amused her—on a cynical level—that as she hopefully coordinated her next move it would be in the backyard of the people who had hung Black Wasp out to dry.

The park was open from midnight to 11:59 P.M. every day. A legal quirk mandating closure for rehabilitation of every public facility was the reason for the one-minute shutdown; the park was quasi-excepted so protesters would have a place to go that was not the fence around the White House.

There were about a dozen people out and about as Mann pulled up. She motored around until she found a spot where she got a signal, on H Street. It was like the eye of a storm, she hoped: if the NSA or Fort Belvoir were listening for her, they would get a faulty, incomplete signal at best.

Exhaling the tension that had been present all day but had been exacerbated by Hao's call, Mann used her government phone to call Grace Lee.

The young woman answered after the second beep.

"Yes?" The single word was clipped and cautious.

"Lieutenant, this is Ann Ellen." The captain hoped the informality would assure her this was not a trap, a forced call.

"May I put you on speaker?" Grace asked.

"Who is there?"

"Friends. Allies," she answered cautiously.

"All right," Mann replied.

"What did I have for breakfast this morning," Lee asked.

"Almond milk, yogurt, and granola."

"Captain—are you all right?"

"So far."

"*Where* are you?"

"Near Lafayette Square."

There was muted conversation. "All right, stay there. We will—"

"I think I should come to you," the captain interrupted. "I'm in the ISV, not exactly incognito."

"I see," Grace said. There was more conversation. "Drive to Logan Circle. I will meet you there."

Mann agreed and ended the call. She sat for a few minutes, waiting to see if anyone had come along to watch or listen or follow. It did not appear so and she set off. She wondered then how many military vehicles ever showed up in the streets of the nation's capital. Probably very few, which—despite the kicks and shakes it took—that told her something about the rockbound nature of American democracy.

Logan Circle was easy to spot, even in the dark. It was a large, floodlit spoked-wheel design rendered in cement with a fountain in the center. She could not quite make out the green-patinaed figures in repose, spitting up geysers of water, but they reflected the four radii.

It was not a time to sightsee, though many people were doing just that on the chill but not unpleasant spring night. Mann did not drive around, concerned that she would draw attention, but idled on Rhode Island Avenue in view of the circle. She slipped her right hand in the deep pocket of the puffer jacket, felt the grip of the 9mm handgun.

Several people walked by, none of them familiar, including the man who suddenly turned and came toward the passenger side of the ISV. Mann did not quite draw the firearm but was ready to. The man was short, broad, and seemed to be admiring the vehicle and not her—

"He's with me," said a familiar voice from the street.

Mann turned and saw the welcome face of Grace Lee. It was half-hidden under a baseball cap that announced some chicken take-out service. The lieutenant noticed Mann's eyes.

"Borrowed," Grace said with a grin. "Jaz picked it."

Mann relaxed. "God, it is good to see you," she said.

"Likewise. The gentleman is Jay Paul with Trigram."

Mann turned and nodded.

"Very happy to make your acquaintance," Paul said. He seemed sincere.

"We walked here," Grace explained. She told the captain to turn the corner at P Street then gave her the address. "We'll meet you in front of the house. The gate will be open and you can pull around back."

"Well concealed," Paul said. "We have to assume the army will want their vehicle back."

His airy manner did not conceal the fact that he was right: Angie Brunner had pulled the guard off. But if word reached the president and he countermanded the order given in his name, the search would be on for the ISV.

The destination was an easy two-minute drive. Mann's first impression was that the spy game paid well. Either that, or Berry had grifted enough from the Op-Center budget to buy the place while he was still a government worker. It had always struck the captain as improbable that so many politicians and their associates had estates as well as vacation homes. She had never seen that in the military, even among top brass.

Maybe there were as many honorable officers as she had always hoped there were.

Lieutenant Lee came over as Mann got out. She saluted the captain.

"I wanted to do that in the street but didn't dare," Lee said, smiling. "Major Breen was the master of anonymity and caution."

"God rest his soul," Mann said, returning the salute. "And your parents, Lieutenant. I was very sorry to learn of that."

"Thank you, sir." The smile vanished then. "What of Admiral Williams?"

"Still held, still alive, but not in great shape," Mann said. "We'll talk more inside."

They went in through a back door that opened into a pantry adjoining the kitchen. Paul was already inside, still at the counter, working on his laptop. Berry was microwaving chicken leftovers—which explained the hat Grace was wearing. He looked over as the women entered. So did Rivette.

"Sir, welcome!" he said from the living room, throwing off a sharp salute.

"Lance Corporal," she replied, saluting back.

Berry offered his hand. "Captain Mann, it is an honor to meet you. I was in the West Wing during the Black Order situation."

"Coup attempt with a second act of attempted mass murder," Grace said.

"The lieutenant doesn't approve of genteel euphemisms," Paul said without looking up.

"They have their time and place," Berry affably disagreed. "Not everything in life should be a screaming tabloid headline."

Grace eased around him and slapped the cap on the counter beside the empty chicken bucket. "That's all I saw growing up in New York," she said. "The *New York Post* and ugly hardship. If the Taoists and Buddhists who trained me had their way, I never would have enlisted. I just could not reconcile their visionary hope with reality."

"You had to try and fix it," Berry said.

"That's right."

"Peace through strength," Berry said as the microwave announced his warm dinner. He lingered a moment. "Tell me something. Your actions in China. Did they support that theory or contradict it? Would you do the same thing again?"

The room and the people in it sagged under the weight of the question. It was blunt, unexpected, and confrontational.

"Allow me," Captain Mann said, touching Grace on the shoulder and stepping closer to her. "No one, not even the sharpest minds in the proudest think tanks in Washington can see into the future. Soldiers on a mission—are different. They are given a task to fulfill. It could be to take a road or save a hostage. And then something else joins the equation—not the call of duty but a call *to* duty. Something that drives a soldier against the odds, against reason, to do what they know is right. I myself have turned from battle. I ran, I hid, I sought God, I *found* God, and then I went back to do what I was sent to do."

"Your service record, commendations, and sacrifice are known to me," Berry said.

"Known but not understood, Mr. Berry. Your question is lousy with cynicism. I believe that even if she had foreseen the outcome, the terrible price she would pay, Lieutenant Lee would have done exactly what she did—her duty. And I have read Admiral Williams' report, sir. He went out of his way to praise the compassion that was evident in Lieutenant Lee's debrief. Not just for Dr. Dàyóu, who was being held captive and would have suffered terribly at the hands of General Zhou Chang, but for his wife, his daughter, and finally, the son she tried to save. Lieutenant Lee was under no obligation to make that attempt. That was her own mission initiative."

Berry did not reply. This was a time to be politic, not for him to furnish a lesson in geopolitics. He would do and say—or not do and say—whatever was needed to move forward.

"Mr. Berry, I suggest you eat your dinner before it cools to rubber," Mann said. "But know that at the risk of losing this shelter and your support I will not tolerate armchair generaling from someone who is not even a military officer. And never was, unless I missed it in all those heralding announcements in the press."

Grace's eyes were damp and Rivette had only half lowered his salute before his arm seemed to stick in shock and awe. Paul did not look up from the computer but was breathing hard through his nose.

Only Berry seemed relaxed. He moved between the women to reach the microwave.

"Lieutenant Lee," Berry said as he removed the plate of chicken. "Your actions required courage, a lot of it. That is not in question. But this calls for courage too. And you didn't answer my question."

The young officer's jaw tensed as she peered through her tears. "No. Not if I had known."

Berry regarded Ann Ellen Mann. "Everything you said,

every word of it, Captain, is true and heartfelt and I respect you for saying it. You bear the scars of service, and now Lieutenant Lee bears her scars. The reality of my world is simpler. What can *I* do, what leverage can I secure, what information can I collect to avoid putting people like you in a position to make these choices? Words, Captain. Ideas. Threats. Blackmail. Even a dead Chadian assassin. What is the minimal price I can offer for the greatest result?"

The room was now tense as well as heavy, two separate worlds with different rules occupying one small space. The gravity the Black Wasps felt was enormous.

"Come on," Captain Mann said to Grace, taking her by the arm. "Let's sit down and talk."

"Before you do that," Berry said, "allow me to play the son of a bitch once more. Mr. Paul?"

"Two hours and forty-two minutes," he said. "Scrolling that backward, I'd say two hours and ten minutes, give or take."

"Until what?" Mann asked.

"Until it's too late to do anything about Chase Williams," Berry told her. "I intend that my friend *not* be delivered to Beijing. I believe that is your purpose as well?"

Mann nodded.

"Then I suggest we get to planning. As Mr. Paul said, we haven't much time."

CHAPTER THIRTY-FOUR

P Street NW, Washington, D.C.
March 23, 9:24 P.M.

Matt Berry had been on what he called the "active sidelines of conflict" for his entire career. An undergraduate from Florida State but a PhD from Princeton, magna cum laude, in international affairs, Berry had risen to the position of under secretary of state for arms control and international security affairs. From there, he was invited to join the Midkiff administration, where he served for both terms.

Berry had gotten to know Williams through Op-Center's director of operations, Brian Robert Dawson. It was Dawson who kept things humming when the secret government division was still the National Crisis Management Center and it was considerably larger and more complex. Berry and Williams were unalike in every way, which was one reason they had gotten along so well. Each respected the other's challenge to his belief system. As Berry had demonstrated to Captain Mann and Lieutenant Lee—perhaps at an inconvenient time but no less necessary for it—he liked having to defend long-held positions.

His days were usually full and the attention to detail had usually sapped him by this time. On a day that had cost the life of one colleague and the liberty of another, he felt especially burdened—and, worse, responsible. Dylan Hao was his man. But, with the able skills and resources of Jay Paul to lean on, he would make it through this crisis. After all, Berry reminded himself, one way or the other this ended at midnight.

The five occupants of the safe house were seated in the living room, facing the center in a spacious but tense huddle. Mann had told them about the assassination attempt and then her back-to-back conversations with Angie Brunner and Dylan Hao, which left Berry a little less sour than before.

"I know the man and he's getting desperate," Berry said.

"About what?" Rivette asked. "They've got the admiral and they'll have the Dàyóus."

"But he won't have what the Chinese want more, to save face for Black Wasp having cut a big, public path through their homeland. I'm not just referring to the lieutenant's work but also the trafficked young women rescued by Lance Corporal Rivette and Major Breen."

Rivette seemed to puff a little at the compliment.

"What does it look like, Hao becoming 'desperate'?" Mann asked.

"He tried to get you to come to the embassy," Berry said.

"To hack one of my devices, I assumed."

Berry shook his head. "They failed to kill you; they would want to ruin you. He most likely wanted to have video of you freely coming and going, outside, inside, and most importantly with Chase Williams. You would not have been permitted to get close to him. The images would suggest that you were uninterested in him, perhaps a part of the conspiracy against Black Wasp. They would suggest a power play between you and Williams."

"That's ridiculous," Grace said. "No one would believe that."

"And no one could disprove it. The result would be the same—the decapitation of Black Wasp."

"That would still leave me and the lieutenant, though," Rivette said. "We hurt the Chinese, not the captain."

"You would have been shipped back to your units, Black Wasp disenfranchised before the end of the week. A lieutenant and a lance corporal with the regular airborne and marines? The intelligence division of China's Central Military Commission would have found you before the ink of the transfer printout was dry."

"All right," Mann said. "What do we do?" There was a contrite quality in her voice. It was not an apology for what she had said before but rather an acknowledgment that her monologue did not tell the entire story.

"If we want to really hurt them and kick the president in his weak knees, we have to do what we all want to—keep Chase Williams from getting on a plane to China."

"How, shoot our way in?" Rivette asked.

"That's a negative," Jay Paul said, a tablet on his lap. "A ten-man team from Arrow is on board. That's the strike force attached to the Beijing Military Region Special Forces Unit. They are armed and all have diplomatic immunity."

"How do you know the squad is on the plane?" Mann asked.

"One of our contacts at the National Reconnaissance Office informed us that January Dow asked for an ID of the aircraft coming to pick up the Dàyóus."

"Standard operating procedure for any foreign aircraft with a military complement," Berry said. "If we field—let's call it an honor guard, we don't want it to be larger than that of the foreign force."

"Letting them save face?" Mann asked.

"Caution," Berry said. "If they are unsatisfied with the resolution, the Chinese may look to provoke an incident to show not only how brave they are but also to hit us on our territory as we hit them. It's an idiot little game, but it mustn't become a deadly one."

"Or a bigger idiot game," Rivette said.

"That too," Berry agreed.

"Then to your earlier point, how do we keep Chase Williams from being put on that plane?" Mann asked.

Berry replied, "We grab him before he gets to the airport."

The boldness and commitment of the statement killed any lingering resentment Black Wasp had for the man.

"To do that," Berry continued, "we have to identify the vehicle he will be traveling in. That means eyes on the Chinese embassy as soon as possible."

"I'll go," Grace said. "They know my name but maybe not my face."

"If you've ever been in a school yearbook or martial arts competition, they know your face," Berry said.

"They don't know my face," Captain Mann said. "And as I said, your friend Dylan Hao invited me to come to the embassy. If I can get the information you need, I don't care what it does to my career."

"Hao won't let you out of his sight," Berry said. "You will be walked through the building like a mouse in a maze. Besides, you already turned him down. If you call and tell him you changed your mind, he'll know something is up."

"It sounds like you're telling us to suck sand, Mr. Berry," Rivette said. "You said yourself we've got to do something."

"We will. Mr. Paul?"

"I think I can do it."

"Do what?" Mann asked.

"I've been looking at the aerials of the embassy compound," he said. "They've got walls like a prison, but there are trees around them, especially at the front. They were put there to absorb a potential car bomber ramming the walls. We'll know within a few minutes of when they leave for the airport. We know that they'll be in an armored vehicle that can accommodate at least two passengers, two security men, and the driver."

"That's a stretch limousine, not a sedan," Berry said.

"Correct," Paul said. "And they won't want to have a limo gap. They know the U.S. officials—January Dow and two bodyguards, according to protocol—will be arriving with the Dàyóus."

"Six people, a stretch limousine," Mann said. "My God, do the games never end?"

"In diplomacy and public appearances? Never," Berry said.

Rivette leaned forward. "Let me see if I got this. The limo leaves the embassy, Mr. Paul lets us know, and we do what? Attack an anti-explosive-plated vehicle with bullet-proof windows—on a public street? And with what?"

"I'm just the intelligence man," Berry said, sitting back. He glanced at his phone. "You're Black Wasp. You tell me. How do we pull this off within the next two hours?"

CHAPTER THIRTY-FIVE

The White House, Washington, D.C.
March 23, 9:50 P.M.

In a day of meetings President Wright wished he did not have to sit through, this was the most onerous. He was about to meet with January Dow, a young Chinese interpreter, and the Dàyóu family.

He had met Yang Dàyóu, his wife, Dongling, and their daughter, Ushi, when they had arrived in the United States. The president had expressed his deep sympathy for the loss of their son, Wen. The college student had died in a Chinese prison, a direct result of the defection of his father.

The Dàyóus had agreed to come to the United States because the chief engineer had been wrongly blamed for the explosion of China's new hypersonic missile. At best Yang Dàyóu would have been executed within the week; at worst he would have spent his life in prison. Seeking asylum at least gave Ushi Dàyóu a future unclouded by disgrace.

That was less than five weeks ago. Today, the Dàyóus' world would be inverted yet again. According to January, the engineer had taken the news of his return stoically and without comment. John Wright wondered if he and his family would have more to say now.

Wright was not a devout man but, privately, he prayed they did not.

They were announced by the president's assistant executive secretary, and they entered; Dongling first, followed by Ushi, Dr. Dàyóu, the young male interpreter who worked for the State Department, and then the national security advisor. January appeared more somber than usual. Wright wondered if she truly felt that. He respected the woman's judgment and leaned heavily on her skills when it came to navigating the Washington bureaucracy with which he and Angie Brunner were unfamiliar. But there were times he wondered if January ever felt anything, really.

This was one of those times.

The guests were shown to seats and offered tea, which they declined. The interpreter accepted a bottle of water. January remained standing off to one side, her tablet clutched to her chest.

"Thank you for coming," the president said. "I am sorry it is under these circumstances. I wanted to express my regret that détente compels this policy shift."

The translation made, the president waited while Yang Dàyóu responded in a voice barely above a whisper.

"I am sorry as well," the young man said on behalf of the engineer.

"Your pretty words do not alter the reality that my beloved son Wen died for nothing."

The president was taken aback by the bluntness of the statement; he knew he should not have been. The Dàyóu family were commodities in the game of state and they knew it.

"Once again I offer my profound sympathy. But at great personal peril, one of our troops did try to secure his release."

Dr. Dàyóu spoke and the interpreter said, "Wen was in Qincheng Prison because I was freed. Had you done nothing he would still be alive. We return to an uncertain future and a grave to visit."

The president looked to January, whose expression did not change. He folded his hands. "Sir, the Chinese killed four astronauts as they reentered the Earth's atmosphere and launched retaliatory attacks on our homeland. Today, one man was killed, another beaten nearly to death. I am sorry, sir, most genuinely sorry. But if anyone is to blame for this regrettable . . . situation, it is your countrymen."

When the interpreter was finished, Dr. Dàyóu stood and spoke.

The interpreter said, with reluctance that was apparent, "It is a weak leader who blames his own failings on the actions of others."

The interpreter rose when he was finished and bowed to Dr. Dàyóu, indicating that he was done. The engineer turned toward the door of the Oval Office and January jumped ahead of him to open it. Dr. Dàyóu was followed by his wife and daughter, the interpreter—who apologized quietly to January—and then by the national security advisor herself. She showed the president a look of practiced consternation as she shut the door. It was the look of someone who watched a mugging with disapproval but kept on going.

At that moment, John Wright felt close to no one except the forty-odd people who had sat in this very office since 1800 and made decisions like this one. He sat there thinking about Adams, Lincoln, the two Roosevelts, others. He stone-skipped through the campaign, all the effort it had taken for him—and for Angie—to *get* here. The feeling of triumph.

How did it go so far south so fast?

The part that gnawed was that the president could not blame Dr. Dàyóu for his pain and he did not blame himself for his decision. He was not even distressed by the way January Dow had put on a mask of self-preservation, distancing herself from the decision, leaving it to sit on the president's desk and there alone.

That was when the door opened and transformed the president's Chinese concession into a potential crisis.

CHAPTER THIRTY-SIX

Embassy of the People's Republic of China,
Washington, D.C.
March 23, 10:00 P.M.

Tree, my ass.

Jay Paul drove his personal vehicle to International Court NW, parked there, and walked south to Van Ness Street NW. The Chinese embassy was across the street at 3505 International Place NW. There was a police car parked down the street and tape limiting traffic on that side. Outside the gate was still an active crime scene, though no one was working it at present.

Paul would in fact be watching the building from outside the University of the District of Columbia Van Ness campus where he was friends with the CIA spotters who posed as students, professors, or the homeless. Nellie Friday, who would be there now, was a "professor" and also an occasional lover. He did not want to share that information with Black Wasp. It was not because Paul did not trust them; it was because, with the exception of Matt Berry, he did not trust anyone.

Not even Nellie, though she was nearer to that line than any-one else in his life.

That was why he told them he would be in a tree. Where he would be, and with whom, was none of their business.

For Jay Paul, keeping secrets was an old habit, frequently reinforced. It began with his name, which was not Jay. He was christened Jabez, his evangelist mother telling one and all, "As his name itself announces, God will increase his bounty." It was a cranky, unwieldy name that he stopped using in kin-dergarten.

Sophia Paul was fanatical, loud, and unwed. She worked for a preacher who had a big tent and bigger visions in Downs-ville, Louisiana. Jabez suspected the Reverend Toomey, who stood five-two, was in fact his father.

Jabez took a lot of teasing about his parentage and his mother's perceived lunacy, which was what turned him to soli-tude and bodybuilding. Upon graduating from high school, he spent the next six years on the professional circuit. His ac-tivities brought him to the attention of the CIA. Competing around the world, he had access to venues in Tehran, Beijing, Moscow, and even Pyongyang, and that was of interest to the intelligence agency. He was recruited after an interview that took place outside the Roosevelt Hotel in New York, across the street from Madison Square Garden.

The young man's tendency toward secrecy became his bedrock policy. Paul took pictures for them, eyeballed gro-cery stores—bare shelves were always a measure of local

discontent—and chatted up local interpreters. When he suffered dual inguinal hernias, Paul was forced to give up the
sport. He accepted a variety of federal positions analyzing
data until his thirtieth birthday.

Matt Berry became aware of Paul when he applied for a
job in the Midkiff administration. Berry found a place for him
on the national security staff. As Berry later said, a CIA agent
who stood five foot one and had strongman swagger was too
fascinating not to have around.

Paul had dressed in a white sweater and matching trousers. Spies wore black; that was who the Chinese would be
looking for. Nellie wore black, but that was because it hid the
shadows of the switchblade she kept in the right-hand pocket
of her blazer and the 9mm she wore in a custom holster tucked
in the small of her back.

Nellie was glad to see her former coworker. Not just because she liked him but because, together, they looked like a
pair of professors who had stayed late and were having a chat.
Though they had not seen each other in several months, they
texted several times a week.

She greeted him with a crooked smile between her high
cheekbones. "Well."

"Well," he replied. "Been here long?"

"Two hours and change," she said. "Missed all the action.
Nothing to post on 'Undercover Instagram.'"

The last was a private joke of Nellie's, the notion that the
first spotter who started a social media site for secret government surveillance would be rich.

"On the run but at least traveling first class," was the motto she had suggested.

Paul was glad to see that she had missed the van. Nellie had never been in the safe house, had never seen the vehicle, but there was always the chance that she had followed him on streetcams, MapQuested him, knew more than she let on. Like where he went after leaving her apartment.

Nellie turned her eyes back to the embassy. "I won't ask what's up because I know you won't tell me, but maybe we can play twenty questions to pass the time."

Paul did not respond so she proceeded.

"I'm guessing the scuffle earlier in the day and the habeas corpus tonight are cause and effect," she said.

Paul shrugged.

"That wasn't a 'no,' so there's a connection, just not a direct one," she guessed.

He shrugged again.

"One person is murdered every one-point-four days in D.C.," she said. "There were two homicides today, starting this morning in Lady Bird Johnson Park. Related?"

He shrugged.

"The destruction of *Phoenix One*," she said. "Chinese action for sure. The precipitating event for today's body count?"

"Is that what the CIA thinks?"

"That's what everyone from CNBC to Newsmax thinks," she replied.

He shrugged.

Nellie smiled. "All right, that's all I've got. Not very

impressive for a woman who has been standing out here since eight. Can you—will you—add anything?"

"Wish I could," Paul told her. That was only three questions. She seldom got to four, let alone twenty.

"Maybe I've seen something that can help *you*," she said.

"Possibly," he admitted.

"Got any questions?"

"Want to hook up tomorrow?" he asked.

She grinned. "You're slipping."

"How?"

"You just told me you know you'll have free time tomorrow. There's a ticking clock on whyever you're here tonight."

Now Paul's mouth twisted. Nellie was not wrong.

"What does the agency know about Yang Dàyóu?" he asked.

"He defected. Wright's spine turned to soup. He's—" Nellie bit off the rest of the sentence. She took her eyes off the embassy for a moment. "They're bringing him here?"

"No," Paul told her.

"Berry wants to know when they're leaving to *get* him." Paul shrugged.

"Why?" Nellie asked, knowing she would not get an answer. She looked back at the embassy. "Jay, I want to work for Trigram."

Jay Paul gave her hand a little squeeze and moved on. "See you on the way back," he said.

"You're slipping," she said again. "That's the way you came."

He had only gone a few paces. He turned. "And?"

"The carport is on that side."

"The wall's too high to see," Paul told her.

"But you've got great hearing," she said. "How many doors will you be listening for?"

He smiled approvingly, shrugged, and moved on.

CHAPTER THIRTY-SEVEN

The White House, Washington, D.C.
March 23, 10:01 P.M.

It was uncommon for Angie Brunner to leave her door open. Overheard conversations, especially incomplete snippets of them, were weapons in Washington. She did not like furnishing arms to the likes of January Dow.

But eavesdropping was a double-edged sword. When the Dàyóu family had passed, trailed by January Dow—who did not look over—the sour look on the face of the national security advisor told her the brief meeting had not gone well. That was reinforced by the appearance of the interpreter. The young man who had passed her door a few minutes earlier had been proud and erect. The man who left was a slouching, fidgety shadow of that.

It was one of the sick, sad truths of the federal government that however it impacted the nation, bureaucrats and elected officials savored the misfortunes and setbacks that befell others. Even if they did not know someone, ascension by any individual inspired jealousy while failure caused joy.

Whether she liked it or not, Angie fit right in with that mind-set. It had been the duality in Hollywood; it mattered even more here. And no one deserved a kick in the seat more than the national security advisor.

Which means John Wright is probably hurting right now, Angie thought. *Good. He screwed up.*

The mistake was not necessarily in the decision he had made regarding the Dàyóus. Throughout her career, every movie was a potential smash until it opened and it was not. One used their sharpest instincts, their best guesses.

Wright's mistake was showing his trusted, loyal lieutenant the door. The woman who was widely credited with having won him the White House was sidelined for a new model. Someone without a deep well of smarts but a wide web of connections.

She fought the urge to go to the Oval Office and knock on the door. She cared for him and believed in their work. But he would have to come to her. That meant her curiosity about what had gone wrong would also have to wait.

Angie went to the mini refrigerator in her office for a small bottle of orange juice. She got a granola bar from a cabinet. She did not get to enjoy either of them. Her phone rang before she sat back down, and she grinned, half expecting it to be the president. It was not.

Knocking the door shut with the toe of her shoe, she answered the call and sat on the edge of the desk.

"I hope I'm not interrupting anything," Ann Ellen Mann said.

"No. Never. Talk to me."

In the moments before Mann continued, Angie felt a surge of confidence. The rush surprised her. She had taken a chance on the captain earlier in the evening; she felt, without quite knowing why, that risk was about to be justified.

"Ms. Brunner, Black Wasp is not going to let the Chinese take Chase Williams to China."

The statement was audacious, and it momentarily threw the chief of staff. But there was nothing uncertain in the caller's voice. To the contrary. "What—what are you planning?"

"I am not at liberty to share that," Mann said. "But it will not please the Chinese and that will blow back on the administration. Admiral Williams said you have been a friend of Op-Center and I have seen that myself today. I wanted you to have this opportunity to prepare the president."

Angie's heart was drumming, but her mind was in neutral. She had no idea what to say or do.

"I—can you say—are you going to the embassy?" she asked the captain.

"No. This will, this must, be executed on American soil. Forgive me, but we have suffered heavy casualties today. The consensus is that the president will not protect American citizens, not to mention those who come here with a legitimate need for sanctuary. Black Wasp will."

Angie was still mentally frozen and now mute as well.

"This is happening one way or the other," Mann went on,

"but there is one thing you can do for us—for the nation—if you will."

"What's that?" she managed to ask.

"Advise the president to get in touch with the Metro police," she said. "Tell them to avoid the route the Chinese will take to the exchange."

"What if—they may do the opposite. Bulk up."

"We are a go regardless," Mann said. "The attitude here, for what it's worth, is that either the president is for us or against us. Whatever he communicates to the MPDC, Commissioner Mackenna will follow his lead."

The captain was not wrong. Commissioner Mackenna was former Navy SEAL Charlie Mackenna.

"You said 'here,' Captain. Where are you?"

After a short, muted conversation, Mann replied, "Where we won't be found or stopped. Thank you, Ms. Brunner, for everything you did—and tried to do."

Mann ended the call.

Ann Ellen Mann had told her the truth, there was no doubt about that. The situation with Chase Williams was never going to stand. The intercept was going to happen. Yet what Angie was facing went deeper than that: she wanted it to happen.

What has come over you? she wondered. *Principle?*

Angie sat there, suddenly aware that the heat of her palm had softened the granola bar. She put it aside as if it were radioactive, did not want to consider anything that was not *this*.

No, she thought. *You should not* consider *anything.* She never had. It was a leap from the trivial to life and death, but she made it. As a producer, she had never read a script or made a movie based on considered factors or a list of projections. It was always: What did her gut tell her?

It was her instinct that worked like a puppet master now. She slid from the desk, went into the corridor, and stopped by the door of the Oval Office.

"Anyone in there, Parand?" she asked the assistant executive secretary.

"No, Ms. Brunner."

Angie entered and shut the door behind her. The president was seated behind his desk, staring at the coffee table. No refreshments had been provided, save for a bottle of water; it had not been that kind of a meeting.

"Sir?" she said.

"Yes?" he said without looking up. "Sorry. I'm stuck in this loop of how did things get so out of hand?"

"We were inconsistent," she said, "something we never were on the campaign trail."

"I would say, instead, we were green," he replied.

"The Dàyóu? We were ambitious."

"Have it your way. In any case, we jumped into the deep end and China dragged us under."

"You want to get out?" Angie asked.

He finally looked at her. "How?"

"Don't react. Just listen."

"Okay," he said warily.

She came forward. "Mr. President, Black Wasp intends to rescue Chase Williams."

He scowled. "You know this—how?"

"Captain Mann just phoned."

"Where is she?"

"I don't know—with the rest of the team."

Wright exhaled, hard. "This is real."

"Yes, sir. They are going to intercept the vehicle that is going to take the admiral to the airport."

"And do what? Hijack it? Shoot it up in the middle of a major thoroughfare? Are they insane? Are you?" He jabbed a finger at Angie.

"Incredibly, sir, they are not," Angie said. "You do recall, sir, they *have* done this sort of thing before."

"And got us into this mess!"

"No, sir. We got us into this mess. We wanted intelligence about a missile system. They brought back the mother lode."

He shook his head. "My God."

"Mr. President . . . John . . . you asked if I was crazy. I'm not. Hear me out. Yes. We drew first blood last month. China hit back, raising the stakes considerably. If we call them, if we hit back hard, we will ensure that this kind of brinkmanship does not occur again."

"*Or* they will unleash hell."

"It's possible but unlikely. This is a just and targeted response. Our decision now is actually pretty simple. Do we support Black Wasp or do you alert the police and end up with American forces fighting American forces in our streets?"

"We've had domestic terrorists strike before—"

"We haven't had uniforms versus uniforms, the police fighting the military." She leaned on the desk. "But think about this. What kind of a message does it send to China about American unity if we have the police stand down and let Black Wasp fight for their founding commander?"

He shook his head. "Now you think I'm out of my mind. Angie, this is an attack on diplomatic personnel."

"And what the hell is Chase Williams? You want it in raw numbers? How about all of your military officers and most of our troops. Abandon him and you will never have the trust or confidence of any member of the no-man-left-behind brotherhood."

He sat very still for a very long moment. "It's been a long day and—thank you. Thank you for the courage it took for you to walk in that door. Thank you for the wisdom it took for you to kick me in the ass." He stood. "Dammit, yes. What can I do to help?"

Angie told him.

Wright picked up the desk phone. His eyes met those of his confidante and friend. He was wildly unsure now about his own sanity, but he trusted this woman and was ashamed he had forgotten that.

"Parand? Please get police commissioner Charlie Mackenna on the line. Tell him it's urgent."

CHAPTER THIRTY-EIGHT

P Street NW, Washington, D.C.
March 23, 10:46 P.M.

"You know what?" Rivette said to the others. "This is exactly the kind of planning we do for every mission. And you know what? Things never go the way we plan."

The Black Wasps and Matt Berry were still in the living room, only now both Rivette and Grace were preparing to rescue their former leader. They were both in what they called "final countdown" mode, sharp and eager to launch.

The two were kneeling beside their backpacks, which were on the carpet. Berry watched the lance corporal with his gun, Grace with her knife. Mann would be at the wheel of the ISV. She was old-school military, a talent she had honed in Afghanistan. She was studying every possible route to and from the embassy to the airport, as well as turnoffs that would hinder possible pursuit by the MPDC. Although the military vehicle had a sophisticated GPS, she did not know whether their course or an electromagnetic pulse might slow or kill its effectiveness.

Together, the three had all come up with a plan of attack that had the best chance of success—especially if they did not have to deal with the police. Berry was excited for them and proud of them.

The Trigram officer was busy checking intelligence leads as well as waiting for word from Jay Paul. Berry suspected he was probably more on edge than all the others. He was not an advocate of violence or vengeance—except as an object lesson that served a larger purpose. This escapade was neither. He wanted Hao taken apart but would settle for him being taken down. It would take considerable damage control if word got out that this trusted, reliable man had been a double agent who had not only fooled Berry but had seized one of his best friends. And, worse still would be if Hao escaped justice and decamped to China.

Saving Chase was the justification for this adventure. For Berry, for Black Wasp, that was the heart. But Hao was what intelligence referred to as a "highly critical objective." In most cases, that ranked higher than coming back alive.

"Excuse me, Mr. Berry," Rivette said. "It occurs to me— you happen to have any grenades here?"

"I do not, sorry. Why?"

"Well, the car is gonna be armor-plated for sure, a tank built by Mercedes." He held up the gas canisters Mann had brought, the ones they had been using in their drill only that morning. "But it'll also have bulletproof windows. These pack a kick, but a vest full of them may not be enough to bust through."

"Most likely but bulletproof is a misnomer," Berry said.

"Cars have bullet-*resistant* glass, thirteen-sixteenths of an inch thick as a rule. It's lighter than you'd find in government buildings under the theory that the car will speed off before repetitive impact fatigue causes complete degradation."

"Oh," Rivette said. He believed what Berry had said even if he did not entirely understand that.

"Anyway, I've got that covered," Grace said, reaching into her grip and pulling out a solid steel four-knuckle ring. She slipped it on and fired out a from-the-chest jab.

"Pretty, but I saw guys use those in San Pedro and they're great on jaws and noses," Rivette said. "Plus, those dudes were big with arms like telephone poles."

"I'll get through," Grace assured him.

Mann closed her tablet. "It's coming up on eleven. I think we should move out."

"Driving around D.C. in that ISV, you said you felt conspicuous," Rivette said.

"I did. It was still daylight. Also, I want to run the route I think they'll take, check to see if there are police around and, if so, where they patrol."

"The expensive home streets," Berry said. "That's where you'll find them. There aren't a lot of those on the way to the airport."

Grace looked over at the captain. She gave Mann a concerned look. The older woman smiled reassuringly.

"I'll be fine, Lieutenant," she said. "I'm not having PTSD of my last mission in Kabul. I was with you in Philadelphia, don't forget."

"And she put down the Chinese bomber on some *very* short notice," Rivette reminded her.

"I haven't forgotten anything," Grace said. "To the contrary. I'm taking a moment to honor our new teammate. I'm grateful that she is the one on whom our lives and this mission depend."

The remark was unexpected. Mann should have learned by now—but had not—that each culture she had encountered had its own rules and guidelines and that respect for experience was a cornerstone of Chinese heritage.

The captain nodded in appreciation. "I'm going to make sure we're not bringing anything we don't need, keep us light."

"I'm not big on changing tires," Rivette said, "and I don't think we'll have time for that anyway."

"My thought as well." Mann smiled as she left by the pantry door.

The room fell silent again, the collective temperature rising as H-hour loomed. In turn, both Black Wasps put on the charcoal-colored spandex tactical outerwear they had brought. They allowed for mobility and did not have sleeves or cuffs that could snag on anything.

"Mr. Berry, sir," Rivette said, "how about you getting us some of those new Gen 6 Nanophotonic Refraction Stealth Operator Suits I read about. Be nice to have for our next mission, if there is one."

"I'll see what I can do," Berry laughed.

Grace made sure there was a place on her person for everything she needed and that she could move freely with all of it. Rivette did the same with his weapon and spare clips.

As they were finishing, Captain Mann returned. She was smiling. "We're set, and I don't mean just the excess baggage."

The other three looked over. She held up her phone.

"A text from President Wright," she said. "Not Angie Brunner but the commander in chief himself." She glanced at the phone and read: "Speaking for myself and for the MPDC, Godspeed Black Wasp."

As one, the Black Wasps seemed to grow several inches. The moment did not break even when Berry's device chimed; if anything, it seemed to be extended.

"Call from Jay Paul," the Trigram officer said. He put it on speaker. "Go ahead, Jay. We're all listening."

"The target is an Audi Armored Pullman Premier," the caller said. "They must know or assume someone is out here watching and want to rub our noses in it. Instead of using the side entrance they rolled the stretch around front. I believe they mean for us to see Admiral Williams being hauled off."

CHAPTER THIRTY-NINE

Embassy of the People's Republic of China,
Washington, D.C.
March 23, 10:57 P.M.

Dylan Hao waited until Wang Jing informed him that the flight from Beijing was in its final approach before he put his end of the handover in motion. Jing had also texted that the American emissary, national security advisor January Dow, had notified him that she and the Dàyóus would be under way at 11:30 for a midnight exchange.

The deputy director did not comment on the day's setbacks. Hao was not surprised by the omission. Jing was most likely preoccupied with the two most important events outstanding: repatriating the Chinese citizens he had come to collect and making a permanent new "citizen" out of the man behind that affront. Hao did not think Jing would mind that it had been necessary to break Williams like a dog or a horse as long as the admiral was alive.

Dead he is merely a memento, Hao thought. *Alive he is a trophy.*

Before their departure, Hao summoned the embassy physician. When Dr. Fulin arrived, the injured man was conscious but willfully uncommunicative. The medic provided a quick examination. His assessment of Williams' injuries—without benefit of X-rays, he cautioned—was that the injuries were apparently not life threatening.

"I will do what I can to make sure they remain so," Dr. Fulin said.

The doctor realigned the minor break in their guest's nose and used a cyanoacrylate surgical compound to repair the deep cuts in the upper chest and along the throat. If he was shocked by the wounds or by the size of the welts and bruises surrounding them, he did not show it.

"Please see that he uses his seat belt," Dr. Fulin said. "Turbulence may shake these simple repairs loose. I will send along a first aid kit should bleeding resume while you are in flight."

Hao thanked the man. So did Williams, in Mandarin. The American was sitting on the foot of the bed, looking straight ahead. It was the only word he uttered.

Fulin wished him well before departing.

Hao did not offer Williams a change of clothes, nor had he offered to have the bloody garments washed. To him, this was the uniform the American had chosen. He would wear it so that the CIA operative who was stationed across the street, posing as a student or professor or panhandler—depending on the shift—would photograph him in it. He would wear it straight through to Qincheng Prison.

Five minutes after the hour, Hao summoned two security guards and instructed them to walk Williams to the limousine parked out front. The drive would take around a half hour. The plan was to walk Williams onto the plane after the Dàyóus had boarded. Jing did not want the family to see the prisoner, or his condition, until they were out of sight of any observers. There was no telling whether the family had succumbed to the Stockholm syndrome during their time in America, surrounded by Western trappings and fawning kindness.

When the guards arrived, Hao instructed them to bring Williams around to the driver's side.

"I wish him to be seen from the street," Hao said. "We want to make sure the CIA documents the last maneuvers of an old soldier."

The men went to escort Williams to his feet. He wrenched his arms free. They grabbed him again, tighter this time. The admiral let his legs go limp, made himself dead weight. He was determined not to go, not to face a slow, degrading death. He must try to escape again or perish in the attempt.

The men hoisted him up, grunted as they tried to pull the much bigger man forward. The tops of his feet dragged on the floor. Hao watched with impatience, then disgust.

"Get a wheelchair from Fulin, quickly!" he told one of the men.

The guard left in a hurry. The other remained and put Williams back on the bed. Hao bent close.

"I see this spark, this flame in your eyes," the agent said. "I assure you, there will be no chance for you to take your own life, so put that from your mind. And if you believe you have nothing left to lose, consider this. You can cooperate with us and sit quietly in a prison cell or you can fight us and be beaten so severely that you cannot sleep or sit or lie down for the pain. The choice is yours."

Williams remained silent. Even when Hao swore and struck him, he did not react. When the wheelchair arrived, he allowed himself to be dumped in it because there was nothing left to fight with. No target, no strength. His only hope was that there would be an opportunity between the embassy and the airport or the airplane and Beijing for him to do something that would result in his death.

As a final precaution—or insult—Williams was blindfolded before he was wheeled out, the cloth knotted tightly behind his head. The wheels squeaked as they turned and the sound of the floor changed from tile to carpet and back again, and voices he had heard in the distance fell silent as he passed.

His eyes teared behind the blindfold, but that was all right, Williams told himself. It had been a good life and he was proud of what he had accomplished—even the mission that had led him to this place, this end.

Most of all, he was proud of the two young minds he had helped to shape as members of Black Wasp. Whatever his fate, whenever it came, he knew that a part of him—his code, his sense of duty—would live on through them.

CHAPTER FORTY

Van Ness Street NW, Washington, D.C.
March 23, 11:15 P.M.

Traffic on the thoroughfare was typically light at this late hour. But this night whatever traffic Captain Mann encountered in her two lanes was uncommonly thin, unusually watchful, and exceedingly slow.

She remarked on it as she drove.

Matt Berry, on the other end of an open line, said, "That's probably got something to do with the speed traps front and back. The order to execute came over on the police radio a half hour ago."

"Won't the Chinese be listening too?"

Berry snickered. "You bet. And they'll assume it is because of them, the arrogant pricks."

Grace and Rivette were in the back seat. They were quiet and watchful. Neither was thoughtful. A disengaged mind was the lieutenant's contribution. When she and the lance corporal first began training, she explained that the mind had no jurisdiction in combat.

"Only the first of the five spirits should govern your moves, your five senses."

It sounded like mumbo jumbo to Rivette until the first time they drilled. He killed two cardboard cutout civilians in the training house; she killed none. After that, she taught him exercises to silence the "nattering monkey brain" and focus on the task at hand.

They were doing that now as the cooling night air blew around them. The canvas top of the Infantry Squad Vehicle had been rolled back, leaving the four roll bars exposed. There was one around the windshield, one in the back behind the storage area, and one each behind the front seats and rear seats. There were no doors on the gunmetal-colored vehicle and the turbo-diesel engine furnished a muscular 275 horsepower capable of reaching sixty mph in just over six seconds. The multimatic dynamic suspension made for an extremely smooth ride while the Mud Terrain T/A KM3 tires—designed for all terrains—was untroubled by the imperfections of urban asphalt.

It was a ride Jaz Rivette once said he could sell for retirement fund numbers back in his home surf and turf.

The ambient sounds of the city were muted as midnight encroached and, to the three passengers, sounded increasingly distant. There was a bond between them, one that had absorbed Captain Mann as if she had been with them on every mission they had undertaken. The connection was partly the result of their shared purpose, partly a shared background of hazardous military duty.

The trio drove past landmarks without quite noticing them, stately structures that blended into a quilt of alabaster and marble. All three were eyes-front on the large GPS monitor in front that showed a red dot crawling, bug-like, nearer and nearer to the green square representing the Chinese embassy compound.

"You'd better slow," Berry said. "You overshoot, they'll see you when you turn back."

"Roger that," Mann replied.

Before they left Berry had alerted them to the likelihood that guards at the front gate would be watching for Black Wasp or anything looking like them. Mann slowed from thirty-five to twenty-five miles an hour.

"Well, it is a school district," Rivette remarked, looking at the college just creeping into view on the map.

It was the lance corporal ice-breaking; the women ignored him. Energy was pulsing through their chests and along their arms. The ride was abruptly different from other rides the Black Wasps had taken: this was for one of their own. Despite the fact that they were crawling along Van Ness, the trio felt a forward momentum that had not been present on any other speeding car or boat or aerial transport they had ever taken.

Suddenly, the voice of Jay Paul broke through the thick, watchful silence.

"DEFCON two," he said in a careful, articulate whisper. "I repeat, DEFCON *red*. The passengers have just been loaded. The target is blindfolded, bandaged, and in a wheelchair. May be fragile. Stand by."

After digesting what had just been reported, Rivette snarled, "Goddamn them. Goddamn them all."

This time he spoke for everyone. All three knew that the admiral was not a delicate man; that had not been Paul's meaning. He meant that Williams was injured—to what extent could not be known—and was being wheeled instead of walking under his own steam.

"That could be his cussedness," Mann said. "You want me, you're going to have to hand-carry me."

"Update," Paul said. "Target resisted being put in the car."

"Give 'em hell, Admiral," Berry said over the phone.

"Matt—Hao just got in," Paul confirmed.

The lights of the compound were coming into view. Grace began breathing from the abdomen to power all of the meridians in her body. She sat up taller to align her core with the universe.

And she slipped on the steel knuckles.

A white BMW boldly passed them, momentarily blocking their view. It had diplomatic plates, but it was not going to the Chinese embassy. When it was gone, Black Wasp could see what Jay Paul was just reporting:

"DEFCON one," the spotter said urgently. "I say DEFCON *white*. The target has left the compound. Zero accompaniment. Low profile."

"You ready?" Captain Mann asked the others.

Rivette had the powerful .45 in his lap. He was holding it lightly, respectfully, like it was the hand of a girlfriend. "I'm good."

Grace said, "Go."

Mann put her foot to the gas—not gently as she had while she was pacing their approach but with the ferocity of a charging tiger. The four fat tires gripped the road and hurtled them forward. They quickly overtook the BMW, which honked in protest. It did not concern the captain that the Chinese driver might hear through the muffled comfort of the limousine. The growl of their engine would announce their approach.

The black Audi loomed nearer, faster. The ISV was in the left lane, the target in the right. They blazed past Jay Paul and a woman who looked like she was taking pictures with her cell phone.

"Your ass is so ours," Rivette said through his teeth. "Ours."

If this were a training mission, Mann would have told him not to be overconfident. But it was not a training mission. She was tearing through the streets of the capital, mindful in the event there were bicycles or pedestrians, headed toward a showdown that was measured not in hours or hypotheticals but in seconds, and for real.

Grace was behind the passenger's seat. Rivette was sitting back in the seat.

"Remember," he said. "You gotta give me—"

"Room. Quiet."

The woman flexed her small fingers in the knuckles. It was a good fit, like her bones had been moved to the outside. The lieutenant's balance was impeccable as she sat forward and got her feet under her. She did not rise, not yet; she merely sought to center herself before rising. She would not hold the roll bar; that would both take and crimp energy that she could not afford to spare. Her stance would embody a crane, rising from the water and being alert to every current, to the wind.

The ISV closed in on the limousine, which responded not by speeding up but by slowing, assuming it meant to pass.

"Perfect, asshole," Rivette said. He raised the .45 to the height of the driver's window. The rest was up to Grace.

The military vehicle overtook the Chinese. The windows were blackened, impenetrable, but that did not matter. Not knowing where Williams would be seated was the reason they had targeted the driver in the planning stage: there was no question where he would be. They considered the possibility that the man was probably armed—"with a pussy .38 in a shoulder holster," Rivette had guessed—but he would not risk lowering the window to fire.

Mann was no stranger to ISVs and braked with firm but measured pressure. Grace and Rivette had expected the hard slowdown when the target was achieved, and both were ready for it. The lieutenant waited to stand until Mann had matched the speed of the limousine.

Grace's entire world was a pane of glass-clad polycarbonate and, in particular, a section of that pane near the top of the doorframe. The power for what she was about to do would not come from the hip. A swivel like that burned up half the energy of a punch just delivering it. It would not use the muscles of the shoulder; they had the limitations of all flesh and sinew.

She needed to drive 100 percent of her force forward. And not at the window. She visualized a driver behind it. The head of the driver. A man who would be looking ahead and not to the side.

Core energy was something Grace visualized as crackling static and vapor. The one represented aggressive yang and the other fluid, irresistible yin. Together, inseparable, perfectly balanced, they were the Tao, the unity of the entire universe—

With a cry that functioned like an afterburner, Grace released her fist forward. It flew like a winged dragon, the embodiment of the five ancient Chinese elements, metal, fire, air, earth, and water. The steel knuckles struck the glass with an impact that shook the limousine on its careful suspension, that generated a sound like a waking volcano, that ended on the other side against the scalp of the person who was sitting there.

With equal resolve Grace immediately returned the right arm to chamber, elbow cocked back, the straight-ahead forearm pulling the fist back through the opening it had made.

The strike took less than two seconds. When it was completed, and in a continuing, fluid movement, Grace poured her body down like a waterfall, squatting on the floor of the ISV, giving Rivette a clear shot at the hole she had made.

The lance corporal could not see inside the cantaloupe-sized hole. All he saw was shadowy movement and a hint of blood briefly illuminated by a streetlight flashing by. He fired once above the dark, moving mass that was the driver. The sound rang through the street, a tympanic soundtrack for the suddenly shuddering, swerving trajectory of the limousine.

Mann slowed as the all-wheel drive of the Audi struggled to stay on course. As the report of the .45 faded they could hear shouts inside.

"Hao's telling the driver not to stop," Grace said.

Mann acknowledged and turned the wheel to the right, bumping the car toward the sidewalk. A dogwalker screamed and jumped as the limousine scraped the side of a parked car with diplomatic plates. The heavier limousine did not bounce back into the road but plowed ahead, the fender punishing the front wheel well of the car and causing it to swivel from the curb. Locked on the chrome of the Audi, the parked car twisted the limousine toward the sidewalk where it slammed a concrete bench and came to a crunching, uneven stop.

Mann angled the ISV beside it, boxing the limousine in. She stopped short of blocking the driver's side doors.

Rivette jumped over the door of the transport and took up a position to the left of the gently sloping hood. He targeted the hole, though from there he was also able to cover the back door. Grace leapt over her side, swung over the trunk, and stood by the back door on the passenger's side. That was where Hao was sitting. If he emerged, she would knock him back in.

Captain Mann got out, touched Rivette on the shoulder to let him know she was coming around. She walked in front of the ISV and went to the front of the limousine. The driver would be able to hear her but not shoot her.

The instructions were simple. Even if they did not speak English, the occupants would understand the message.

"Get out!" she snapped. She raised her hands, framing a severe expression. "This way."

Two doors cracked open, both on the left side. The driver eased out, hands raised, the side of his head bloodied where Grace's knuckles had impacted. No one emerged from the back. There was just a voice that floated from the darkness.

"I know that tone," the speaker said.

•   •   •

Chase Williams had never tasted air so fine nor heard words so welcome as those spoken by Ann Ellen Mann. He pulled off the blindfold. The admiral believed he could exit under his own steam, but that was not what he did, not yet. Beside him, Dylan Hao sat trembling with his phone in his hand. He had punched in 911 and was about to speak to the operator when Williams said, "While you're at it, tell her an American has been kidnapped."

The dispatcher heard the comment and asked again what the caller's situation was.

He ended the call.

"They'll be showing up now anyway," Williams said to him.

"I have immunity," Hao said confidently. He looked at the admiral. "Your team has created an international incident. There will be grave repercussions."

Williams managed to snicker, even though it hurt his nose. "You heard what the captain said. Open the door and get the hell out."

His eyes and manner defiant, Hao unlocked the door and pushed it open. His face was met by the bottom of a foot. It belonged to Grace Lee. The kick lifted Hao from the seat and sent him sliding against Williams.

"Sorry, Admiral," the lieutenant said as she reached in and pulled the agent out by two fistfuls of shirt, tie, and jacket lapels.

The woman twisted at the hip, the momentum bringing Hao with her. He stumbled as he tried to find his footing. Grace helped him remain upright by continuing her turn full circle and slamming him spine-first into the front passenger's door.

The façade of diplomatic immunity crumbled like the bullet-resistant glass and his long face showed fear—along with the blood that was running from his shattered nose.

While Grace held the man in place with her left hand, she drove the palm heel of her right hand into the nose she had already shattered. She did not immediately withdraw from the strike; she shook off the steel knuckles and those fingers became claws, the claws raking down from his forehead through his eyes and down along the bloody cartilage in the middle of his face. He screamed from the mauling, his hands rising in a disoriented attempt to block further blows.

Grace released him and let him drop. He landed on the

concrete, fetal and shaking. Only then did she notice Mann to her right and Williams to her left. Across the hood of the car, Rivette stood with his gun on the driver.

"He'll be chewin' Tylenol for months," Rivette said.

Grace looked from her victim to her commander. Mann was smiling and nodded. The lieutenant turned to Williams. She threw him the proudest salute of her career.

The admiral looked hurt and drawn, his appearance also being compromised by the unflattering backlight of a streetlamp. But there was a smile about the mouth and in his eyes.

Williams returned the salute smartly, and then—after a brief hesitation that was broken by what-the-hell laughter—the two embraced. Captain Mann turned to help Rivette with the driver. After patting him down, she firmly indicated for him to get the hell back up the street toward the embassy. He departed with a small bow of acknowledgment, and in haste.

The admiral broke the hug and, wavering, had to steady himself on the side of the limousine. He looked out at the street.

"No siren," he said.

"No siren," Grace laughed. "The MPDC is babysitting. President's orders."

"Wright?" Williams said with surprised gratitude.

"Actually, Angie," Mann said.

The captain was walking over with the phone, trailed by Rivette. The lance corporal looked down at the quivering Hao.

"The order even has a name," Mann went on. "Matt?"

"It's called Operation Escort," Berry said. "Charlie Mackenna came up with that one. I'll give it a few minutes before I have him come in and clean this up."

"You were part of this rescue?" Williams said.

"With Jay Paul," Berry said. "He just called to say everything went A-OK."

"Best spotter ever," Rivette said.

Williams looked over at him with gratitude and the men exchanged a salute.

"Captain, sir," Rivette said, "does our mission have a name too?"

"Not yet."

"Good, because I'm giving it one now," Rivette said. He glanced down again at the agent by his feet. "I'm calling it, 'Operation Good Thing You're Lying There, Piece of Shit, 'Cause Otherwise—Target Practice.'"

"You exceeded my expectations, Lance Corporal," Mann said.

Williams was overcome, not just by the actions of his team—his extended team—but also by the compounded fear and emotional burdens of the day. His legs wavered and Grace stepped up to support him.

"No, it's okay," Williams said. "Thank you."

She stepped back wearing a look of concern. "We should get you to a doctor ASAP."

"Chase, do you think you can hold off on that?" Berry asked.

Rivette walked toward the phone as if Berry were standing there. "What was that?"

"This was not the only situation playing out tonight," the former deputy chief of staff reminded them. "There is one other."

Mann understood before the other Black Wasps. "He's right. Matt, what's the play?"

"I'm going to call the president," Berry said. "What I need you to do is get back in the ISV for a short drive. One that I think will have a sense of déjà vu for the lieutenant and the lance corporal."

CHAPTER FORTY-ONE

Washington Dulles International Airport,
Loudoun County, Virginia
March 23, 11:56 P.M.

The jet from Beijing had arrived on time, as did the small con-
voy from Washington, D.C. The 737 taxied to a remote area
of the field that was reserved for foreign leaders. A newly constructed chain-link fence with iron slats formed a barrier on
three sides, making it the most secure sector of the airport. As
soon as the 737 had come to a stop and the engines fell silent,
a motorized stairway was driven over by a ground crew with
top security clearance. The staircase was moved into position
and the door of the aircraft opened. All ten members of the
PLA emerged. They formed an honor guard on the tarmac,
their rifles across their chests. In the echo chamber that was
the receiving area, every step, every move of a weapon, every
command had been amplified.

Wang Jing stepped into the doorway and remained there.
That was the prearranged signal for January Dow to move up
with the car containing the Dàyóu family. January had been

informed that the respectful show of soldiery was to assure the Dàyóu of their honored status. Whether she believed that, or suspected it was a face-saving, chest-thumping photo op crafted by the People's Liberation Army—to stand, weaponed, on American soil—did not matter. In a few minutes, the unfortunate nightmare would be ended.

January went to the back of the stretch limousine to open the door and allow Dr. Dàyóu to exit first. Before she could do so, however, there was a commotion on the field coming from the direction of Flight Line Road. There was a military vehicle rushing toward them followed by two cars from the Metropolitan Washington Airports Authority Police Department. Their sirens were on and so were their top lights. The odd thing, to January, was that the ivory-tone vehicles were in pursuit. They were behind it, lateral to each other, like an escort. A fourth vehicle trailed them: a department Fire and EMS Ambulance.

The military vehicle blazed past the two other cars that had been part of January's group and stopped alongside the limousine. The doors remained shut as the national security advisor stalked over to the ISV.

No one in the vehicle rose—until, slowly, the man in the passenger's seat stood. The flashing lights of the police cars threw him in alternating flashes of red and blue.

"Admiral Williams?" the woman said. Her look, which had been one of scowling disapproval, went blank and numb.

"We have someone who needs a ride home," Williams said.

At that, the black-garbed Jaz Rivette stepped from the car. He held his .45 in his right hand, pointed down. In his left hand, he accepted someone who was pushed over by Grace Lee. The man in the middle wobbled where he stood. If Grace had not been holding him still, he would have dropped.

Grace looked toward the 737. Mann got out to help support Hao so Grace could approach the aircraft. Raising her hands to show she was unarmed, she shouted loudly, in Mandarin, "We bring you Dylan Hao, with the compliments of Admiral Chase Williams! Send two men and you can have him! Otherwise, we'll leave him here."

It took Jing a moment to decide. Grace could tell that this development was news to him, that he obviously had not yet heard what had happened. No one would until the driver made it back to the embassy and the news went out to all system personnel.

With the handover at stake, he decided to accommodate the woman—whom he knew was certainly Grace Lee, she who had attacked them in Taiyuan.

With a short command he sent the two closest men to collect the agent. They ran over—impressively, in lockstep—and accepted the man without ceremony or honors.

"He got a little damaged," Rivette said in English. "Sorry."

As the men took Hao's arms he looked over at Williams. "This is not over."

"Intrigue never is," he replied. "But I think you are."

The PLA troops walked the man back to the aircraft and, at a gesture from Jing, helped him up the stairs.

When they were gone, January Dow regarded Black Wasp as a group before her gaze returned to Williams.

"I'm glad to see that you are safe," she said thickly.

"There's more," Captain Mann said.

January looked over as the woman walked toward her. The captain's hand was out. Her government phone was in it.

The national security advisor looked at the ID and, her brow knitting deeply, she put the phone to her ear.

"Ms. Dow, I'm calling off the handover," the president said. "You will come back with the Dàyóus. Angie is already informing Ambassador Qiang of our decision, and of our deep disapproval of the action Hao and his people have taken against our citizens."

"Sir," January said, "what has happened tonight will likely trigger a new response—"

"I have put that on the calendar for tomorrow," he said. "Right now, let's end this on our terms and get some sleep. Everyone needs it."

"Yes, sir."

January returned the phone to the captain. She looked again at Williams and his team.

"I don't like this and I fear that the situation will escalate," she said.

"Not for the Dàyóus," Grace said. She pointed at the limousine.

Dr. Dàyóu was standing beside the open door. As Hao and then Wang Jing retreated into the aircraft, the engineer put his hands together in a prayerful gesture, held them to his chest, and bowed over them toward Grace.

The lieutenant bowed back, her eyes misting. It struck her that she had wept more today than she had at any time in her life. But this moment, at least, was not in mourning but in profound gratitude.

The officer turned back to the ISV, January Dow blowing past her without a look or comment.

That, in itself, was comment enough for Grace.

CHAPTER FORTY-TWO

P Street NW, Washington, D.C.
March 24, 12:05 A.M.

While the plane was fueled and prepared for departure, the January Dow caravan drove off. The mood was not celebratory, nor did anyone comment on the success of the mission. They had lost Major Breen, and Grace Lee's loss was even greater.

Williams was shown to the ambulance. He did not require any help and declined the gurney. Before entering, he motioned Grace over.

"I'm terribly sorry for your loss, Lieutenant," he said. "I never had the privilege of meeting the Lees, but I can tell you this. Today they would have been proud of you."

"I believe they are, sir," Grace said. "I truly believe that."

"So do I, Grace," he said sincerely.

A minute later Williams was on his way to Walter Reed. The president had requested that trip when he had called for the Metropolitan Washington Airports Authority PD escort.

Black Wasp departed when the Chinese 737 taxied for

takeoff. Only then was there a real sense of relief and a stand-down order Captain Mann was grateful to give.

Rivette asked to take the wheel of the ISV, claiming he was too juiced to sit still.

"The police may still have their checkpoints set up," Grace said. "You get a ticket, you pay."

"Not gonna rush," he assured her. "I just want to feel in control of something for the first time since I brushed my teeth this morning."

Mann got in the back with Grace.

"Say, where're we going, Captain?" Rivette asked. "Back to Belvoir?"

"No," she said. "Matt Berry asked us to swing by the safe house, if we're not too tired."

"I'm good with that," Rivette said.

"Did he say why he was asking?" Grace wondered.

The captain shrugged. "I just met the man, I have no idea what he wants. But I'm in no hurry to get back to the base. Spent a lot of time there today."

Grace nodded her assent and the ISV set off across the tarmac, the police cars trailing.

They drove through the gate of the safe house. Jay Paul's car was already parked beside Berry's car. There was barely room for the ISV, and Rivette backed out.

"Where're you going?" Mann asked.

"Street. They didn't pick up the van yet," Rivette explained. "If the Chinese come looking for the ISV, it's his ass."

"They won't come," Grace said as he swung to the curb.

"Why do you say that?" Mann asked.

"Dylan Hao was an exception," Grace answered. "Beijing isn't reckless. They'll expect a trap if they see this most-wanted vehicle parked in the street. No one would be that cavalier otherwise."

"I don't know that word, but I probably wouldn't like it," Rivette said as he parked. "I look at it another way. They left with their asses kicked. They don't want more."

Grace got out. "We were burned too, Jaz."

"Lieutenant, you know I didn't mean any disrespect—"

"I know," Grace replied. "But we didn't come out of this clean."

Mann said, "Every squad I've ever served with knew that was a possibility. You accept the reality and move on. There's nothing else *to* do."

Grace did not agree. There was something else to do and, as they walked to the house, the street refreshingly still and quiet, she moved it from her "to-do" list to active duty.

Berry welcomed the trio with the first smile they had seen on the man. Even Paul was not bent over his laptop. He had a beer in his hand and wore an easy expression. He raised the bottle to the three as they entered.

"What can I get you?" Berry asked, no longer the tactician but the affable host.

Rivette asked for a beer, Grace and Mann for iced tea. Berry served the drinks then tossed a bag of tortilla chips on the table.

"Yeah, I don't like steak and potatoes after a mission," Rivette snarked.

"Time for that later," Berry said. "Sit, please."

Grace and Rivette took their previous seats, Mann stood. The ISV had cramped her leg, challenging the old wound. It felt good to be back in action—except for the stiffness that resulted from too many years of inactivity.

"As if your actions—tonight and in previous missions—did not say enough about your abilities, Chase Williams has applauded you to me many times. The admiral is not a man to swing wide to praise anyone. You earned it."

Berry had been considering many of his next words all day, ever since Grace and Rivette had come to his office. He remained standing as he spoke.

"It is my belief that tomorrow, two things will happen," Berry continued. "First, to pacify what are sure to be some very angry Chinese, the president will announce an immediate investigation into the 'intolerable' and 'un-American' actions of this evening." The former White House official made a show of putting air quotes around those words. "The investigation will be high profile and will last for—about a week. Then, at the instructions of the press secretary, they will vanish from the media. Not slowly but overnight. As much as the investigating panel will have been for show, the fast fade will let China know that, in fact, they deserved what they got and there will be no legal requital."

"Sound and fury signifying nothing," Mann said.

"That's right." He regarded the captain. "You're familiar with that, I think."

Mann nodded. "Been the poster child for older, crippled women soldiers. Interviews, congressional testimony, the works."

"Resulting in?" Berry pressed.

"Me being propped in a chair until Chase Williams rescued me."

Berry gave her a sympathetic look—practiced but not entirely insincere.

"You said two things," Rivette pressed.

Berry grinned. He was not accustomed to being interrupted or pushed. This entire experience might be beneficial to him as well.

"The second thing is that the president will have to decide, and quickly, what to do about Black Wasp."

"Why quickly?" Mann said. "If the probe is destined to come up empty-handed—"

"That's external," Berry said. "There will be resumed internal pressure to shut Op-Center down entirely. January Dow miscalculated tonight, but she's not one to go down from a single thunderbolt. She'll be electrified. She has mistrusted Chase and the rest of the organization from the start. She has enemies, but she also has friends. I believe that Wright will give January her way on this."

"Okay, now that's a thunderbolt," Rivette said. "We win—again—and you're saying we'll be out of a job?"

"I'm saying Op-Center will likely be shut down, or at least remade in January's image—whatever that is." He paused to make sure his next words were heard. "I am saying, Lance Corporal, Lieutenant, Captain—that by this time tomorrow you will have received orders to return to your previous commands."

The pronouncement settled on the group like mourning—unwelcome, bleak, and deeply personal.

Mann broke the long silence that had been punctuated only by Rivette's quiet oaths.

"Why are you telling us this?" the captain asked.

"In my business I always anticipate likely next moves," Berry said. "Those are what I think the White House will do. We have no control over them. However, we do have control over what we do."

Grace was the one who broke Berry's dramatic pause. "We?" Grace said.

"Right," Rivette picked up on her remark. "How are we 'we'?"

"I have a proposition," Berry said. "Call it preparedness. Over the years I have seen—and you have witnessed—people like January Dow, and by extension John Wright, act in the best interests of political survival and party agenda. The needs of the nation are a distant third. You've seen it yourself, Captain Mann. How many navy fliers did you see digging trenches in Afghanistan?"

"A few," she admitted.

"Why were they there?" Berry asked. "Because military budgets are guided by having boots on the ground, in the air, walking a deck. There was no real need for those personnel. We won World War II based on just twenty percent efficiency. That was an unacceptable number then, it's worse today."

"It's dumb and wasteful and all that, but what's it got to do with us?" Rivette asked.

"The reason Trigram is in business, the reason we are effective and successful, is because neither I nor my partners play that game," Berry said. "Once in a while—rare, but unavoidable, really—we get taken in by a Dylan Hao. But our number of efficiency is ninety-nine percent. I want to start spreading that around."

"How?" Mann asked.

"You're sounding like a mob kingpin, the kind of man my dad used to call 'a band leader,'" Grace said.

"I won't deny there are similarities," Berry said. "You can't deny that people like January Dow also have those qualities. It's called palace intrigue, ladies and gentleman. Some people, like Chase Williams, are experts at negotiating the machinations and double-dealing. A few of us take a parallel but separate route."

"The fifth column," Mann said.

Berry smiled. "Exactly, Captain."

"What's that?" Rivette asked.

"Spain, 1930s," Mann said. "Armies marched toward—Madrid, I think it was. People were focused on those four columns, unaware that a fifth was already inside the city, spying and softening the enemy for their military."

"Perfect description," Berry resumed. "Trigram has confidential sources. We have insiders giving us leads. We have double, triple agents. We have hackers. What we do not have are warriors." He went from face to face. "I want Black Wasp to come to work for us. Based in this house, doing what you've been doing but answerable only—and I emphasize the word 'only'—to Ann Ellen Mann."

"You surprised me," the captain said.

"Which part?" Rivette asked. "The whole thing?"

"I thought you were leading up to Chase Williams," she said.

"I was wrong, before," Berry said. "I have three predictions. I know Chase Williams well, and while I would of course ask him to join my operation, I believe that the retired admiral will become the retired, retired admiral."

Captain Mann was a cautious woman by nature, and it remained to be seen whether the events predicted by Matt Berry were in part or in whole correct. Which left the job offer still hanging. The topic needed debate and reflection—but not until his projections had been proved right or wrong.

"Mr. Berry, I don't know what your idea entails either personally or logistically," Mann said. To the Black Wasps she said, "I don't think we should say anything until we've slept."

"Okay, but I just want to say I like the idea of moving here," Rivette said. "That part is solid."

"Lance Corporal, I invite you—all of you—to stay here tonight," Berry said, pointing to the floors above. "We can talk more in the morning or whenever you like."

"I think we'll go back to Belvoir," Mann said. "That's still where we're stationed."

Berry nodded in understanding.

"How about we talk again after the president has had

time to sleep on things," Mann suggested. "I appreciate the offer and I respect it, I do. But I'm not one to walk away from my oath—or, frankly, my pension—because the commander in chief wants to send me to another command."

"Fair," Berry said. "I wouldn't expect you to do otherwise. As I said at the outset, I just wanted to put the proposition out there."

Jay Paul rose. "Sleep seems like a good idea. I'm heading out."

"You don't live here?" Rivette asked. "Why the hell not?"

"We all need to get off the treadmill sometimes," Paul said. "Anyway, this place is for folks who need to go stealth. For what it's worth, after today, I hope it's all of you."

"Thank you," Mann said.

Berry turned to his assistant. "Was that Nellie Friday on duty tonight?"

"It was."

"See you—what time tomorrow?"

"I'm thinking lunchtime."

Paul left by the back door and Rivette watched him go. "Captain Mann, sir. You have my vote already."

Grace rose. "I think I'll drive. Captain, if you wouldn't mind sitting up front there's something I want to talk to you about."

"Of course," Mann said.

Together, as a unit, as soldiers bonded by duty and combat, they left the safe house for an uncertain future.

CHAPTER FORTY-THREE

Fort Belvoir North, Springfield, Virginia
March 24, 7:41 A.M.

Ann Ellen Mann awoke to the uncommon sound of silence. The house was unnaturally quiet and, save for the grounds crew repairing her backyard, the usual noises of a residential community on a spring morning were absent.

The captain dressed and went to the kitchen. She had smelled the coffee, and under her navy mug sat a handwritten note. It was legible; it was from Grace.

"Sir, Jaz and I requisitioned a car and have taken a drive. We will be back tonight. Regards, Grace."

The officer did not wonder where they had gone. There was one bit of business that had been left unfinished. The lance corporal had gone with her for moral support. Grace would not need any other kind.

Mann folded the note and set it down.

"Do the right thing," she said quietly. The captain did not know if her thoughts would convey across a great distance. She knew from experience in Afghanistan that such things were possible. And if anyone could hear her, it would be Grace Lee.

The captain poured a cup of coffee and then checked her phone for messages. There was a text from Angie Brunner. It came in nearly two hours before and asked the officer to call when it was convenient.

"That doesn't sound urgent," Mann said aloud.

She walked to the living room, sat in the sofa, and winced from the pain in her leg. The sciatica tightened and she had to straighten the leg and roll slightly to her right to relieve the discomfort.

"No more urban street fighting for you," she told the unhappy limb.

She punched Angie's name and the phone called. The chief of staff answered on the third beep.

"Good morning," Angie said pleasantly.

"Good morning. You were up early."

"Who needs more than two hours' sleep? What about there? Everyone sleep well?"

"Like little lambs," she said. The captain decided not to mention the road trip the other two had undertaken.

"Have you seen the news?" Angie asked.

"Not yet. Anything I should know about?"

"The attack on the Chinese embassy car is the top headline globally," Angie said. "The ambassador is furious with us, and Beijing, we hear, is furious with her. It's being called a political attack by parties unknown, probably Taiwanese patriots."

"Are the reporters saying that or—"

"No, the Chinese themselves," Angie said. "They're trying to turn their misdeeds and tactical blunders into an asset. Sympathy, it seems."

"What else could they do with it?"

"They can and have blamed the MPDC for the ticketing blitz," Angie said. "Complained it created a 'window of opportunity.'"

"Well, there's some truth to that," Mann said. "Any mention of the Dàyóus?"

"Not from us and certainly not from them," Angie said. "It's all about spin now, and there's no way that works for them."

"Sounds good," Mann said. She took a sip then said, "So where's the other shoe?"

Angie snickered. "The president has promised the ambassador a full investigation of the attack," the chief of staff said. "They both know that a panel will come up with theories and likelihoods, but it will not lead where we and the Chinese know the story starts and ends."

Score one for Matt Berry, Mann thought.

"All of that aside, Captain, Black Wasp made the president look good internally. There are some puffed chests among the top staff. They don't all know who or why, only that it was our side and they performed heroically. January Dow is not happy and, far from retreating and nursing her bruised ambition, she is still pushing for some kind of immediate rapprochement, which in her mind must include the return of the Dàyóus."

"What does the president say?"

"I can't share that, but I will tell you that the family is back in Silver Springs and the only travel plans are to a permanent safe house somewhere in the Pacific Northwest, which was their original request."

Mann was glad to hear that.

"There's more, though, yes?" the captain said.

"Unfortunately, there is," Angie admitted. "The furnace needs to be fed."

"January Dow?"

"She's still national security advisor and she has a lot of— well, not friends. But she has allies of opportunity, let's call them. She wants Op-Center's head."

"Will she get it?"

"The president hasn't decided," Angie said. "January aside, his own concerns are valid. This could just as easily have gone another way. And however guilty the Chadian was, John Wright is not in favor of cartel-style executions. I can't say I disagree."

"Are we getting the boot?"

"I honestly don't know. He will decide today, most likely. January is like a dog with a bone about that topic."

Score two for Matt Berry, Mann thought.

"But however this goes, Captain, I want to add how impressed I am by how you handled this and how grateful I am that the country has patriots like you."

"There are millions of us," Mann said. "China, Russia,

North Korea, wherever and whenever—all you ever have to do is call on us."

"I know. And thank you," Angie said.

The call ended. So too, the captain believed, had the career of Black Wasp. At least as a military unit answerable only to the president of the United States.

It was a bittersweet moment. Triumph and defeat, somehow bundled as one. What would Grace have said? The yin and the yang of all things, vice and versa, bound by their inherently opposite natures.

"And, dammit, this had to be the briefest command in American military history," she said, raising her mug to toast herself.

She would miss the team and a central part of her would always mourn Major Hamilton Breen. But it was all right. If Wright decided against them, there was still a path forward.

For now, the matter of Trigram was still open-ended. Though as she sat there enjoying a well-earned pause in matters of consequence, she could not help but wonder one thing:

Was Matt Berry's third prediction correct?

CHAPTER FORTY-FOUR

Walter Reed National Military Center,
Washington, D.C.
March 24, 11: 53 A.M.

Being driven to Fort Belvoir was an emotional moment for Chase Williams. It climaxed a morning that, in itself, had been both powerful and humbling.

He began the day with an outpatient medical examination at Walter Reed National Military Center. A series of X-rays, supported by a CAT scan, were taken to determine if there had been serious damage to his chest, throat, or skull due to the beatings delivered by Dylan Hao.

Any other aftereffects were still to be determined.

While he waited in a small conference room for the results of the tests, Williams knew that events that brought him here had also left the future of himself and of Op-Center—together and separately—very much in the air. More than any medical issues, questions, indecision, and uncertainty about his future weighed on him as never before. Williams had been around Washington long enough, and John Wright more than enough, to know that while he could take up sailing, squash, or Bible studies—the pastimes he personally enjoyed—the future of Op-Center was not his to control. The events of the previous day were not just an elephant in the room; they were the room. Until he saw and reckoned with the fallout, until he knew the repercussions—if any—the only thing he could do was prepare.

That was why he had placed a call to an old friend, someone whose good word had helped him to secure the directorship of Op-Center. General Mike Rodgers was a casual friend and a longtime admirer of the admiral, and the feeling was mutual. The former deputy director of the National Crisis Management Center and commander of the Striker military unit was surprised and happy to hear from him.

"I spend most of my time on a boat, in the Gulf of Mexico, fishing," Rodgers told him. "How are things in my old stomping grounds?"

"Last time I looked, proud and secret." Williams hesitated. "Well, mostly secret."

Rodgers chuckled. "That's my Op-Center. You okay? It's been, what, about a year and a half?"

"Something like that," Williams said. "I'm fine." It was difficult enough sounding normal with a badly swollen jaw; now he found himself choking up and he did not want to. "I was thinking about Paul Hood earlier, but I have a question for you."

"Shoot."

"Mike—do you miss it?"

"Oh boy," Rodgers said, then answered without hesitation, "I miss it every damn day. I used to mark them on the calendar—how many days 'since.' I stopped after a year."

"Why?"

"Don't laugh, but I saw this yogi on some streaming thing—"

"I'm not laughing."

"Good," Rodgers said. "Anyway, he said that living in the past is like holding a leaking bag of garbage over your head. It ruins the present, each moment of it. He was right. Chase, the years I was in uniform, particularly at Op-Center—they were great. Some were rough, heartbreaking. Others were— Christ, they were big and global and I felt like I was doing what I was born to do, serving my country. But I had my innings. It was time to be grateful for that and move on."

Williams laughed so he wouldn't weep. "Fishing?"

"There's the contradiction," Rodgers laughed. "I loved it as a kid, down at the pond near my home. That and feeding crackers to ducks."

"Living in *that* past is okay, then?"

"Different," Rodgers said. "Second childhoods are permitted. You can't do that now, by the way."

"What?"

"Feed the ducks at Guilford Riverway. Last time I went there, the Department of Environmental 'Something' had posted a sign that said feeding the waterfowl would disrupt their migratory habits and possibly lead to dietary injury and death. I fed 'em anyway."

Williams chuckled. "I don't think I'm quite at that level of curmudgeon."

"Probably not. You Annapolis guys—so well-behaved."

"That must be it."

Rodgers waited. When Williams did not speak, the retired general pushed.

"So what is it, Admiral? You thinking of hanging Op-Center up? Or is that information above my security downgrade?"

"I'm thinking of a change," Williams said.

"Do you think you can handle being without the routine, the service—the sense of being plugged-in?"

"I don't know. That's why I'm calling."

"Except for service—and you can always find ways to contribute—the rest always mattered more to you than it did to me. But then I was only deputy director. The buck stopped with Paul Hood. You like the buck."

That was true. He had been unhappy for the few weeks that Ann Ellen Mann had been running Black Wasp. For that to be permanent—

"Tell you what," Williams said. "If I decide to turn in my suit, I'll make my way down to Bayonet Point. You can help me catch a marlin, something to write home about."

"That's a deal," Rodgers said. "Hey, let me know what you decide."

"I will, Mike, and thanks."

After Williams hung up, he used a finger to deal with pesky tears. The hospital would have a car waiting to take him home to the Watergate as soon as he had his results. While the admiral sat there, he saw that he had a text from Matt Berry. It was on the only device he still had, his government phone; two and a half hours old.

One day you'll learn to work this damn thing, he told himself. He winced when he thought that it might not be necessary.

He called Berry. The man was a cynical optimist; if nothing else, Berry would be good for sarcasm and polemics.

Berry sounded unusually chipper, answering with a hello that rose at the end.

"What's the diagnosis?" Berry asked.

"You know where I am?"

"Do you have to ask?"

"Stupid of me," Williams said. "I'm waiting to hear. The doctors and technologists didn't think anything was badly amiss."

"Very glad to hear. I've got to tell you, Chase, you should be insanely proud of that team you built. They are amazing."

"They're special," Williams agreed.

"I've offered them all a job."

Williams had never underestimated Berry's ability to surprise him. The very fact of the downsized Op-Center and his Defense Logistics Agency with its secret cash reserves was evidence of that. But this caught him entirely off guard. There was an uncharacteristic strut in Berry's tone. Williams was not sure how to handle it.

"Do they need one?" Williams asked.

"Likely," Berry said. "If they accept, I'd like you to come with."

"We've had this conversation," Williams said. "You enjoy the private sector and its intrigue—"

"I do, but when we had that conversation Wright was moving in and I was moving out. More to the point, you still had your position."

"As far as I know, I still do."

"Touché, my friend," Berry replied. "Then let's consider this discussion—how do we describe it? Ended or tabled?"

Williams considered the question. "Premature," he answered.

"Nice. I can live with that. Look," Berry went on, "the reason I wanted to talk to you was twofold. First, to apologize about Dylan Hao. We'll talk about that some other time. I screwed up and—I'm sorry. That's all I can say at the moment. But second, to tell you . . . to *thank* you . . . for enabling me to be part of one of the most exceptional experiences of my life. I say again, you should be proud of that team. Each of them has a part of you, a strand of military DNA."

"Thank you," Williams said.

"Call me when you get the test results?"

"Sure thing," Williams said.

The admiral closed his jaw gingerly. He was glad to stop talking. The entire left side of his face was sore. The only thing that made it feel better was how god-awful Dylan Hao felt not only outside but inside. Williams, at least, still had friends.

He sat there waiting for his doctor, thinking about Berry's

comment regarding his DNA. It was not just his training, his example that was manifest in the actions of Black Wasp. It was Breen's DNA, and through them it was DNA that went back to John Paul Jones and George Washington. It was special, despite the efforts of too many pundits who tried to say it was not.

Before he saw Berry's message, Williams had been thinking about calling Captain Mann. He decided to wait. As his emergency contact, she would have been notified about the trip to Walter Reed, and the results. The rest of what they would talk about—this was not the time. Berry's offer, if it came to that by necessity or choice, was also something she and the team should decide on their own.

Nor would his own decision have anything to do with theirs. If he elected to continue with his career, with a career— that was one course. That choice was easy. All he had to do was keep doing what he had been doing since he was a teenager. The other choice—

"Admiral Williams," said a young woman who entered the room with a stack of X-rays and a scrolled printout held together with a rubber band.

"Yes, ma'am," he said.

"There's good news and bad news," she said. "The good news is you've only got a mild concussion. The bad news is that after a week at home you'll be able to resume your duties, full-time."

She ended the medical soliloquy with a grin. Williams did not mind the questionable bedside manner. He could not begin to imagine the number of times this woman had been forced to deliver actual bad news.

"Thank you," he said.

"I'll forward these to your personal physician. I'm told you have a car waiting out front."

"I do. Again, thanks."

The woman held the door and Williams followed the exit signs to the main lobby. As he made his way into the sunshine, his mind returned to the thought he had left unfinished. The one that no old soldier wanted to face.

If he did not have Op-Center and declined the offer from Berry, what form of fading away did he want to pursue from day to day to day . . .

CHAPTER FORTY-FIVE

New York, New York
March 24, 2:27 P.M.

Powered by purpose and by coffee, with lingering adrenaline to spare, Jaz Rivette drove north through moderate traffic, beneath sunny skies, and with a mostly mute, thoughtful passenger beside him.

The lance corporal would have preferred something other than a Honda for the journey, and something newer than on-its-last-legs, but as long as they made it to New York and back he was content.

Rivette had left his weapon behind. Grace had said twice in the first five minutes of being in the kitchen that his presence was not a command and this was not a mission. Before leaving the residence, Lieutenant Lee told him she appreciated the ride but had cautioned, "More than that, I do not want you to be a part of it."

"The getaway driver *is* a part of it," he had replied.

"As far as you knew, we were going so I could make funeral arrangements," she said.

"Whatever you say," he had told her. "But you know, you're the only grown-up I know who doesn't drive."

"A lot of New Yorkers don't."

"Maybe so, but I'm going to instruct you when we get back."

Grace had neither resisted nor accepted. The lieutenant had already said she was not making plans beyond the drive north up Interstate 95.

Lance Corporal Rivette was concerned for his colleague and—she had said it for the first time, though he had always known it—for his friend. He knew they were not going north to plan for a funeral. Grace had shown him the email she had received from the Department of Defense, notifying the lieutenant of her parents' death through her official detachment at U.S. Army Special Operations Command (Airborne) in Fort Bragg, North Carolina. The email had come during the night and offered both condolences and the mandatory offer of leave-taking.

Whoever sent it did not know that Lieutenant Lee was not in North Carolina. Black Wasp was a secret operation. Physical mail was forwarded to a PO box Chase Williams had set up. With the unit presently in limbo, with her physical home in New York a shambles, with her family destroyed, Grace was not sure where she belonged.

"Behind bars, probably," she said when they saw the first signs indicating New York City. They were the first words she had spoken since they left Fort Belvoir.

"What the what?" Rivette said.

"Just thinking," she answered.

"I don't think I like the direction of your—contemplative nature," he said. He used a phrase Major Breen had once employed to describe the lieutenant—when she was not pounding, slicing, throwing, or kicking an adversary.

She did not respond.

"I've been contemplating too," he boasted. "I wasn't too keen on that Jay Paul guy when we first met him, but he came through. So did Mr. Berry. I don't know what this means for my enlistment or pretty much anything else, except I think I'd like working with them full-time."

Grace smiled faintly. "What you liked were the thick towels in the safe house bathroom, Jaz."

"That too, no doubt. I would not mind living there—and don't tell me you wouldn't either. But I'm thinking about the future. You know how you always say that you learned in martial arts that the best students never stop learning, that the best teachers never stop learning?"

"It's true."

"Well, I feel like I—we—have gotten sharper and done some good things and seen some weird-ass places I never expected to see—hello, Sana'a, Yemen. But I don't know that I've grown. What's strange? I still feel like I'm closer to San Pedro than I am to the future. Talking to Little Guillermo, I felt like I did when I started doing stakeouts for him ten years ago. You feel that way?"

Unfiltered by her habitual focus on a moment, any moment, she said, "I guess I do."

"The military, it's kind of a pyramid, right? Fat at the base where the grunts live, narrower at the top the bigger the brass. But it's a straight line, like the perfect shot. Wind, gravity, the target is moving—the things that you have to think about when you shoot are not even factors. We do, we behave, we perform, we rise." He was silent for a moment. "So here's a question."

"Is it affected by wind or gravity?" she asked.

"No, and that's what bugs me. What we did yesterday, what we've done so far as Black Wasps. Does that get me corporal or am I gonna be busted? Straight up or straight down?"

"Good question. I don't know."

"Right, we don't. So I'm thinking—maybe we should be prepared to accept Mr. Berry's offer, ask to be discharged, before we get kneecapped by the president. The admiral probably has the suction to get that done."

"What do you think he would advise?" Grace asked.

"If he's smart?" Rivette said. "He tells me, 'I'm still learning, kid. You tell me what you want.'"

Grace looked at him. "Jaz, there are times when you positively astound me, and it has nothing to do with your marksmanship." She grinned. "You've grown in ways you don't even realize."

That was her last comment until they reached the Holland Tunnel that passed under the Hudson River, taking them from New Jersey into Lower Manhattan. Chinatown was due east.

It was the first time Grace had been back to the city of

her birth in two years. Being present again, physically, had an impact she had not expected. Her roots, her childhood, her joyful adolescence giving way to training and skills and at least some wisdom hit her like a returning faith. The bricks, the asphalt, the faceless people moving here and there, the traffic, the towers—many of them new and unfamiliar but typifying the sinew of this place—she was overwhelmed and had to struggle to retain her composure.

Rivette did not intrude on her moment. He had no idea where he was or where he was going and followed the GPS. He had been to New York exactly once, for a shooting competition, and recognized the spire of One World Trade and the Statue of Liberty as they came into view. Looking toward Midtown he noticed the towers in Hudson Yards—they were new. His peekaboo glimpses between intervening buildings also revealed the spires of the residential skyscrapers farther uptown on Billionaires' Row.

It was nuts, he thought. Like he had never been here at all. Then he crossed Broadway, and his focus returned. A voice told him that his destination was at hand.

"Grace?"

"Columbus Park is ahead," she said. "I trained there. A lot. Bayard Street is at the north end."

"Yeah, the map voice told me that."

"Sorry. I wasn't listening," Grace said.

The woman was lost in something Rivette had never seen.

"Tell me about training," he said.

Rivette wanted her present; he was not sure she should be

making decisions now that were going to affect the rest of her life. The drive had been hours of mostly silence, and the reality of why they were here hit him hard. This was not a military maneuver, sanctioned by the president. This was to be murder.

A small, wistful smile settled briefly on the lieutenant's face. "The pavilion on the north side of the park—people would sit on folding chairs and play stringed instruments. The erhu, mostly. Like a violin. Others would play checkers. South of that, there are the soccer fields, basketball courts . . . and the grassy areas where we trained. Pickup groups, mostly. A buffet of ancient arts. Sirens from the police station across the way. Vans coming and going with prisoners. The smells from food carts." She looked around. "Funny, isn't it? The memories are more vivid than being here now."

"I'm thinking that maybe we should get out, let you walk around—listen to some erhu."

"No."

Her rejection was firm, absolute, like when they were on a mission. Which they were.

"Say, Grace—"

"I said no, Jaz."

"I wasn't gonna argue. Just wanted to ask—uh, maybe you want to go to . . . what was that? Mulberry Road first?"

"Mulberry Street," she said, the name tasting bitter. And—again—no. First I want to get this done."

"Right. Well, about that—"

"Don't!" she snapped. The rebuke was hard; she quickly softened it. "*Please* don't."

The reality of her parents' death and the weight of what she was about to do replaced the feelings of nostalgia, camaraderie, Taoist philosophy. It dampened everything in her soul and mind other than hurt. The only thing in her mind, in her mind's eye, was the face and name of Bruce Chan. She had looked him up online. It was not difficult finding him: he had an extensive rap sheet, mostly related to vehicular theft and stripping parts from parked cars.

He must have been highly recommended and well paid to do what he did.

The energy inside the car sank and Rivette slumped; he did not maneuver through the traffic but poured through it slowly. He made his way east on Canal Street, was glad that Centre Street went the wrong way for him, and continued his slow plow to Mott Street. He turned right.

If this was not the beating heart of Chinatown, Rivette could not imagine what was. It was stuffed on either side with old tenements and restaurants and shops—and everything was colorful and active. He did not get to admire anything in particular; he was too busy watching the road and, peripherally, looking at Grace.

"What's the plan if the target is not present?" Rivette asked.

He used the tone they used on missions, hoping that got through.

"He'll be there," Grace said.

"How do you know?"

"He killed some people yesterday," Grace replied coldly. "His masters will want him to lie low."

"Makes sense. You plan to knock on the door?"

She did not reply.

"Kick it in?" he pressed.

"I don't know, Jaz."

"He could be armed."

She gave him a look that said, *How is that different from anything we've ever done?*

"Okay, I just want to put things out there. It's not a mission, right, but I'm still wheelman. If he's not there? Gotta check parking signs—"

"We wait," she answered. "You can let me off at the corner of Mott and Bayard. Actually, no—there's a spot in front of the Buddhist temple. See it?"

She was pointing to the east side of the street.

"I see it. Says 'no parking.' There's a hydrant."

"Pull in. You've got military tags. The police won't bother you."

Rivette looked around. "Lotta delivery trucks. What if one of them tells me to move?"

"He'll be speaking Mandarin. Ignore him."

"If I can't?"

"Circle the block. I'll find you."

Reluctantly, Rivette did as she instructed, parallel parking as only an Angeleno could. Then it hit him.

"Wait," he said. "I have to stay with the car, then."

She popped the door. "That's right."

"Uh-uh," he said, shaking his head in emphasis. "I'm going with you."

"You're not. This is mine."

"*Lieutenant*—nothing has been 'yours' alone since I met you."

"Well, this is," she said, shutting the door, putting her hands in the pockets of the red hoodie she was wearing, and heading down the busy street full of tourists and the lunchtime crowd.

The address was a four-story building of rust-colored brick with faded yellow fire escapes out front. There was a skin care center to the west and, beyond it, a massage parlor with drawn shades and a neon, red OPEN sign in the window. Memories, familiarity, home, sadness moved through Grace like the powerful vapors of energy her *sifu*s always talked about. Her hands felt charged, her heartbeat matched the quick pace of her steps—she practically charged toward the worn-out stoop with its three steps and rusty iron railing that led to a door with flaking green paint around a window half covered with old stickers advertising locksmiths and computer repair.

She looked at the names on the buzzers to the right of the door. She found S. Chan, J. Chan, and—there it was: B. Chan, 2F.

"To hell with you," Grace said to the entire list of names. She grabbed the knob of a door that required a key to enter. She held it, put her left shoulder to the wood, and concentrated her energy on a sharp push. The jamb split at the faceplate, and the bolt moved enough so that she could enter the dark, mosaic-tiled foyer. The flooring must have been beautiful, once. She crossed it toward the staircase. If anyone in a street-level apartment had heard the crack, they did not come to investigate.

She took the stairs two at a time and found herself at 2A. She moved down the corridor dimly lighted by a single bulb behind a dusty fixture. Her destination was at the end. Rivette's caution flashed like a neon sign of its own. If the target was there, he could be armed. If he was not there—

He *was* there. Someone was. She felt it with a sixth sense a lifelong apartment dweller possessed. With a deep intake of breath Grace ran at the door, arms pumping, step high. She hit the featureless gray panel and went through it like an artillery shell, her hands pushing the door hard to the side, the impact tearing the flesh of her palm heels. She heard gasps, a shout, objects falling—glass, a table or chair, the things of a New York apartment.

She stopped, dead-halt, and stood like a Shaolin bull ready to charge again.

Before her was a small room, a living room with a window to the right, a kitchen to the left, a bedroom ahead. There was a sofa made up like a bed. There was a man lying in it and a woman on the tattered rug before it. The woman was older, on her back with pieces of the smashed furnishings around her. She wore an old housedress and a look of fear. The man on the sofa was dressed in a bathrobe and slippers. He was Bruce Chan.

Grace regarded him with fire in her hands and throat. The blood from her palms dripped to her fingertips. The bull had become a dragon, its claws red.

"You stole a van yesterday," Grace said in Mandarin. "You used it to kill my parents."

The man looked up at her. He had not yet reacted to what she had said; he was still frozen in shock at her explosive arrival.

The woman on the floor moved first. She seemed to be in pain. Without taking her eyes off Bruce Chan, Grace stepped forward and extended a hand to the woman.

"What is this?" the woman asked, ignoring the hand of the intruder. The question was for Bruce, not Grace.

It was Grace who answered. "This man was hired by a criminal named Dylan Hao to drive into a building on Mulberry Street. It was reported as an accident. It was an assassination."

The woman's look of fear shaded to an expression of horror. Still on the ground, propped by her palms, she looked over her shoulder. "Son?"

The man's eyes did not leave Grace. He was breathing heavily. His lips started to say something, but he could not seem to find the words.

The woman turned slowly. She looked back at Grace, whose hand was still stretched toward her. The woman accepted it—but not to rise. She clutched it tightly.

"Miss Lee," she said, "what you said—it is so?"

"It is."

The woman began to sob. "I—I read of it. I did not know. I honor you and I apologize for my son."

Grace took her eyes off Brace Chan and looked at the pale, poor face below her. It was a small journey but a profound one. It doused the flame that had consumed Grace inside and out. She lowered herself to a knee so her face was level with that of the woman.

"We . . . it's money, not . . . not hate," the woman said, her voice trembling. "I . . . do not know what else to say. Except . . . do what you must."

Grace released the woman and stood. She went over to the man, who had not moved.

"I came here to kill you," she said. "You took my parents from me. I give you to your mother." Grace turned.

The woman touched Grace's leg as she walked past, stepped over the wreckage of the door and the broken lives she left behind. Broken but perhaps not irreparable.

Grace ignored the faces of those who had braved a peek from behind their door chains. She heard honking from the street as she descended the stairs. Her eyes adjusted quickly to daylight, saw Rivette waiting for her in the Honda, holding up traffic and not seeming to care.

"I thought you might need to make a quick getaway," he said through the open window. "Actually, no. I didn't really think that. What I thought was that you might need a friend."

Grace waved at the line of cars to shut up, like she had done so many times for so many years. She ignored their gestures, too, as she went around to the passenger's side. She climbed inside. As she sat, Rivette noticed her bloody fingers.

"It's mine," she assured him, opening the glove compartment and locating a soiled shimmy.

"Never thought I'd be happy to hear you say *that*," he said, exhaling.

Grace wiped her hands, replaced the cloth, and stared ahead. She seemed to be somewhere else; Rivette was not surprised.

"Thank you for doing this, Jaz."

"You're welcome."

Tears formed in the woman's eyes. She turned and gave her companion a look that only comrades in arms would understand.

"I couldn't do it," she admitted.

He smiled at her, his own eyes damp. "Not a surprise."

"It was to me," she said. "If you don't mind, I'd like to see my parents before we leave."

"I don't mind at all," he told her.

"Go back to Columbus Park, east side. I'll direct you to the funeral home."

Putting the car in motion, Jaz Rivette drove them toward the one certain destination in an uncertain future.

ABOUT THE AUTHOR

JEFF ROVIN is the author of more than 150 books, fiction and nonfiction, both under his own name, under various pseudonyms, or as a ghostwriter, including numerous *New York Times* bestsellers and over a dozen of the original Tom Clancy's Op-Center novels.